FOUR OF A KIND

KELLIE BEAN

ISBN-13: 978-1-988902-05-0

Patchwork-Press.com

Cover Design by Cormar Creative Edited by M.M. Chabot Junior Editor: Katie Sanchez, Philippa Atwood, Talyn Legler

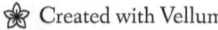 Created with Vellum

For my sister
I'm so glad there aren't three of you

CHAPTER 1

I DON'T KNOW ABOUT HOME sweet home, but after nine hours in the car, we're finally in Fairview. The drive was too long, but at least I got to ride shotgun for the entire drive because my sisters were too hung-over this morning to fight me for it.

It's probably the combination of exhaustion, anticipation, and a massive bag of sour jelly beans talking, but I'm somehow more excited than nervous to be here. A new town, and a chance for a whole new Reagan—as cheesy as that sounds.

Reece and Reilly start to wake up as the car slows down, from the off-ramp, we merge onto Main Street, the not-so-originally named central street of Fairview. Trying to stretch their legs, someone kicks the back of my seat. Before I can say anything, an impressive looking brick church catches my eye. Next to it is a tiny bungalow that's been painted a bright shade of purple, and beside that there's an ice cream shop, which looks like it's been in the same spot for around fifty years, complete with a chalkboard sidewalk sign advertising their newest flavor, Midsummer Ice Cream. This place looks more like a movie set than a real town, like a single gust of wind could knock the church over to reveal a structure made from cardboard.

We're really here. Back in Fairview.

The four of us are dead silent as we take in the rows of mismatched shop fronts and mid-afternoon shoppers. Even Mom, who's been here twice already in the last month, seems a little awestruck by the town where she grew up, as the sun shines through a cloudless sky above us.

Fairview is the kind of place you'd see on scenic post-cards, not a place where people actually live. But we will. Even though it may as well be a million miles away from the city where we've spent most of our lives so far.

Reilly's face reflects in the rearview mirror, her expression purposefully neutral. I don't have to see Reece to imagine the scowl smeared across her face; she will not be won over by small-town charm today. But while I'd never say it out loud to either of them, I have a good feeling about this place.

"Ready?" Mom asks, turning the car onto our street, Oakridge Boulevard.

I force away a smile, because as far as my family knows, I'm still pissed about having to move in the middle of summer vacation with almost no warning. My sisters are all angry, so everyone assumes I am too. And really, siding with my sisters is easier. Even if I don't say anything at all, everyone will just assume I agree with them.

In the past couple weeks, things have been less tense. There were no more screaming matches about forcing someone to move against our will. The move was coming, no matter how many people still thought it was a bad idea.

Rhiannon still refuses to talk to Mom, but everyone else at least mostly moved on. For a while. Once the reality of our move sunk in, everything came right back up to the surface on moving day.

"We're looking for number one-fifty-one," Mom says as though we haven't all spent the last month staring at this house on Google Maps.

The street is ridiculously long due to a mixture of large front yards and the winds and bends of the road. We're going to be living right at the end of the cul-de-sac, just before a narrow pathway that cuts between houses as a shortcut to the park.

As the gray house we're about to live in comes into view, so does a boxy, white news van.

We're still a dozen houses away, but it's impossible to miss—and something I definitely didn't expect. All at once, I'm not that excited.

I wasn't supposed to have to talk to actual people I'm not related to today, let alone put on my publicity face. My heart races as a million possible scenarios spin through my head, they could ask me anything, and I might say something to make myself seem like an idiot.

"Looks like we've got company," Mom says, slowing down the car.

My body slumps down in the passenger's seat. I'm trying to hide even though we haven't been spotted yet.

"Seriously?" Reece snaps from the back. She only got about two hours of sleep the night before, and I don't imagine she's in the mood for surprises, even if there is a photographer involved.

"Mom," Reilly adds, a trace of a whine in her voice. "What are they doing here?"

"I'm sorry," Mom's eyes dart around nervously, looking for a way around being spotted. "I had no idea they'd be here. I don't even know how they knew *we'd* be here." She pulls the car over to the side of the road, hiding us behind a minivan.

I inhale slowly, willing myself to stay calm. It's not like we haven't dealt with the media before, but it's been years since anyone has really cared about the 'Fairview Four.' It's what they called my sisters and I after we were born—four identical baby girls born in a small town. When we were little, there were a couple of news features about us, as well as a half-hour documentary for some silly reality TV channel. Most people didn't care about the random identical babies at all, but there were also enough people cared *way* too much.

At least, by the time we were old enough to search for ourselves online, there was almost no one left who made a big deal about the anomaly of our birth.

Groaning, I bang my head back against the headrest. I want to be in my new room, in my new bed, organizing my bookshelves. I really just want to be anywhere but here, about to have to answer pointless questions about myself and how it feels to be back after all these years.

"They can't see us like this!" Reece shrieks, probably realizing that it's been almost a full day since she's even thought about applying lip gloss. "We look like we've been living under a bridge."

I didn't even think of that, now it's one more thing to worry about. We've been sitting in this car for hours, and we probably smell like it. Plus, I'm still wearing pajama pants. This is not exactly the first impression I was hoping to make.

"All right," Mom says after a minute, starting up the

car's engine again and simultaneously cutting off the whining in the back seat. "I've got a plan." Without saying anything else, she turns into the closest driveway, backs out, and takes the car back down Oakridge the way we came.

"Is the plan 'go back to Richmond'?" Reece asks, still sounding like she could use more sleep. "Because that's something I can get behind."

Mom backs up the car, and all at once, the tension in the car evaporates as we sneak back off the street, we're all on the same team again.

"That's a no. But at the very least you get some time to stretch your legs, eat, and get changed. If the Gazette is this eager to document our moving day, I expect they'll be willing to wait a little longer."

"Why do they even care about this?" I ask.

"People in Fairview loved being part of your story when you were little. I'm sure they're just excited you're back," Mom says.

"So, a slow news day, basically," Reilly says.

"Slow news day," Mom agrees. The sleeve of her sweat-shirt slips back down to her wrist as she makes a turn, and only then do I realize that she looks as frazzled as the rest of us. When she got in the car this morning she was stone-faced and unwavering to everyone's complaints, but it looks like the long ride has taken a toll on her too. Or maybe the welcoming committee.

She probably doesn't want them to see her like this any more than we do. Her hair is normally stylishly bobbed and obviously dyed, with thick blond and red streaks line her brown hair. By it's current disheveled state, I doubt she even thought to run a brush through it before we left Richmond this morning.

We park at the first fast food joint we find, a local mom-

and-pop-style diner called Lizzie's, immediately we go in to find food and spruce ourselves up. We have enough stuff with us for when we get settled. Each of us had a backpack of clothing, long enough to last until we unpack the rest of our stuff.

Reilly and Reece take half an hour to put on makeup, forcing their hair into identical messy buns. While their hair looks deliberate and styled, mine looks more like a tangle of brown hair that's sitting lopsided on top of my head.

"How do I look?" I ask, half joking.

Reece makes eye contact with me in the bathroom mirror, grimacing sympathetically. "Here," she says and turns toward me.

She takes only two minutes to transform my pathetic excuse for a hairstyle into a bun, one that looks exactly like hers and Reilly's. Without taking her eyes off me, she sticks her hand out behind her to Reilly, snatching frantically until she hands over the lip gloss to Reece. Within minutes, we all look like carbon copies of each other—which really doesn't take that much work. Anyone who doesn't know us will see three identical girls with long, brown hair, light-brown eyes, and slightly upturned noses. Somewhere on the road behind us is number four.

Reece, Reilly, and I aren't a complete set. Not without Rhiannon.

A few minutes later, we leave the bathroom to find Mom sitting with the food she ordered for us. We sit down around a pale-blue diner table and start to eat, it doesn't take long to realize that everyone else has noticed us. I focus all my energy on not looking anywhere beyond our table. I'm pretty sure ninety percent of the people here are just sitting and watching us eat, I try to avoid making eye contact with anyone beyond our little circle. They know who we are.

"We should call Rhi and give her a heads-up," Reece says with an exaggerated smile. She's seen our audience as well, clearly enjoying the attention way more than I am.

Mom pauses for a moment before fishing her phone out of the purse she had tucked between her and Reilly. "Hi, baby," she says so softly that she hardly sounds like my mother. "I just wanted to let you—"

When she pauses, I already know what happened. Rhiannon handed the phone over to Dad as soon as she heard Mom's voice.

"Hi," she says finally, her voice back to normal. "Yeah. It's fine. How far out are you? I just wanted to give you guys a warning about a news van in front of the house. I imagine they want to do a feature..."

While the two of them talk, I pick abandoned fries off everyone else's plates. When Mom hangs up, she looks defeated.

"Did Dad have any advice about dealing with the media?" Reilly asks, forcing a smile.

It's enough to force a genuine laugh out of all of us, giving our group an excuse not to talk about the cloud hanging over our mother. Even now, a month after having been told that we were moving back to Fairview, she's still taking Rhiannon's reaction hard. Mom loves being the good guy, the superstar, but this move didn't win her a lot of points.

For the first few days, we were all too angry to talk to either of our parents, it took less than a week before we were talking to Dad again. One by one at Reilly's urging, we all caved and started talking to Mom again too—grudgingly, in Reece's case. Rhiannon is still just as pissed off at her as she was a month ago.

She hasn't exactly been fun to live with. No one even

put up a fight when she said she wanted to ride with Dad in the truck, because that meant none of us would have to deal with her for nine blissful hours.

Fed, dressed, and feeling at least a little more in control, we pile back into the car without complaint. I still don't want to go through whatever is waiting for us, but I suspect I won't have to do too much. Reece and Reilly have never had trouble dealing with the spotlight. All I'll have to do is stand there and be a part of the set.

The crew see us as we pull into the driveway. Two men, one holding a bulky camera, and a woman wave frantically, as if maybe we didn't see them lying in wait. This is probably the entire staff of the small, local newspaper.

For a moment, I let myself forget them. We're here. A house three times bigger than the one we used to live in is sitting right in front of me, complete with dusty, blue paneling and a wraparound porch. It looks slightly crooked, but in a way, that makes it special instead of creepy. It's even prettier than the pictures we've seen.

For the first time, I can really imagine us living here. Once we get rid of our uninvited guests, that is.

"Ten minutes, a few smiles, and they'll get out of our hair," Mom says, bringing me back to the current predicament.

It's only once I'm out of the car that I realize there's a fourth member of the news group, someone I didn't spot before. Sitting cross-legged on our lawn, hunched over a composition book, is the slightly gangly form of a teenaged guy. There's a *guy* on my lawn! Okay, I'm definitely glad we stopped to get changed before showing up here, but his unexpected presence only increases the anxious static forming in my mind.

Whoever he is, he's completely absorbed in whatever he's scribbling down into his notebook, letting me stare for a moment too long. He looks tall with long, brown legs sticking out from a pair of old board shorts. Brown hair sits almost straight up with a few streaks of lime green visible from the back. It's hard not to wonder what he looks like from the front, even if part of me is even more nervous because there's someone my own age here now too, ready to welcome and judge the Fairview Four.

Look up...look up...look up, my mind chants at him as my eyes continue to bore into the top of his head. He doesn't look up; I'm not sure he even noticed when we pulled in.

Reilly tugs at my wrist, pulling me away from the guy and toward the three waiting adults who *have* noticed us. "Reagan, come on." She tilts her head sympathetically like she thinks I'm lagging, trying to avoid making small talk and getting my picture taken.

Mom waves us over from the front porch where she's standing with a perfectly coiffed blond woman in a dark-green suit.

We stop beside Reece on the stone walkway that leads up to the house. "And this is Reilly and Reagan. Girls, this is Mindy Harris with the Fairview Gazette."

"It's so nice to meet you both," Mindy says, her eyes only meeting mine for a second before they dart past us and back to the car. It's easy to see exactly what—who—she's looking for. "We seem to be one short." Mindy scrunches her lips together as she takes us in.

One, two, three. Not the four she was hoping for. I'd like to point out that we're actually two short, since my dad isn't here either, but like always, I keep my mouth shut.

"Rhiannon made the drive up in our moving truck with the girls' father," Mom says like she's apologizing. She has nothing to apologize for, especially not to this woman who gave us no warning she'd be here. "We didn't quite expect this today."

"Of course, of course! No trouble at all, Elaine." Mindy smiles, showing off a row of perfectly white teeth. "Will they be arriving soon?"

"Unfortunately, no. They're at least two hours behind us. We'd be happy to sit down with you tomorrow though, once the girls have had a little time to settle in."

I almost laugh at the comment. We moved out of the city, to an entirely new state, and it's only going to take us one afternoon to get settled in? Yeah, okay.

"If there's really no way to get Rhiannon here, I *guess* that will be fine," Mindy says. "Everyone is so looking forward to seeing the girls together in Fairview again. We did want to do this before the new school year starts."

"When's that?" Reece asks Mindy.

"September second." Less than two weeks. "Assuming the girls will be going to Fairview High." She can't be bothered to speak to us directly. Apparently, we're just supposed to stand here and smile for the cameras. Which isn't so bad, now that I think about it.

"'That's the plan. They'll be sophomores this year."

"Oh, wonderful. My son Kent is starting his sophomore year too." Mindy claps her hands together once. "He keeps a busy schedule, but I'm sure he'd be happy to show you around!" She beams at the three of us like we should be weeping with gratitude that her darling boy is willing to play tour guide.

Rolling my eyes is tempting—until someone shoulders his way past Mindy and sticks his hand out in front of me.

It's *him*. The guy with the green hair. Kent, Mindy's son. It makes enough sense that I already feel kind of dumb for mocking him in my head. It's not his fault his mom has ruined my day.

I blink slowly, looking back at him. From the front, he's even better than I imagined. His eyes are the same warm brown as his skin, they crinkle up a little as he smiles at me.

"Hi," he says, looking down at his hand expectantly. I'm still fixated on the near golden brown of his eyes, and the way they stand out unnaturally bright against the even tan of his skin. "I'm Kent. Welcome to Fairview."

Right! Hand-shaking. Frantically, I grab on to his hand, bouncing it up and down a few times before he moves to Reece and then Reilly.

"Nice to meet you," I mumble.

I don't think he hears me, but a second later, his eyes lock on mine. For a moment, he just looks at me. I will myself to do something, anything. His eyes almost seem to be teasing me. I can't help but smile before we both glance away. "Welcome to Fairview," I hear him mumble again. He's already moved on to shaking Reece's hand, but there's something about the way his head still tilts in my direction, clearly suggesting that maybe she doesn't have his full attention.

After he introduces himself to Reilly, the four of us all hang back as Mindy and my mom keep chatting about everything from the drive, to the move and the weather. No matter how short Mom's answers are, the questions seem to keep coming. Mindy is obviously hoping that if she holds us here long enough, she'll be able to wait out Rhiannon. But no one can out stubborn our mom.

The boy—Kent, I silently remind myself—smiles back at me, before getting dragged back into a conversation with his mother. I'm already reliving our entire interaction, trying to point out all of the ways I've already embarrassed myself.

But all in all, it wasn't terrible. We've officially met someone our own age in this own. And he's officially cute.

CHAPTER 2

I DIDN'T THINK I'd get even a wink of sleep the night before school starts, all of my obsessing must have taken more out of me than I'd realized. I wake up to the screeching noise Rhiannon has set as her alarm; It's supposed to be some sort of post-alternative-something-or-other music. It's awful.

Everything is awful.

I don't want to be awake.

Ugh.

I open my eyes to see my sister already flitting around the room. She offers me a half-apologetic shrug when I sit up a few minutes later. She's well aware of how I feel about her need to wake up this early. Every. Single. Day.

Once she turns off the shrieking alarm, my brain gradually begins to function again. I glance down at my phone. I could sleep for another half hour, and still manage to wake up with more than enough time to eat and get ready. But this is our first day at Fairview High, and now that I'm up, I'm wide-awake.

Rhiannon already has a cup of black tea sitting on her

dresser, the biggest kick of caffeine Mom will let her drink. I keep trying to tell her, sleeping in past six thirty is another way to gain some extra energy, but she never listens. No, she has too much to do and too little time to do it. Or something. Even when we don't have school, she can't possibly have any extracurriculars, and she doesn't know anyone besides our family in the entire state, Rhiannon always finds a way to stay busy.

Me? I'm a night person through and through. If my parents would let me, I could stay up until four every night playing City of Ages, reading, and talking to my friends online. Except then I'd sleep until noon every day. It's a trade I'm more than willing to make.

"Get up, get up, get up!" Enthusiastic fists bang against our door from the bathroom, connecting our room with the one Reece and Reilly share.

I groan in response and throw my pillow at the door. How is everyone functioning this early?

"We're up! We're up!" I answer when the banging refuses to stop.

Rhiannon walks over and opens the door, sending Reilly flying into our room.

"You're awake!" she announces, as though this is somehow news. "I've thought of something." She's already poking her head around in Rhiannon's closest. "What are you wearing today?"

I do a double take, considering that maybe I mislabeled whom I'm talking to. Usually Reece is the one who acts as the fashion police for the rest of us.

No, that's definitely Reilly. I can tell by the waves she's worked into her hair and the softer tone of her voice. Anyone who really knows us rarely has trouble telling us apart. Genetically, we might be the same, but we all have quirks and tells that mark us as individuals.

"No idea," I say, even though I have three outfit options sitting in my top drawer, ready to go. I just don't want my options picked over this early in the morning. "Why?" Suspicion clear in my voice, an inevitable side effect of pre-dawn fashion dilemmas.

"Not you, Reagan," Reilly says, not unkindly. "Rhiannon. I figure you'll be wearing your usual?"

"Pretty much the same thing you always wear," Rhiannon adds.

I stick out my tongue.

The two of them start talking, holding up various pieces of clothing for inspection to each other. I get out of bed—a decision I immediately regret as the floor is cold. Everything is cold.

In my dresser, all three outfits are exactly where I left them. Giving them another look over, I have to admit that they're all basically different versions of the same jeans-and-T-shirt combo which I wear most of the time. Still, I was going to put in at least a little effort for the first day of school. Maybe I'll throw on earrings or something.

Our new school isn't exactly huge, so odds are this is going to be my first impression with pretty much everyone I'll meet this year—an idea that equally excites and terrifies me. And maybe a second chance to make an impression on the one guy there I have been introduced to already. I hadn't seen Kent again in time since we'd moved in, but he's still ranking number one on my list of things to like about Fairview. I pop in a set of silver, star-shaped earrings. Why not?

"Ray!" Reece says. "Are you even listening?"

I'm clearly not. I didn't even see her come in the room. "No. Sorry. What's going on?"

"Well, I was thinking about it, and I talked to Reece."

"Yes..." I motion for her to speed things up. I don't have the patience for this stuff, especially before seven a.m..

"We need to squash this whole identical thing right off the bat. This town is way too into it already. We can't be too matchy or anything, and the first day is going to be the most important day to start doing that." She's wearing skinny jeans and a tight, forest-green tank top with a more generous V cut into the front than I would ever be brave enough to try. Not exactly what I had been planning to wear.

"We need to make a statement," Reilly continues for her, proving that the two of them have obviously discussed this before. "We need to dress like four different people and not the Fairview Four that everyone remembers from a million years ago."

"We're not even in that many classes together," I argue for the sake of arguing, still wondering why this is even a discussion. Being dressed similarly would have taken a major coincidence for any of us. And if anyone we meet today actually wants to learn to tell us apart, all they have to do is pay attention. To the way Reece is always moving in some way or another, or how Reilly is nice to absolutely everyone.

But it's the first day, and we've already obsessed over every other detail. I guess this is the only thing left.

"Yeah, but other people will have classes with more than one of us. We don't want to be mistaken for one another," Reece counters. "Then no one will ever learn to tell us apart."

"I think they will probably notice that we all look the

same." I peek over to Rhiannon for support, but she's too busy tying her hair back into intricate braids to chime into the conversation.

It's bugging me that they've put real effort into not looking the same. Yeah, I want people to be able to tell us apart, but looking alike is part of our identity as well. It's not like we'd ever really be able to hide it.

"Obviously." Reece says, "But we don't need to add to the sideshow."

"Which brings me back to my original question," Reilly says. "What are you guys wearing?"

We all end up dressing pretty much like we always do. It's been a long time since our parents have been able to force us into matching outfits. All of our styles have developed in protest of the years we had to spend in identical pink outfits. Though, if anything, my style is a lack of style.

If she can help it, Reece tends to wear what everyone else at school is wearing. Rhiannon practically picks a new fashion sense to play around with every month—for starting the new year, she mostly just looks badass with dark jeans, a halter top, and a fair bit of makeup. Reilly is the only one of us with a specific style. She likes light fabrics, loose-fitting clothes, and way too much floral print. I tend to go for jeans and T-shirts with random nerd references on them.

Too soon after, our outfits sorted and breakfast eaten, we head off to the Lion's Den.

Fairview High is about half the size of our old school, Ashmore, where we went freshman year. We step out of Mom's car and onto a long stretch of grass in front of the school. And it hits me—this is it. The move happened so quickly, but the wait to get to this very moment has taken forever. We've spent the last week living in a bubble, unpacking our things and going through many overly friendly neighborhood introductions. High school is a different game entirely.

From the looks of it, all my sisters are genuinely excited in spite of everything. Even Rhiannon seems ready for this. In the last week, she's been better than she was back in Virginia before we moved. A little less miserable, a little easier to be around, a bit more like old herself. She grunts a "thank you" to our mom before she pulls away, keen to start to her first day as Fairview's resident M.D. Even she can't hold a grudge forever. Besides, Mom seems genuinely happy to be back, which is always a plus.

Mom's new job is the reason we had to move back to Fairview in the first place. Like she keeps telling us, this town is a little... eccentric, and things don't always go the way you'd expect. There are a couple of smaller practices for family doctors scattered around the area, but the Fairview town council also employs an official town doctor. Even the house we live in—one my parents couldn't afford on their own—is a perk of getting that job. The house, the job, all of it has been around since the town was founded along with a few other bizarre traditions I thankfully have never had to participate in.

"Ready?" Reece asks.

People are already staring at the four of us standing outside in a row, not doing anything. If we're trying to keep a low profile, this might not be the best start.

No, nope, and no way are the only thoughts that cross through my mind at her question. I'm nowhere near ready, but I refuse to say that out loud. Instead, I work to convince myself that this isn't a big deal. It's school. I've done it a million times before. But no matter how many times I tell myself that I'm excited about this and things will be different here, when push comes to shove, I'm the same old Reagan I've always been.

If I let myself think about anything else—the people, the expectations, all the non-stop staring—I'll never move from this spot. Mom will come back at the same time tomorrow and find me right here. That's not going to happen.

Someone squeezes my hand. I glance beside me to see Reilly offering me a small smile as though she can tell exactly what I'm going through. That's kind of her talent—she knows what you're feeling without having to say anything, and she knows what to do to make it better.

"As ready as I'll ever be," I finally answer. "Let's do this."

———

I managed to swing my schedule so I am in a class with each of my sisters, something no one else managed to pull off—probably because they all picked their classes based on what they genuinely wanted to take and not based not wanting to be alone in a classroom full of strangers. Unfortunately, I only have three sisters and Fairview High has a five-period schedule. So I'm stuck with biology and lunch by myself.

Surprisingly, when lunch rolls around and Reece waves goodbye before heading to gym class, I'm not that worried. Lunch I can do.

At Ashmore, lunch involved brown-bagging my food and eating it as quickly as possible before meeting my best friend Nadine in the library. We would spend forty minutes reading or hanging out online whenever there was a computer free. My habits don't have to change now just because there's a whole new group of students to avoid.

The cafeteria is easy to find. I already saw it twice when navigating between my morning classes. This school really isn't that hard to figure out. There are a few hallways branching off in different directions from the main hub where the gyms, cafeteria, and administration offices are. The east side of the building, where most of the English, math, and science classes are, has a second floor, but everything else is all on the ground level.

I pull my lunch out of my bag, dropping the rest of my things onto the first free expanse of table I find. As soon as my butt hits the chair, I catch myself doing the same thing I did in history and then again in geography—looking for that telltale streak of green hair. But I'm one of the first handful of students to reach the cafeteria for third-period lunch and can tell right away that Kent isn't one of the many students already filling the space around me.

The cafeteria gets crowded quickly, countless backpacks and endless chatter, and soon enough, there are people heading right for me.

"Hi!" a voice chirps from directly beside me. "Which one are you?"

I turn to face a black girl wearing an impossible amount of jewelry and sitting way too close to me.

"Uh, hi. Reagan. I'm Reagan."

"Reagan!" another voice chimes in, this one belonging to a lanky guy in the process of planting himself down on the other side of what is supposed to be my corner of solitude. "The oldest one, right?"

I stare back helplessly, my mouth hanging open a little. Another person joins us at the table, but I don't even bother looking over.

"Sorry!" the guy says. "I'm Tom. Welcome to Fairview."

I shake my head slightly, trying to force my brain to

work again, trying to fight all of my instincts that are currently telling me to grab my stuff and run out of the room as quickly as possible. Which only seems like a plausible option until I realize that I would never live it down. Fleeing from the cafeteria isn't a great way to make friends.

"I'm Reagan," I say, blushing immediately. Of course I'm Reagan. That's literally the only thing I've said so far. Now I'm supposed to come up with something new. "Sorry. Today has been a little crazy. Hey."

"So was I right? Are you the oldest? Tell me I'm right." Tom asks, grinning.

"You're right," I agree. This isn't the first time I've been quizzed about birth order. But I am the oldest, and that gives me something they seem remotely interested in talking about, so I just go with it. "Then Reece, then Reilly, and then Rhiannon."

"Told ya!" Tom cries out, pumping his fist in the air. "My mom is obsessed with the Fairview Four. She's been talking about you guys since she learned you were moving back."

"Well, she should try watching soap operas or something," I say without thinking. "They're way more interesting."

Damn it. Insulting people—or their mothers—probably isn't the best plan. I was better off keeping my mouth shut, instead of opening my mouth like an idiot.

Thankfully, Tom laughs instead of getting insulted on his mom's behalf. "Ha! Yeah, I know it's kind of weird. But she loves all of those shows about weird families and stuff, so she always loved that you guys were from here."

"You're calling my family weird?" I ask, enjoying the joking nature of the conversation. And maybe the attention.

"No way," the girl beside me says. "It's cool. Four iden-

tical sisters? That's gotta be really rare. They're special."
She's staring at me. Why is she staring at me?

"Thanks?" I say, attempting a shaky smile.

"So, like, can you guys tell each other apart?" she asks.

I don't even know what this girl's name is. I should probably find this whole thing annoying, yet I somehow don't. I
will need to meet people in this school eventually, and I
might as well do it here and now before everyone here realizes we're really not that interesting. These three, random
people who I didn't know existed five minutes ago are
watching me like I have got something interesting to say. I
try to be as worthwhile as they seem to think I am.

"Of course!" I say with forced enthusiasm. "Pretty much
anyone who has known us for a long time can tell us apart.
The only people we're related to who can't are my dad's
parents, but they live in Ireland, so we almost never see
them. None of our friends had any trouble with it..." I say,
which isn't exactly true. Even our parents make stupid
mistakes sometimes, but that seems too complicated to get
into right now and would end up with a lot of me pausing
for way too long as I figure out how to explain.

The Q and A goes on for the rest of our lunch period,
and by the time the warning bell rings, I haven't even
touched my sandwich. I eat half of it in two bites.

"Crap." I swallow down the last bite of my food and look
up at the clock before starting to shove my leftovers back in
my bag. "I still don't know where my next class is."

"What do you have next?" Someone asks, briefly
distracting me from the building panic in my chest.

"Bio with Mr. Floren. In room..." Where did I put my
schedule? "341A. What does that even mean?"

"Don't worry about it," the guy sitting closest to me, Erik,
says. He seems nice enough, nodding along to the whole

Donovan family intro for the last hour and ten minutes like he actually thought it was anything other than dull. "I'm in that class too and can walk you there."

Grateful to him I exhale, relieved. I haven't exactly been looking forward to going by myself. Now, I have a kinda-sorta friend to go with.

By the time the four of us get up and split off in different directions, I'm feeling almost like I'm right back at Ashmore, surrounded by people I've known for almost my whole life. If I managed to start making friends after only half a day, I can do this.

I can totally do this.

Erik slips seamlessly into the crowd of students rushing between classes, I try to follow as close to him as I can without literally holding on to his body, but somehow, every move I make seems to go against the flow of traffic. I get shoulder-bumped by someone in front of me, and my heel gets stepped on by someone behind me. Twice. The second time, I almost lose track of my guide.

Right. Left. Left. I do my best to keep track of the route between the cafeteria and our destination, barely.

"Reagan!" a voice calls from directly beside me. I keep moving but whip my head around, turning to figure out who it is I've met that can already tell me apart from my sisters. "Hey!"

I lock eyes with Kent, who has his hand raised in a wave. He's already a few feet behind me, but the crowd won't let me stop. I start to smile, something I usually have to remind myself to do—note to self: look friendly—but someone bumps me from behind, propelling me forward. I have to turn around to keep myself from tumbling to the ground. By the time I glance back, he's gone. And now he probably thinks I'm a complete bitch.

But I don't have time to think about that now—though I'm sure I'll obsess endlessly about it later. Erik has stopped next to a puke-green door, our biology class. One more class without one of my sisters, and then the hardest part of the day is done. Probably even the hardest part of the semester since at least I won't be doing any of this for the first time ever again.

Here goes nothing.

CHAPTER 3

"MISS DONOVAN?"

I look up from the notebook I've been scribbling in to see the entire classroom staring at me, yet another downside of being the only Donovan in the room—extra attention.

I'd bet that, if I were any other new kid, the teacher wouldn't already know my name.

"Yes?" I answer, well aware that I should already know what it is Mr. Floren is asking of me.

My biology teacher is a large man with dark hair, with a face covered in scruff. He's the first teacher of the day who didn't make me stand up and introduce myself to everyone, like some kind of exhibit. I like him so far—or at least I did until he decided to call on me, pointing a giant neon arrow right at the new girl.

"Well, what do you think? Why is biology one of the most important studies for mankind?"

I blink. That's what we were talking about? I wasn't listening at all. It had all been the usual introduction to a new class stuff and my mind had started to wander without my permission.

This should be an easy one. Mr Floren has given me a softball question, but all I can focus on is that everyone else in class is waiting for me to give an answer. Mr Floren doesn't say anything, he just waits. He might as well crucify me right here in front of everyone.

A piece of paper shifts over to my desk.

This classroom is set up with two rows of double desks that also act as lab stations. When I first saw it, I wanted to turn around and wait to go in until the last possible second, so I could just take whatever seat was free rather than having to ask people if they'd mind sitting with me. But I didn't show up alone, and I couldn't exactly ignore Erik, so we sat together. It was that easy. Now he was feeding me the answer to Mr. Floren's question, via the piece of paper.

"Because we're essentially studying ourselves," I answer, attempting to look up as soon as I've read the paper. "Biology teaches us about how we work and what happens when parts stop working."

Mr. Floren's mouth twists up into a small pucker. He knows. He definitely knows what just happened. It takes every ounce of willpower I have to stop myself from breaking eye contact with him, tempted to stare intently at the textbook I've been ignoring all period.

"Okay," he says finally, his face relaxing into an easy smile. "Mr. Lagaor, can you name three areas of study that also utilize biology?"

I sigh in relief before looking over at Erik, mouthing a "Thank you." I can already see myself spending more time with him and his friends—hanging out at lunch and after school, studying for bio exams etc. He offers up a quick nod of acknowledgement.

My sisters will be pretty damned shocked to learn that I met people on my first day. Hell, my best friend from back home, Nadine, won't believe it at all. Between the two of us, we only made one new friend in our first year of high school. In Fairview, I've already potentially made three—and the day isn't over yet.

I should learn my lesson here and pay attention to the lecture, instead, I uncap my pen and scribble a note to Nadine. Last year, we had already memorized each other's schedules, and I probably would have been able to pass this to her between classes. This year, I'm going to have to wait until I get home and then type it up to e-mail to her.

I'm still writing when I hear my name. I look up to see Mr. Floren looking right at me—again. This time, there is no kindness or patience in his eyes.

Shit.

"I'm sorry you don't find my class worthwhile enough to hold your attention. May I ask what is so important?"

Shit. Shit. Shit. I look down at the paper in front of me, scrambling for ideas. "Notes?" I offer, but I know I sound pathetic.

"Fine. Let me see." He beckons toward me with his hand.

I would give every penny I have to actually have biology notes in front of me right now, every penny and probably all of my sisters'. I'm that desperate.

"I'm sorry," I say, all but confessing my sins. "It won't happen again."

"We have rules in this school, Miss Donovan. And those rules apply to new students and local celebrities alike. Mr. Shevaz, please bring me the notebook in front of Miss Donovan."

Erik winces apologetically but grabs my notebook without question. There's no time for me to do anything, and I couldn't if I wanted to. I'm glued to my seat.

When he clears his throat, my heart stops completely. He's going to read it out loud.

He's going to... I... this is the worst—what did I write? I can't remember what I wrote. Everyone in this entire class is about to hear it word for word. Suddenly it hits me. I absolutely want to die. That would distract them.

I can feel the blood surging through my body, every inch of me flushes a deep scarlet. They're going to hate me. Every single person in this room is going to hate me.

Please don't do this.

"Nadine,'" he reads, his voice perfectly clear. I try to stop myself from listening to focus on burying my head in my hands and blocking out the rest of the class, but it doesn't matter. "'I miss you! How's Ashmore? How's Elise? Tell me everything. I've already met some people, which is hard to believe. Reagan Donovan doesn't make friends—Reagan hides in the corner and plays City of Ages.'"

Oh god. I'd already forgotten I wrote part. So much for anyone here ever thinking I'm cool enough to hang out with. And the rest of it is coming back to me quickly. The worst part is yet to come.

"'Not sure what you'd make of Fairview. It's a really pretty town, and the people seem nice. The news crew when we got here was only the tip of the iceberg. Everyone at the high school is obsessed with us. They know our birth order, who our parents are and they care way...'" Mr. Floren pauses, clearing his throat. The entire room is perfectly still and quiet. "Well I think that's enough."

My heart is racing. My fingers are clutched onto the side of the desk and my eyes are glued to the whiteboard behind the his head. Is it over now?

No one is speaking. I can feel them all looking at me.

I have to do something, so I move my head and make eye

contact with the girl across the aisle from me. Then the girl beside her. I don't need to look any farther. No one is watching me with curiosity or wonder anymore. Now I can't tell what they're thinking. I can't bring myself to make eye contact with Erik. I can't bear to see what he thinks of me now.

Everything is ruined.

My eyes settle on Mr. Floren as he's closing my notebook. He won't look back at me. Maybe he realizes what a colossal dick he has been, mortifying the new girl on her first day. Maybe he'll look back on this moment for the rest of his life and remember my face. But it doesn't matter; the damage is done.

Get out. Get out. Get out.

I fumble for my bag as every nerve in my body screams, convinced I'm going to die at any moment. My mind is too focused on getting the hell out of there to think straight.

Fight or flight... I'll choose flight every time.

My chest constricts as soon as I reach the hallway and I break into a run, to getting some distance from that classroom. I can feel sweat dripping down the side of my face even though I'm shivering. Getting free of the room only does so much to calm me. There's no taking back what just happened.

I'm alone for now. How long until the next bell rings? I don't want anyone else to see me like this, and I sure as hell can't go back to class. I can't think clearly or do anything besides relive the last few minutes.

Heat rises in my cheeks again as I gasp for a much-needed breath. For almost a full minute, all of my effort goes to making myself inhale and exhale. Inhale. Exhale. In. Out.

Breathe, Reagan. Keep breathing. My body struggles to listen to anything I'm telling it to do.

I can't go back in there. Ever. Those people hate me now—hell, they'll all probably tell their friends and then everyone at this school will hate me and my sisters. Stuck up, self-involved—I can hear the whispers already.

I won't be returning to that science class, so what's Plan B? Coming up with something to do next helps my heart rate to slow back down. I'm starting to feel like a person again. Barely.

More specifically, I'm remembering that I'm a person who knows where the guidance office is.

I have to fix this!

"Excuse me," I say to the impossibly petite lady manning the desk when I get to the administration offices. In the distance, I hear the bell signaling the end of fourth period. "I need to drop a class."

"We don't rearrange schedules once the school year has started," she responds with a grainy voice. She doesn't even look up at me. She must get these kinds of requests all the time.

Damn it. At Ashmore, they could switch classes around for up to two weeks after a new semester started. This place has to be able to do something for me.

"Please..." I say. I have nothing more to add. I'm willing to beg if I have to.

At last, she glances up. I don't know if it's the desperation in my voice, or the Donovan-ness of my face that makes her take me seriously, but she lets me in to see the next available counselor. Within minutes, I'm free of Mr. Floren and sophomore biology.

Unfortunately, I know that the glares and whispers will follow me anyway. If only there was a way to transfer right out of this school.

I don't bother going to my last class of the day. Fifth period has already started by the time I finish dropping biology, replacing it with ... drama class. Oh god, did that really happen too? I can't even think about that right now.

That will be tomorrow's nightmare.

The last thing I need is to barge in late in the middle of class. With my luck, everyone from that bio class also has math fifth period, so I would be surrounded by familiar, judging faces as soon as I get in the room.

Rhiannon texts me within ten minutes, asking where I am. I'm surprised she hasn't already heard what happened. I tell her that I'm not feeling well and that I'm going home early, so they won't wait for me at the end of the day. While I'm walking my phone buzzes with new messages, but I don't bother to look at them. I have nothing to say for myself right now, and there's nothing they can tell me that will make this any better. They might even hate me too if people end up judging them for the fact that they're sisters with a socially inept moron.

Since I get lost and have to turn around three different times, the walk home takes me twice as long as it probably should. The town is small, but I still don't know my way around and so many of the houses look similar. Thankfully, Dad isn't home when I get there. Otherwise, I'd have had to offer up some sort of explanation about what I'm doing home already. Instead, I slink up to my room, crawl into bed, pull the covers up over my head, waiting for the world to end.

CHAPTER 4

"HEY. I BROUGHT YOU SOME DINNER." Rhiannon slips into our bedroom, closing the door behind her.

Since the school day ended earlier, none of my sisters have been up to see me. It's not the kind of thing that happens by accident, so they all heard what happened. They've been giving me my space.

I've been on my computer for the last five hours—playing as Kinsey, my level-seventy Wood Elf Witch in City of Ages. Being her makes it a little easier to forget about being *me*. At this point, I wish I could step through the screen and stop being myself entirely.

When Nadine logged on, I told her all about what happened. Failing miserably to laugh the whole thing off, I brought myself to tears all over again as I gave her the play by play of everything that happened.

At least I didn't have to sit through dinner with our parents asking all of us a million questions about our first day. If we had a good day, what our teachers are like and what we think of the other students.

It's awful., the teachers are miserable old assholes, and

everyone hates me. Not exactly the report they were looking for, but it's the best one I've got.

"Thanks," I say, before pushing my keyboard out of the way to make room for my plate.

I expect Rhiannon to put the food down and leave me to my solitude, instead, she sits on the bed beside me.

"Not really in the mood to chat." I keep my face purposefully composed, but Rhiannon doesn't even seem to notice. She stays put, sitting and waiting for me to crack first. "Seriously. I assume you heard about the note in Biology, I don't want to talk about it. At all. Ever. I'm an idiot."

"It's not that bad, Ray."

"Not that bad? I insulted everyone who has been remotely nice or interested in us—publicly. I just permanently killed my own social life in Fairview, now everyone probably figures we're all snobs who think we're a big deal and the center of the universe. Best first impression ever."

"Okay, it sucks. Maybe we could have saved the theatrics until everyone got to know us all a little better, but something like this was bound to happen with people watching us like this. To hell with anyone who says you're full of shit and that no one cares about the Fairview Four, because they *are* watching us that closely, and it is creepy. But you probably didn't need to say it out loud."

"Thanks," I mumble. "I feel much better now."

"Let me finish. I promise everyone will get over it. Probably faster than you'd think. This is the same old drama that happened at Ashmore, but now, you're the one getting the brunt of it."

"Except everyone in Fairview was already watching our every move. Now, everyone in that class is at home, telling their parents what happened. And then they'll tell their friends, who will tell the people they work with, and then everyone in town will assume we're awful and Mom will lose her job and..." I've run out of steam with this particular worst-case scenario, but there are a dozen more I've been playing through in my head.

"You might be overthinking this," Rhiannon says with only a hint of a smile in her expression.

For the first time today, I consider that I am. Rhi isn't one to try to make people feel better. She tells you what is on her mind and doesn't waste time pulling punches. Sarcasm is a different story, but there's never any question of what Rhiannon is trying to say. At least until recently.

"Really? You don't think people will still be talking about this—about me—tomorrow?"

"Oh, no, they totally will be. But the day after that, a few less people will be talking about that, and a week later, no one will even care anymore. It's cliché, but it's cliché for a reason. As for Mom, they begged her to take this job. They aren't going to take it back over some high school drama."

"Okay, so I find a way to avoid going back for a week or so?"

"Mom and Dad will absolutely go for that plan. School? Pah! Not that important."

There's the sarcasm.

"Do you think they've heard yet about what happened? They might take pity on me."

"Well, seeing as Reece gave them all the gory details at dinner, I'm going to say yes, they've probably heard about what happened."

I throw my head back, letting it smack against the back of my computer chair as I groan. Why is this my life?

"Well, I'm voting no on the whole 'you skipping a week of school' thing anyway," she adds. "I went through the entire day barely talking to anyone besides Reece at lunch.

You and I were supposed to have a class together, instead, I ended up having to sit by myself in all four of my classes for this semester."

I'd never say it out loud, but I'm not surprised Rhiannon didn't talk to many people today—in spite of all the extra attention our family has been getting. She has this vibe about her that warns people off, and her expression is always dead serious. For people who don't know her, it can still be kind of intimidating.

For people who have known her for her entire life, it can be kind of intimidating.

"You like sitting by yourself," I point out. Rhiannon means business when it comes to school, getting annoyed with anyone who tries to distract her in class since she was eight.

But I feel bad anyway. I'm not the only Donovan sister who's most comfortable keeping to herself. I get how important it can be to have someone who you know isn't silently judging you.

Now I'm a moron who doesn't know when to keep her thoughts to herself, *and* a crappy sister.

"Fine," I throw my hands up in defeat. "I'll be there tomorrow." It's not like I ever really had a choice in the matter. "So, tell me about it... What did I miss? Was it pretty much like any other math class ever?"

"Too early to tell," she says. "I'm getting the impression that all of our classes here are going to be easier than the ones at Ashmore."

"It's a little sick that you seem disappointed at that."

"Shut up." Rhiannon reaches over and pelts me with one of my throw pillows, narrowly missing my dinner, which I still haven't touched.

"When I got to class, there were only two seats left

together, against the wall in the back. Since you never showed, some random guy ended up sitting beside me. He didn't seem to get the hint that I wasn't interested in talking or hearing all about how... never mind. It's stupid."

"By any chance, was a guy with a green streak in his hair there?"

"Um. I don't think so. Why?"

Hope falls flat into the pit of my stomach. "Never mind. It was random. Where's my seat? There had to have been at least one left since I wasn't there."

"Two rows up."

"Trade with me," I offer. "You know you'd rather be sitting closer to the front, I'd rather be the one hiding in the back—even if that means finding new and creative ways to avoid overly chatty people. Also, I'm your favorite sister and you want me to be happy."

After the day I've had, I guess I'll be going out of my way to hide out in the back of any and all classrooms from here on out. If Rhiannon can help give me a head start, then I'm all for it.

"You make a compelling argument," she says, laughing. Her smile looks just like our dad's, whereas Reece, Reilly, and I smile more like, well, each other.

"This will sound incredibly cheesy," I warn her, "But it's kind of nice to see you like this again. You were so pissed for so long, so I wasn't sure if you'd ever get back to normal. Not that normal you smiles that much either."

At first, she scowls at me, but the expression quickly melts back into a grin. "I know," Rhiannon says. I'm glad I didn't send her spiraling back into miserable-bitch mode. "I'm getting there. There was just so much going on that you guys didn't know about."

My eyes widen a little before I can stop myself. There's news, and I want to hear it.

"What is it then?" I try to keep my tone casual, but this is the first thing all night that has truly taken my mind off what happened. There's a chance that pity alone will be enough to get her to start talking.

We've all asked Rhiannon about what has been up with her, and as soon as we do, she clams up, making it clear the conversation is over. Maybe, if I don't make a big deal out of how she's been acting these past weeks, she'll open up. Either that, or she'll do it to take my mind off my own personal misery.

Is it wrong to hope for that? Probably.

Rhi takes a deep breath, and I have no idea if she's bracing herself to explain everything she's been going through, or about to tell me to fuck off and mind my own business. I'm prepared for either.

"You swear you won't go blabbing this to anyone else?" she asks.

I can barely wrap my head around what I'm hearing. My first instinct is to squeal, pinkie swear, and promise to do whatever she wants if she'll just tell me all her secrets. That would be the wrong approach—Rhiannon is like a baby deer, always skittish and overly cautious. Anything could scare her off.

Honestly, I'm surprised it isn't Reece she decided to confide in. Reece has a code, and she'll never tell on one of her sisters or share any of our secrets without permission no matter how many times the rest of us screw up on that particular note.

"Of course," I nod solemnly.

"There was this guy." She pauses, considering her words. "There is this guy. I met him three weeks before

Mom told us we were moving, at that art festival I went to. You remember—the one I had to go to on my own because Reilly was sick and you guys wouldn't go with me."

A guy. All this time, it's been a guy she's been pining for.

I think my mind may have just exploded or I've somehow been teleported to a bizarre alternate dimension.

I swallow hard and try to come up with something to say. The last thing I expected was for Rhiannon to confess to anything to do with dating or guys. She's never shown interest in anything like that—guys, girls, dating, serious relationships, none of it. Though now I understand why it isn't Reece she's talking to. Even a hint of Rhiannon's dating would have our most romantically inclined sister dancing around like a moron, teasing Rhiannon behind the rest of our backs. She'd never hear the end of it until Reece had somehow taken over Rhi's entire relationship somehow. Which is, I'm fairly certain, the last thing Rhiannon would ever want.

For a full minute, Rhiannon says nothing. Eventually I can't take it anymore.

"Tell me about him," I prompt. "Who is he? What's he like? Are you guys still together even though..?"

"Yes. We're still together." Her tone is harsher than I'm expecting. "Just because we don't live in Richmond anymore doesn't mean we're not together. We still text almost every day, and we keep trying to Skype each other, but our schedules never match up."

My plan hadn't been to put her on the defensive, and I'm not sure how to undo the damage now. "Okay... I'm trying to be chill about this, but you're killing me here. What's his name? You can at least give me that!"

"Derrick," she says and then cracks a smile. It's the most

genuinely happy I've seen her look in a month. "He's a student at VSU. He writes music and works at an auto shop."

"Wait, what? How old is this guy?"

"Only two years older than us."

I nod and smile, stalling for time until I can come up with a response. Our parents have strict rules about who Reece can date, but that's because Reece would date pretty much anyone. The topic has never come up with me, and as far as I know, they haven't broached it with Rhiannon either. Yet, I'm somehow still confident they wouldn't be all that excited about her having a secret boyfriend who is already in college.

"Why didn't we ever meet this mystery guy? Derrick." My voice comes out dull and lifeless. I should try and make it sound like I'm teasing her or something, but I can't. It's hard to process any of this. Rhiannon has a secret boyfriend. An older, secret boyfriend. An older, secret boyfriend whose existence has been making her miserable for weeks already. I did not see any of this coming.

No part of me ever would have pegged Rhi for the type to become this obsessed over a guy, but I guess that, if it were me, I'd do the same thing. I can't imagine finally finding someone, then being forced away from them a few weeks later with almost no notice. Leaving him behind must have been awful, it's hard not to wish she had told us so we could help her if possible.

"We were waiting until after our birthday," she says. "Because of the age difference thing. But then Mom told us about the move. Everything got messed up so we never got the chance."

We turn fifteen in four days, something we all always assumed we'd be doing in Richmond.

I pick at my food as Rhiannon continues to tell me about Derrick, though the details all stay weirdly vague. She doesn't tell me where their first date was, how far they've gone, anything like that, but the tone in her voice tells me he's seriously important to her. Even now, two weeks since they've seen each other, he's there at the forefront of her mind—a place usually reserved for boring stuff like classes and extracurricular activities that will benefit her college applications. I've never seen this side of my sister before. I'm not sure what to make of it.

I wish I could talk to Reilly, or even Reece about what has been going on with her. I'm not sure what I'm supposed to do for her to make this better-- to make it hurt less that she has to be apart from this guy I've never met.

Rhi needs to see that Mom isn't the enemy here. Now I can finally understand why she's been so incredibly, relentlessly angry. I can't see a way to fix any of it.

But, I keep my mouth shut both with Rhiannon during dinner, and when I bump into Reece in the bathroom that night. I desperately want to say something, but it's not my secret to share.

CHAPTER 5

WHEN THIRD PERIOD rolls around the next day, there's no question I will *not* be going back to the cafeteria. The mature and socially responsible choice would be to face Erik, apologizing to him and his friends for being an ass, but I'd end up stuttering out something that makes zero sense, before running at full speed to escape whatever disaster was coming for me next.

Maybe we all could have been friends, but that's not going to happen anymore. Whatever, I've still got Nadine and Elise back home, and people I've known online for years. Meeting *new* people isn't really a big deal.

For now, the only logical plan is to hide out at my locker until I finish my sandwich, then disappear to the library. wherever that is. I take five minutes to eat with my head practically shoved inside my locker, during which I don't turn around once. I've somehow managed to get through the first half of the day without making eye contact with anyone, teacher or directly related to me so there's no need to stop now. The day has been mostly painless. I'm starting to think the people in my first two classes have no idea which sister I am, let alone if I'm the moron who had her note read out loud in class yesterday.

Thankfully at lunchtime, the library fills with other students just like me—people with zero interest in interacting with anyone else. I grab a book at random off the fantasy shelf, heading for a desk in the back. Looks like everything is status quo in Fairview after all. Things will be fine. Kind of boring, but fine. I can do boring.

It's when the clock ticks down the last ten minutes of my lunch period that I start to sweat. I may have avoided going back to Mr. Floren's class, but now I've created a whole new thing I need to get through.

Drama.

I'm pretty sure Hell has frozen over, and there are pigs flying around Fairview because Reagan Lee Donovan is now enrolled in the dramatic arts. The only thing worse that I can imagine is having to walk back into room 341A.

So, drama it is.

From what I can tell, most of the art rooms are on the opposite side of the building from the science classrooms. I'm not sure what they're trying to say with that particular arrangement, but it means I don't run into anyone from yesterday's nightmare class on my way to the drama room.

Finding the drama room is all too easy, however, I would have loved an excuse to put this off for just a little longer. Beside the heavy, black door is a bulletin board covered in pictures from past performances and a sign-up sheet for the drama showcase that is being put on at the end of the year. Something I have zero interest in. Still, since there are still a few minutes before class starts, I take some time to pretend like I'm seriously considering putting my name down.

Never going to happen.

The warning bell rings, and my time is up. It's now or well...now. There's no choice but to walk into that class-room—which is probably full of extroverted, obnoxious, hipster kids—and pray I don't end up having to run out of this fourth-period class like I did the last one.

I walk into a classroom with no desks or chairs. It's unlike anything I've ever seen before. The floor is a cheap, gray carpeting and there's a thick, black curtain running along a track down the middle of the ceiling that I assume can be pulled into place, dividing the room into a stage and an audience sections. Which again begs the question of what the hell I'm doing here. I don't even like talking to people, let alone performing for them.

Along the back wall are a variety of wooden boxes painted as black as all the concrete walls, which is to say mostly black but obviously worn down by time. The other side of the wall is covered in a large chalkboard, in front of which stands a man who I assume must be the teacher, Mr. Sullen.

"Excuse me," I say.

He turns toward me, revealing a face covered in a short, silver beard, straight hair, also silver, reaches down to his chin when not tied back into a short ponytail. Not an orig-inal vibe for a drama teacher, but it suits him. His face beams with a warm smile, and an intelligent glint in his eyes.

"I transferred into your class, so I missed the first day." I hand him my transfer slip, which he takes with a smile.

"Well, we're thrilled you've decided to join us"—he glances down at the sheet in his hand—"Reagan. Welcome."

"I've never taken an acting class before," I admit out of nowhere. "I'm not going to be any good at this."

Mr. Sullen looks at me with studious eyes. "Well technically in this class, we study great works of the past as much as we do performance. And I suspect you might do better than you think on the acting side of things. Give yourself a little room to experiment and you might be surprised."

I want to assure him that, no, I really will be very, terrible at this, but before I can, the final bell rings.

"Now, if you don't mind taking a seat with the others, we'll get to work." Mr. Sullen turns away from me to face everyone else, people I haven't had a chance to look at yet.

Even though this is the only class where I'm guaranteed not to run into anyone from biology, odds are every single person in this room has heard about what happened by now. But when I move away from the chalkboard, no one is watching me. All eyes are on Mr. Sullen, who is already animatedly talking about some guy named Godot. I sit down beside a girl with shiny, black hair that reaches to the floor, she even offers me a quick smile before returning her attention to the lecture.

Five minutes into class, Mr. Sullen is passionately discussing something I can only assume is a follow-up to whatever they talked about yesterday—I'm completely lost. Just as I fall deeper into confusion, the door creaks back open, letting a small sliver of light into the otherwise dim room.

At first, I can't make out who has come in, but by the time the person reaches the blackboard, handing a stack of papers to Mr. Sullen, I recognize the lanky form and the green hair stripe. Kent.

I look at the floor, then at the girl sitting beside me and then back at the front of the room. I don't know what to do with my hands. Even when I'm not looking at him, I'm aware of Kent's presence in the room.

Okay, I'm freaking out.

I'm sure Kent hasn't so much as looked at me since he walked in the room. Maybe he's just dropping something off because he has Mr. Sullen for a different period. It's possible he won't stay.

How did I never consider that it was possible he'd be here? This is too small a school for our schedules to be so drastically different that I'd only ever see him passing me in the hallway.

Without once looking back, Kent sits down in the front row beside a short Asian guy and a brown-haired girl with blunt bangs.

Kent is right here, right now, and I had no idea this was coming. I spent the entire day trying to avoid looking at anyone and ignore all the people I'm sure were talking about me. Today, there has been a non-stop replay of yesterday's disaster going through my head, which probably took away from all the other obsessing I'd usually be doing. So I never even considered that Kent might be in this class.

In theory, this is great. In practice... I have no idea what to do or where to look or what to say. Really, I shouldn't be thinking about this. After all, I've spoken to the guy once, so pretending Kent isn't in the room is as good a goal as any.

Despite his presence, I've been close to an ideal student so far. Always perfectly focused on my teachers and what is going on in the lesson—just in case the universe wants to test me again. Of course, no one has called on me for a single thing today, but when they do, I'll be ready. I will not be writing notes to Nadine or to anyone else. I try to adopt that same attitude and give my full attention to the drama less, especially since I'm not sure if I will have to get up and act in front of this whole class at a moment's notice.

God, my brain doesn't even know what to freak out about anymore. There are too many options.

At least once a minute, my eyes dart to Kent's back. He's wearing a blue and white, plaid T-shirt. I didn't catch what was on the front, but there's no question that the pale color looks great against his skin.

Pay attention, Reagan.

I do. Or I try to, but Mr. Sullen has gone off on a tangent about Syria and liberal arts, which I somehow don't think is going to be on any of the tests. When he does get back on topic, it's to give the class its first assignment. Good. Something I can focus on besides willing Kent to turn around and notice me.

The remaining hour of the class is dedicated to flipping through various plays from the bookcase beside Mr. Sullen's desk. Besides smaller assignments and pieces throughout the next few months, the class will split into two groups to put on a performance at the end of the semester, so we can all make our case for what we think the class should do.

I join the huddle of students, careful to avoid brushing into anyone, grabbing the first book that my fingers brush against—a script adaptation of Alice in Wonderland. Then I retreat with it to a corner. For a first drama class, this really isn't so bad. Sitting in a corner and reading is my strong suit. Reading a version of *Alice in Wonderland* I've never seen before? Even better.

After a few minutes go by filled with only a few whispers and the sound of pages flipping, a sharp whistle interrupts my feigned concentration.

"I changed my mind. This is boring!" Mr. Sullen says, throwing his hands up in a dramatic display of dismay. "Everybody, stand up, grab whatever book is closest to you, figure out what it's about, then hold it up in the air for all to see."

At once, the whole classroom springs to life around me

as though something like this were totally expected. I scramble up and do the same, silently dreading whatever's coming next. At least I already know what *Alice in Wonderland* is about. I could go over the plot, point by point, in my sleep.

"Every year, we do this same exercise with the sophomores," Mr. Sullen says. "And every year, it goes exactly the same way. You teenagers are an awfully predictable bunch. Tomorrow, most of you would have come to class with either something written by the Bard, something involving a great deal of kissing scenes, or something totally obscure—and I assure you, many obscure plays are obscure for a reason."

While we're all standing around holding books above our heads, our teacher is pacing around the front of the room, seemingly having forgotten what he asked us to do to begin with.

"Tomorrow, I'd ask you all to tell the rest of the class why you feel like the play you've selected is the best selection," he continues, "You'd make your case while hemming and hawing, half of you only having remembered the assignment during your lunch period. In the end, we'd choose Shakespeare, but one that also works in a few romantic interludes."

"So, let's cut that all out right now, shall we? If you're holding anything written by the one and only William Shakespeare, please put your book down on the floor."

I don't know what he has in mind, but I suddenly wish I'd picked up Hamlet instead. Whatever's coming next, I don't want to be involved.

"Okay. Now, obviously, we have some requirements that will need to be met. If the play you're holding has less than five speaking rolls, put it on the floor."

Alice, Rabbit, The Queen, Cheshire, Caterpillar—I can list five characters in this script without even looking. I keep my book up in the air and hope Mr. Sullen has some sort of objection to anything that Disney has adapted.

This set of instructions takes a bit longer to do. Ultimately, Mr. Sullen ends up helping most of the people still holding books along, telling them which ones fit his criteria.

When the second group of people put their books down, Kent finally looks up and notices me standing there like an idiot and trying to pretend like I haven't noticed him. He raises his eyebrows in silent greeting. I offer a tight smile back because that's all I can manage without turning my face deep scarlet.

As the minutes pass, Mr. Sullen continues to narrow down the selection until only three plays remain in the running, letting everyone else sit down. Alice in Wonderland is still a contender. Across from me, Kent and a guy with impressive-looking dreadlocks are still standing as well.

With each set of instructions, I hoped that my book would be knocked from the running, but, of course, I'm not that lucky. I'm never that lucky. Hell, with my luck, my play will be selected and I'll have to take the lead or something ridiculous like that, simply because I was the one stupid enough to be holding this book when the man teaching our class decided he was bored. The only small concession so far is that we don't have to hold the books over our heads anymore.

"So what do we have left?" Mr. Sullen asks. We each turn our books toward him.

"Twelve Angry Men, Alice in Wonderland and"—he frowns—"The Wizard of Oz. How have we not knocked all musicals out of the running already? There is not one single chance of me listening to you lot try to sing 'We're Off to See the Wizard' all semester. You can sit down, Jermaine."

Finally, I have to look up at Kent. The last man standing and he's already watching me. When our eyes meet, his face pulls itself into a goofy smile. He looks completely relaxed, as though he already feels right at home here in Mr. Sullen's classroom.

"Now, I'd usually make the two of you state your cases, but since you were holding these two plays at random, let's open this discussion up to the entire class. So, what do we think?"

If I had been expecting people to raise their hands to speak in this class, I would have been disappointed. Of course this classroom functions with everyone simply saying whatever pops into their heads. The classroom starts discussion the merits of silly versus serious, costume options, commercial appeal.

I continue to stand in front of everyone like an idiot, casting sideways glances at Kent, who has moved to stand beside me near the blackboard.

"True," Mr. Sullen says, agreeing with someone. "But we could easily have ladies playing the roles of men. A challenge for our costume department, certainly. Not that we have a costume department. Minor detail."

"But why should we have to do a play only about men when there's an alternative that offers both genders roles?" someone says, which is what I was thinking—both my mom and Rhiannon can rant about gender equality for days if someone gives them a chance. The voice of whoever weighed in even sounded a lot like my sister.

The whole class turns to look at me.

Did I say that out loud?

"An excellent point, Reagan." Mr. Sullen is grinning at me.

I'm not sure what compelled me to contribute, but I feel myself stand up a little straighter.

"Okay," Kent says, "but wouldn't it offer more of a challenge to do Twelve Angry Men than a children's book?"

"When you join the Oxford Drama Program, you and your challenge will be very happy together. We're like fifteen, and *Alice in Wonderland* is way more fun," challenges the girl who was sitting with Kent earlier.

Someone laughs, and others murmur their agreement.

"Well, let's take it to a vote then, shall we?" Mr. Sullen announces.

A few minutes later, two-thirds of the class has voted in Alice in Wonderland as our project for the semester, and somehow, I find myself standing in front of the class, once again holding a book over my head.

How did I get myself into this?

"Hey! Reagan!" Kent yells after me as soon as I escape into the growing swarm of the hallway after class. "I saw Reilly and Reece yesterday, but I never got to say hi to you. Now you're in my class!" He seems actually excited by the idea.

I wait for him to bring up the whole reason I transferred in the first place, but the bomb never drops.

"Yeah. They let me transfer in even though classes have already started. Mr. Sullen seems interesting. I definitely never had any classes like that back home," I say. Words are spewing from my mouth without warning. I almost want to blabber on endlessly to keep him here. Standing near me in the hallway, as we get pushed closer and closer together by the throng of moving students. Part of me wants to disappear into that same crowd, so there's no chance of me saying something moronic.

"Then you've never had a drama class before."

"Was it that obvious?"

"Nah. It's just that here, drama classes are always kind of nuts. Mr. Sullen is a lot of fun, and a little moody that's for sure. But you did great."

"Well, no one's asked me to actually act yet. There's still lots of time to self-implode."

"That's the spirit!" Kent says with a laugh. "I've got to get to class. I'll see you tomorrow!" Kent says, smiling and turning away from me.

Yes! I scream inside. And the very next day, and the next day and then all the weeks after that. I will see him nearly every single school day for the rest of the year. Kent actually acknowledged that I exist outside of his mother's newspaper. I try to think of something smart to say but all I do is nod, slightly dumbstruck, watching him walk away.

I never thought I'd see the day where I was looking forward to drama class. Yet, here it is.

CHAPTER 6

THE END of our first week at Fairview also marks the end of our fourteenth year. When classes start up again on Monday, we'll be fifteen—something I feel like I've been waiting forever for.

As we walk home together on Friday afternoon, we try to figure out our long-overdue birthday plans. We've all met people this week, people we could potentially be friends with—even me, which is a small miracle facilitated entirely by drama class. We're all in agreement that inviting anyone over or anything like that would seem desperate this early on, we're better off making this birthday Donovan only, then going all out for number sixteen once we've been here for a while—or Mom has someone been talked into moving us all back to Virginia, where we can celebrate with friends we've known our whole lives.

"Pizza and movies," I suggest not for the first time.

Reece, who is walking beside me, rolls her eyes. "Boring."

I expect her to go on some big spiel about all the things

we could probably convince our parents to do for us out of guilt, but she casts her eyes down and says nothing.

"I don't hear any better ideas," Rhiannon says. "What options do we really have? Everything in Fairview is made for old people. Maybe there's something going on in town, but do we want to go and have everyone gawk at us on the anniversary of the day the Fairview Four were brought into the world? Hell, they probably already have a parade scheduled. Right Reagan?"

Her fingers poke me in the back, "Not funny," I snap halfheartedly. I am so not ready to joke about my rant on Fairview's obsession yet. The rest of our first week was less awful than I'd expected it to be. I still wish I'd kept my big mouth/pen shut.

A gray sky looms overhead as we make the turn off Main Street, towards Apple Road and Oakridge. By the time we reach our house, we're still no closer to deciding what we want to do with our birthday the next day. A few raindrops have sputtered out of the sky, leaving speckles on the sidewalk as we near home.

Eight hours later, the drizzle has grown into a full-on thunderstorm. The wind blows the water away from the front of our house, leaving me cozy and dry on the porch to count down my last few minutes as a fourteen-year-old.

Everyone else in my family finds rain either depressing or massively inconvenient to both style and outdoor activities. Not me. There might be nothing I love more than the sound and smell of a storm, even the feeling of it on my skin when the weather is right is amazing to me. Sometimes, the rain leads me to thinking too much, but tonight, it leaves my mind blissfully empty. A blank slate to start the new year.

"Hey, what are you doing?" Reilly asks, popping her head out of the partially opened front door.

"Rain," is my only answer. I'm half mesmerized by the tiny droplets falling in front of the streetlight and the sound of water pouring through the house's old gutters.

Part of me hopes she'll go back inside, but when she says, "It's almost time," I'm glad she didn't. A thousand thoughts come rushing back into my head as I look over at my sister. Reilly's hair is tied back in a French braid that falls down to her shoulders, where it meets her bright-purple nightshirt.

I can't believe I would have forgotten our birthday tradition. It must be the new house that's messing everything up.

"Which room?" I ask, getting up off the deck chair.

"Yours. Reece is waiting upstairs since Rhiannon is asleep already."

Of course she is. Rhiannon sleeps like clockwork.

As soon as we get back to my room, Rhiannon sits up in bed, "What time is it?" she asks.

"We've got six minutes," Reece answers then shoves herself into Rhiannon's bed with her.

The two of them lie down and snuggle in beside each other, waiting. Six minutes until our fifteenth birthday and I almost missed it, not that my sisters ever would have ever let that happen.

I get into my own bed where Reilly has already curled up at the end like a cat, I slide under the covers, click off the lamp on my night side table and plunge the room into near darkness.

"What do you guys think?" Reilly asks. "How was fourteen?"

"Let's see... We started high school. Literally on our birthday last year. We moved. Reilly had her first kiss," Rhiannon says, listing off some of the more exciting moments of the last twelve months.

Beside her, Reece makes kissy noises. I can't help but giggle, somewhat wishing this portion of the recap would end already. This year, like every year, I have nothing to contribute on the romance side of things.

"I fell madly in love," Reece declares with no hint about who she's talking about. I'm pretty sure she fell madly in love four times in the last six months. "I give fourteen five out of five."

"Seconded!" Reilly calls from her spot at my feet.

"You guys give every year five out of five," I argue. They are both the type of people who will make the most out of every single year of their lives. "I'm calling it a three-point-five. Eventful, but not always in a good way."

"Three stars. Tops," Rhiannon says, I'm surprised it got that high of a rating from her. Although, now that I know she met a guy she actually cares about, that could easily explain the extra stars even if she isn't going to explain her reasoning to Reece and Reilly. "This isn't where we were supposed to be starting fifteen. We went backward instead of forward. Right back to where we started."

From a few feet away, I see the screen on Reilly's phone come alive, lighting up our side of the room. "One minute!" she says, giving my foot a quick squeeze.

For the most part, the year has been good. No complaints—not even one about the move. I'm just not sure it was a year I'll remember ten years from now—minus the whole going-back-to-Fairview thing. Even starting high school didn't end up being that big of a deal. There were a lot more people than there had been in our middle school, but freshman year was a lot like the year before, and the year before that. At least for me. I read a little more, and I started playing City of Ages, spending most of my time with Nadine and Elise. Same old Reagan, same old life.

"Happy birthday!" my sisters yell out together.

I mumble something that sounds like happy birthday once I realize I wasn't watching the seconds count down with everyone else. For a minute, we lie there in silence, thinking about what fifteen would mean for us or just falling back asleep.

"So, any guesses for this year?" Reece asks.

"We'll hit the front page of the Fairview Gazette... again," Reilly says, laughing.

Mindy got her precious interview and photo-op once Rhiannon and Dad showed up that is. Enough for a full front-page spread, including a picture of Mom and Reece moving boxes, Reilly chatting with the neighbors, and me and my sisters sitting in birth order on the front step. I have a sinking suspicion there will be something in the morning's paper, which will only bring my note to Nadine back to the forefront of everyone's minds at school.

"Mom will keep trying to convince us of how great it is to be part of such a close-knit community," I add, using my fingers to form quotes around the last part.

"Dad will renovate every room in the house, starting at least four novels, none of which he'll finish." Rhiannon is probably right, I can't help but wince at that last one.

Our dad had to give up his teaching job at the university back home to move out here for Mom, and there are no post-secondary teaching jobs available within an hour of Fairview. He keeps saying that this is the universe giving him a chance to write his novel, but we all know he'd rather be teaching.

"Reagan will finally kiss a boy," Reilly says, giggling like this is the funniest thing in the world.

An image of Kent flashes through my mind. In my head, he's wearing a shirt that both perfectly ties together the green in his hair and the gold in his eyes while also clinging to the muscles in his arms.

All week he's been making a point of including me in conversations in drama, and introducing me to people. He's acting like we're already friends instead of people who met for ten seconds on my lawn before school started. And that's something.

But not something enough to report back to my sisters with.

"No, she won't," Reece scoffs. "I'm calling it now. No action for Reagan until seventeen and a half."

I try to come up with something to joke back or poke fun at her for, but everything I come up with of sounds a little too mean, and that isn't what tonight is supposed to be about. It's our birthday, and that's important to me. To all of us. Even if I never act like the eldest sister, I came into the world first and I've always secretly worked to make sure our birthday is a day about the four of us together.

"I didn't make the soccer team," Reece says so quietly that I'm not sure I heard her right. I didn't even think about if Fairview had a team.

"What? No way!" Rhiannon cries out, indignant on our sister's behalf.

"I didn't realize tryouts had happened yet," Reilly says. "They're insane if they can't see how great you are. Idiots."

"They happened the day after we moved here, before the school year had even started." Reece says this like it's no big deal, but there's no question of just how big a deal this is. It's Reece and soccer.

"Oh," I say, not sure of what else to add. "Well, that's different then, right? I'm sure you're way better than anyone they've got."

"I guess," Reece says. "But that doesn't make it any

better. I'm going to fall behind. And when it's time to try out for the upperclassman team next year, none of the coaches will have any idea who I am. I might never get to play again."

I want to point out that there might be local teams she can join, but that's not the point. I don't pretend to know the first thing about sports. Playing soccer is where Reece shines. She plays rugby and volleyball too, but she doesn't come alive the same way as she does when she's kicking around a soccer ball. She's good at it. Really good. In a way that makes people wonder what exactly happened to the rest of us. We have the same nature, the same nurture, but none of the talent. Not that I could ever see myself getting into sports even if I wasn't hopeless at them.

Richmond had a pretty big kiddy soccer league when we were little, and my parents tried putting us each on a different team when we were seven or eight. The idea was to give us all the chance to do something away from our sisters, even if it meant driving to four different practices every week.

I fell on my face in front of everyone on the very first day. At first my parents insisted I had to stick it out. Then they saw my first game. Whether it was how miserable I looked or how bad I was at actually connecting my foot to the ball... they never made me go back. Reilly and Rhiannon at least finished out the season. Reece never stopped.

Until now.

I have no idea what to say, and from the sounds of it, Rhi and Reilly aren't doing any better. We go to Reece's games to cheer her on. Okay, Rhiannon and I are usually dragged kicking and screaming to her games, but we and get the basics of how it all works! The only thing is I couldn't tell you about what's involved in moving up the ranks in the high school soccer world. Reece has never said it, but she's thought about playing in college.

When no one else says anything, one by one, my sisters' breathing all takes on the rhythmic inhale and exhale of sleep, leaving me alone with my thoughts. I want to come up with some kind of real prediction about what this year could mean for me, but I honestly don't know. That's kind of exciting all on its own.

A month ago, I would have agreed with Reece's prediction for my love life this year. Like Rhiannon, I'm not exactly known for my romantic adventures, I have a habit of keeping to myself—which doesn't give me a lot of opportunities to meet guys I have anything in common with. Fifteen would have passed unnoticed on the dating side of things. Maybe it still will.

But I'm feeling weirdly optimistic.

I drift off to sleep thinking about Fairview and everything that comes with it, I can't help but think that anything is possible. Anything.

"Rise and shine, girls!" Dad's voice booms into our room.

Startled out of sleep, I flail like a maniac, thwacking Reilly in the head with my foot. She must have spent the entire night curled up there.

By the time I open my eyes, my mom has joined him in the doorway to my room. Both are smiling way too much for this early in the morning, no matter what day it is.

Mom is wearing an oversized sweater and looks more comfortable than I'm used to seeing her. My dad is clean shaven and a little taller than average, the effect emphasized by long limbs. His deep voice never quite seems to match his thin frame. He has light-brown eyes and thin, brown hair that matches mine and my sisters'. With the exception of our noses, which we got from my mom's side, we look like Donovans through and through.

"Good morning," Mom chirps, her short frame is practically bouncing with energy. She's usually more excited about our birthdays than we are, I can't fault her for it—having four tiny people plucked out of your body in one day is no small accomplishment.

The day flies by like all birthdays do—too quickly but full of silly memories like all the years that came before, this time just in a new location. Reilly and Reece make a point of Instagramming the entire experience with me being their camera person. I'm usually the one holding their phones so they can actually be in the pictures they're posting. There's an instance where Reece takes a selfie with all of us crammed into the frame, which I make her send to me.

After dinner, we sit in the living room surrounded by wrapping paper. As expected, Mom and Dad went way overboard in an attempt to appease us about the move, something I'm already all but over.

I got a massive gift certificate to the local bookstore, some new clothes that look exactly like everything else I own, a new video card for my computer, and one of four matching new desks that will go up into the still-empty space in the attic, which our parents have promised we can do anything we want with, but they still heavily imply that we should be using for studying, staying out of their hair. My sisters all got equally overloaded piles of presents. It's excessive by any stretch of the imagination, but I'm not about to complain.

The conversation finally lulls as we all look over our new things and show off our new stuff around in the makeshift circle we're sitting in. My mother, being who she is, can only let the quiet sit for so long before she has to interrupt with her favorite story. It's the story of us.

"It was a dark and stormy night," she starts, eliciting eye rolls from Rhiannon, Reece, and me. Reilly and Dad just smile along, encouraging her—suckers for sentiment.

"And by night, she means afternoon," Dad says right on queue. "The surgery was scheduled for the afternoon because most doctors prefer to book these kinds of things during office hours, and you had a lot of doctors. None of which were more excited to meet the Fairview Four than their very own mother."

"Our," Rhiannon says. "Our mother. We were there, remember? You don't have to tell the story like you're still being interviewed by the Gazette." It sounds snarky, but we all know she's only teasing.

This part of the birthday tradition happens at a different time every year, and it goes more or less than same as it did before—only with different parts embellished depending on how nostalgic my parents are feeling when telling the story.

Our job is both to play along and give our parents a hard time as is our sacred duty as their children.

Before snuggling in beside Reilly on the couch, Rhiannon shuts up. At the same time, Reece reaches over to brush my back with her toes, using her insane flexibility to make a connection between the two of us from our spots on the floor. As my parents go on about our birthday, I revel in my favorite part of the day—the history I share with my three favorite people in the world.

Every year on September ninth, it feels a little like it

must have been during those days and weeks after we were born—like we're all still part of one greater whole. The older we get, the more we all stretch into our own identities, but I'll always love the reminder that we started out together.

CHAPTER 7

THE NEXT MONDAY AFTER SCHOOL, I log into City of Ages as soon as I get home. Monday is dungeon crawl day, it has been for almost a year now. Back when we first started playing the game, Nadine and I had joined a big guild to find people who would help us figure the game, as we had no clue what we were doing. Most of our friends from the group have stopped playing, but there are still five of us that meet every single Monday, and, most weeknights usually playing through some quests.

My obsession wasn't a part of myself that I saw myself sharing with any new potential friends anytime soon— Reece had made it very clear that being a super nerd isn't a selling point, especially when it comes to making new friends.

Once my character, Kinsey, makes it to our usual meeting spot, I spot the others. H3LLFYRE, Frankendogg, and Pizzaz are all in college, and had gone so far as to schedule their classes around having Monday afternoons off since Nadine and I didn't have any real say in when we had to be in school. And sure enough, all three were there waiting for me.

Pizzaz: Hey, Kinsey. We're about ready. Any sign of LuckyBug?

Using my keyboard, I scan the area, noticing that Nadine hadn't arrived. I tell the others I will check in with her. They already know the two of us are off-line friends as well as guild mates. While the whole group sometimes communicates plans over email, Nadine's mom refuses to let her give her number to strangers on the Internet. I hadn't bothered to ask my parents if it was okay, but it wasn't like I spent much time texting anyone other than Nadine. So it would probably never matter.

Reagan: Nadddiiinnneee. Where are you? It's go time.

Nadine: Coming! I'm like five minutes away. I got stuck talking to people after school.

Nadine is freakishly punctual, so I try and shrug it off. She's on her way, that's all what matters. At least, that's what I always remind myself. Most people online appreciate that real life always comes first, but since City of Ages is the closest that we get to hanging out in real life anymore, it's hard not to feel like this should be more important to her than talking to randoms after school.

I'm wearing some heavy-duty headphones, but when Rhiannon bursts into our bedroom like a hurricane, she's impossible to miss.

She ignores the annoyed look I flash at her over my shoulder, digging around for something in her dresser. I turn back to my computer screen, pretending for a second that I'm an only child. It should only be another week or two before dad has the attic sorted out enough that we can move our computers up there, which will free up valuable bedroom space. I'll still have to share the attic space with my sisters, but I'll be able to create my own little corner and pretend like privacy exists in this house.

I wish.

Nadine finally logs in and the five of us set off for the Dungeon of Argrish, planning to battle our way past the spider people before calling it a night. Being here, in this fantasy world lets me believe that nothing in my life has changed. Everything around my character looks exactly like it did when I lived in Richmond. I'm comfortable here. Happy.

But every time I die in game, I still take the opportunity to send a private message to Nadine's character, chatting about my family, school, everything I'm missing back home and whatever else we hadn't already covered while we were texting during the day. It sounds like my old school, Ashmore, is going along business pretty much as usual. Thinking that Ashmore is still there is kind of a nice thought. Ashmore is exactly how it was when I left. But it's also a little lame to think the four of us moving away made no impact at all.

Only halfway into the opening section of the dungeon, just as we are facing off against Phillius the Damned, my computer dies.

Black screen, no power. This is not okay.

I stare at the blackened screen for a second. What happened? The overhead light in my room is still on, so the power hasn't gone out. I poke a few buttons but the computer stays dead.

I'm on the verge of freaking out thinking that my computer is broken, I glance up to see Rhiannon staring at me, horrified. I take of my headphones to hear what she's saying and come in in the middle of a Rhiannon ramble. "It was an accident. I was looking for some of my textbooks from last year and this room is a mess."

It takes me a second to understand what happened, not until I notice her foot planted on top of my power cord. I narrow my eyes at her. "You unplugged my computer?"

"No. I *accidentally* stepped on your power cable and your computer turned off. By accident." Rhiannon had an annoying habit of enunciating every syllable whenever she is being defensive or someone has pissed her off.

"Well, you were accidentally kind of an idiot. Did you find what you needed? Can you just go?"

"We get it, Reagan. You're in drama class now. No need to be such a drama queen. It's not like your game matters anyway. Just plug it back in and get over yourself."

I clenched my teeth, trying to avoid the fight that could become inevitable at any second. I need to get back in game, I don't have time to deal with her attitude. "You're already standing up, at least plug it back in?"

Rhiannon rolls her eyes, and she says I'm a drama queen? But she does as I ask, pushing aside whatever box she'd been looking through to get me hooked up again. I put my headphones back on and make a point of not looking at her. Hopefully if I ignore her she'll just go away—a strategy I've been trying for years, but, so far, I still have three sisters.

───

I'm still texting Nadine apologies for my disappearing act the next day during lunch. It happened at the worst possible moment, leaving my group short one support hero, resulting in everyone dying off within two minutes. By the time I got back online, we were back to the beginning.

Reagan: Maybe we can try again tonight? I'm not doing anything and if everyone else is around, then we can make up for some lost time.

Nadine: Can't tonight, I have plans with Elise and Laney.

Reagan: What? Did Richmond suddenly get more fun once we left?

Nadine: I wish. We're going to make our own fun, getting away from my mom for a night.

That much I get. Nadine's mom can be a lot to take on a good day, she's not a part of my hometown that I miss.

I'm briefly inspired to follow Nadine's lead. There has to be something to do in Fairview that qualifies as fun. Before we moved here, Mom couldn't stop talking about all the events and activities that this town puts on. We missed some end of summer jamboree, but I wasn't crying any tears over that one.

The notion to get out there and try something new leaves me as quickly as it arrived. I'll have more fun playing City of Ages, I can do it just as easily without Nadine. Plus, I have a book I want to finish reading.

Someone sits down beside me at the table I have staked out for my lunch spot since the second day of school. I don't look up until I hear a girl's voice calling my name. "Reagan?"

The brunette girl from drama class has planted herself beside me, dropping a heavy-looking schoolbag on the table in front of both of us. We've never technically met, but she's always sitting with Kent. "You are Reagan, right? We're in Mr. Sullen's class together" I don't answer right away, the girl looked mortified.

"Yeah, I'm Reagan. I should know what your name is, but I'm drawing a blank." I do my best to seem friendly, all while trying to figure out why she could possibly have chosen to sit down beside me.

"Jen," she says, sticking out her hand to shake mine. I'm a little unsure of what to make of the formal introduction from a girl my age, but I'm not about to leave her hanging.

"Nice to meet you," I say, trying to make sure it sounds like a statement and not a question. My lunch period has taken a turn for the unexpected, and I'm not sure I like it. I can already see myself saying something stupid, embarrassing myself in front of a whole new class worth of people.

"Sorry to bug you during your lunch. I would wait until class to ask about this, but when I saw you here, I couldn't resist. You see, we have our first group project coming up next week."

"We do?" I say before I can stop myself. I've been making a point of paying attention in all of my classes, it still looks like I missed something big.

Jen must see how uncomfortable I look, because she quickly shrugs off my confusion. "It was in the syllabus. We're not actually talking about it until class today, I like getting ahead of the game. We're trying to put together a group and we're one short."

I'm dying to ask why she approached *me*, but can't bring myself to do it. "I don't know if you want me in your group," I admit. "I've never done any drama stuff before, I'm pretty sure I will be useless."

Jen nods, studying me. "I'll admit, you're a bit of an unknown factor. When it comes to my grades, I'm not one to take risks. Mr. Sullen isn't your typical grader. Kent, Frank, and I were all in his class last year too, we never managed over eighty-five. At this point, I'm not sure what will win him over, so I'm mixing things up a bit."

I hadn't expected that much honesty, but Jen is clearly

someone I want to work with if I'm going to have any chance of doing well in this class, one I shouldn't have been taking in the first place. "What's involved?"

Jen tilts her head, perplexed. I can already see her changing her mind about me. "Well, it is a drama class. So, you're going to need to do some drama. Acting," she adds when my expression doesn't change.

That's what I was afraid of. But I knew this moment was coming. And I was going to have to try this whole acting thing anyway, so agreeing to work with Jen would mean that I don't have to sit around pathetically, watching everyone in the class chose their friends for their group before the teacher had to assign me somewhere. "I can act, probably." I close my mouth before I talk Jen out of wanting me in her group. "I'm in," I add, before she can change her mind.

"All right, cool. See you in class then?"

"Sounds good."

I wait until Jen has walked away before digging through my backpack, locating the small folder I've been using to keep my drama files in. Maybe it's time to have a look at that syllabus.

———

As soon as I enter the drama room, Kent bounces towards me. Every day since I joined this class, he's made a point of seeking me out and saying hi. When all I can do is fumble an awkward reply, he gives in and goes back to sit with his friends. But today, I'm going to have to be a bit better. I knew agreeing to be in Jen's group meant forcing myself to interact with Kent for more than a few seconds per class, but since that was something I was trying to figure out how to do anyway, it seems like a bonus.

"I heard the good news," Kent says with a lopsided smile. His face was made for smiling. "You know, it's not easy to get an invite like this from Jen. She's kind of intense about the whole school thing."

"I got that impression. I take it she'll be group leader."

"Group leader, commandant, dictator. That's her either way." I move to take my backpack off, to leave it in one of the cubbies by the drama room door, but Kent takes it from me before I can and hangs it up on a nearby hook. "You might as well come sit with us now. No more hiding in the back of the room."

Heat rushes to my face, I hope I haven't spent the last week looking like a total dork, at least any more than usual. My strategy of not catching Mr. Sullen's attention was working so far, but I hadn't even thought to worry that anyone else had caught on to my plan.

I probably over did my attempt at enthusiastic and friendly as I sat down between Kent and Jen, waving hello as they introduced me to Frank. The dark-haired guy gave a friendly smile, then promptly went back to reading the graphic novel he had spread open on his lap.

I catch a glimpse of the cover of what he's reading, getting way too excited way too quickly. "Saga?" I ask. Frank to looks up, his dark eyes wary. "Yeah, volume two. I just started it last week. It's pretty nuts."

"Oh yeah, it gets so much better too. There is some weird stuff in there, my mom was not thrilled when she saw what I was reading, but then she ended up going through the whole thing herself and decided it was worth it. So good!" There was nothing that could bring me out of my shell faster than talking about any of my favorite nerd obsessions. While graphic novels were a new hobby of mine, ever since Nadine's cousin had given her his old collection, I was finding more and more to like. It wasn't often I found someone out in the real world who could talk about any of these things with me.

Frank offers up a quick nod of appreciation before going back to his reading, probably only willing to be distracted from the story for so long.

Just then, Mr. Sullen stood up from his desk and walked over to the blackboard, beginning the day's lesson.

So far, I hadn't had to stand up in front of the class for any more than two minutes at a time, usually doing some improv warm-up for the day. I hoped that because we were getting a big assignment, it would mean I could get away with it for another day. All the while I was hyperaware of Kent's knee only inches from mine. Part of me wants to think I catch him glancing over at me out of the corner of my eye more than once, but I force myself to keep my eyes looking forward. I can't wait to tell Nadine about this.

CHAPTER 8

BED REALLY IS the nicest place on earth.

I'm lying under the covers, listening to Rhiannon getting ready for school, contemplating how I might go about convincing Mom I'm too sick to go to school. The big problem is that I spent most of last night forcing my sisters to run lines with me, getting panicky at the thought of my first drama presentation. Everyone knows what today is for me, which means Mom would need some serious evidence of illness before she'd let me stay home. When your mother is a doctor, actual evidence of being sick is hard to come by.

I drag myself out of bed and tap on the bathroom door. "I'm in here!" Reece yells from inside.

I glance toward Rhiannon for help, but she doesn't' even look up from her phone. Derrick?

Fine, I'm just going to wing the whole faking sick thing because there's no way I'm getting up in front of the class of twenty-five people today to embarrass myself. That's exactly what will happen. I'll have to stand up on the pseudo-stage during class, and everyone's going to realize what a cosmic joke it is that I ever signed up for a drama class at all. As it is, I can barely speak as myself in front of other people.

Trudging down the stairs, I do my best to come off as sickly and pathetic. Sometimes, the best strategy for convincing Mom I'm not feeling well is not to overdo it. More than once, she has filled in the blanks for me on what might be wrong, without my ever having to fake any symptoms. Of course, ninety percent of the time this plan has ended in her declaring that there's nothing wrong with me at all. Despite her talents, it's worth a shot.

When I enter the kitchen, Dad is the one hovering over the stove, cooking up eggs and bacon. "Hey, sweetheart. You're up early." He barely looks up from what he was doing, I'm not convinced he even knows which daughter I am. Dad has never been what you would call a "morning person." Usually Mom gets up when we do and makes sure we eat—cereal and toast, the extent of her culinary abilities—we don't see Dad until we get home from school, at which point my mom is at work.

"Where's Mom?" I ask, trying to keep my voice raspy.

Dad looks up, concern shining in his eyes. "She got called into work around five. Mrs. McCluskey has gone into labor. It's exciting stuff, but it means you're stuck with me this morning."

This changes everything. Dad deals with us so rarely in the morning that he's hardly heard any of our excuses for trying to stay home from school. There's no denying that of our two parents, he's the easier touch. I could actually pull this off. He stands at the stove in the room, studying me. I can tell he's already trying to figure out if something is wrong. Only a gentle nudge would get him where I need him.

But when I open my mouth, I hesitate, surprising

myself. In my head I see Jen's face, frowning down at me from my subconscious. She'll be so pissed if I miss our presentation. Even if can convince her that I really was sick, the chances of her ever asking me to be in one of her groups again is almost nothing. Plus, no matter what happens today, I'm still going to have to do this scene. After all, it's part of my grade, and the rest of my group's grades too. I can only avoid it for so long.

Crap. I do not want to have to deal with this today, or ever. Picturing what it would've been like to walk back into that biology class does the trick, and it's obvious this is the lesser of two evils.

"If getting stuck with you for the morning means getting real food for breakfast, we both know that no one will complain." I do my best to smile without overselling it. "If you've got anything ready, I'll eat now and then go get dressed once Reece has relinquished the bathroom."

"One serving of real food, coming right up."

I stand behind the curtain, waiting for my cue to go out and speak my first line. Our entire performance will last less than a total of five minutes, I wrangled myself the role with the least speaking parts, but it's still way more than I'm really comfortable with. Obviously, Jen has volunteered us to go first.

Five minutes. Soon, I'll be able to go sit back down on the floor and clap politely through the rest of the performances.

Fred practically snorts out his last line and saunters off stage, which is the signal for my character to start her nonchalant walk across to the other side of the room. The assignment was to put a new or modern spin on a classic performance, tailoring it to the style and issues of today. By the time Mr. Sullen had told us to break off into groups and brainstorm, Jen was already handing us our scripts. She had decided that we would be reimagining the classic battle scene from Romeo and Juliet as though it was playing out between a democrat and a republican. Frank had tried to point out that no one in our class could even vote yet, but Jen insisted that issues like these should matter to all of us.

I should introduce her to Rhiannon.

Or my mom. Jen seems like the kind of person that moms everywhere wish their kids would be friends with

I try not to look at the audience as I reach my place on stage, doing my best to embody an outraged, left-wing activist attempting to stage a protest. My first two lines tumble out of my mouth, in-eloquent and probably hard to understand. I stand frozen as Kent and Jen continued their fake romance between two people with drastically different political leanings, finding common ground.

The next two minutes happen so fast, by the time Mr. Sullen dims the lights indicating that it is all over, I'm completely dizzy and can barely remember any of what just happened.

But it's over. No one seems to be pointing and laughing at me, at least not yet. I doubt anyone would call what I had done acting, but I said my lines, stood where I was supposed to, and I didn't screw anything up for anyone else-- a better result than I would've guessed.

My heart continues to race through the next few performances, and it's only as the class is winding down for the day that I feel like myself again. Except, now I'm a version of myself who survived acting for a crowd. If I'm honest, acting wasn't much more uncomfortable for me then having to give an oral presentation. At least this time I had other people up there with me, prying away some of the attention.

I'm collecting my bag when Kent comes up behind me. "We did it. I'm not sure anyone else understood what Jen's point was supposed to be, but it's over. So, whatever. You did great."

I glance down at my feet for a second, unsure of what to say. We both know that what he said was a dirty, stinking lie. "Thanks," is all I can come up with. "But you don't have to say that. I'm sure my joining a drama class was one of my stupider decisions this year, and it hasn't even been a month."

"There's nothing to worry about," Kent says, still smiling encouragingly. "We're all just kind of making it up as we go along, trying not to look ridiculous. Most of the time it doesn't work." Kent casually eyes a scrawny, black guy whose name I don't remember. For his group's performance, he dressed up in several different colors of bed sheets, and a towel on his head. I didn't get the significance, but maybe I wasn't supposed to.

"Well either way, hopefully I'll do better next time. I'm hoping I didn't scare Jen off the idea of working with me. Because let's face it, I don't know anyone else yet."

"Ouch."

"I didn't mean it like that!"

Kent grins. "Yeah, yeah. Actually, that's kind of what I'm here about. We were wondering if maybe you wanted to go into town with us after school. We'll just grab something to eat and call it a celebration of our success," Kent shrugs, "You're welcome to come."

I can't help the smile that pushes its way onto my face, someone is asking me to spend time with them after school. More importantly, it's Kent! If I don't count Elise and

Nadine, this is the first time this has ever happened to me, let alone at this new school. Kent must take my smile as a yes because he's already pulling a notebook out of his backpack, scribbling his number down on a piece of paper. He rips it out and hands it to me. "Awesome. We're meeting at the front doors after next period, but if you can't find me you can text me. I'll find you. You know where the front doors of the school are, right?"

"Yes, I think I can find that much. I'll hold onto your number just in case."

With that, I'm off to math class. All the horrors of my drama performance forgotten with the excitement of my plans with Kent, Jen and Frank. I'm so glad I didn't stay home 'sick', because one, the cutest guy I've met in Fairview wants to hang out with me after school and two, there are people now who have spent a decent amount of time with me and might want to be my friends. That's not something that happens to me often.

As I unload all of my math stuff from my bag onto my desk, I'm trying to imagine what I can talk about to make me seem somewhat cool, or at least not uncool. I wish I had time to talk to Reece before this, although she might have just psyched me out and make me worry more than I will already.

As I think about my sisters, I look around the room for Rhiannon. Her desk near the front is still empty and class is starting in less than two minutes. She comes to math class from lunch, so it's not like she could've been sidetracked by a teacher, which is the only thing that will make Rhiannon late for anything.

Reagan: Hey, where are you?

The response comes so quickly that I know something is up.

Rhiannon: Walking home. Didn't feel like dealing with math today.

I stare at my phone for so long that I have to shove it under my desk when the teacher passes, handing out the day's worksheet. I'm not sure if Rhiannon has ever skipped a class before. If she has, she's covered it up better than the rest of us. Either way, this is completely unlike her.

I move slowly until I can get my phone in my lap so I can text a response. To be fair, skipping classes isn't like me either, I did it not that long ago.

Reagan: Is everything okay?

Rhiannon: Yeah, everything's fine. I had better things to do then go over a lesson plan I've already understood for a week.

She doesn't say anything else, so I stop myself before texting Reece or Riley. I don't know if Rhiannon would want me blabbing that she skipped class to anyone else. If something really is going on, I don't want to be the one to point anyone else in her direction because I know she won't appreciate the gesture.

At the end of the period, I find Riley coming out of her own class across the hall, tapping her on the shoulder. The two of us try to sidestep out of the flow of teenagers trying to escape the building, since the school day has finally ended. Reilly has tied her hair back in a half-ponytail that still shows off the waves she'd curled into her hair that morning, causing her to miss Dad's breakfast. We have the same face, but it's impossible not to notice how much better she makes it look.

"So, it looks like it may just be you and Reece walking home today," I say. I hadn't thought this part through when I'd decided not to rat out Rhiannon to our sisters. They would notice when she wasn't with us to walk home.

"Oh?" Reilly's eyebrows shoot up. "Reece is staying late too. I'm pretty sure there's a boy involved."

Okay, I hadn't thought any of this through. Before Reece inevitably went off to hang out with the friends she already has, the four of us usually walk home together, something I might be able to relate to sooner rather than later. "Are you okay to walk home on your own?" I ask. Part of me is desperate for her to say it's fine because the walk home isn't that long. We were all going to have to do it eventually. Another small part of me knows how much easier things would be, if I let my sister guilt me into keeping her company on the way home. Talking to Riley will always be easier than even sitting in the same room as Kent.

"No, no. I'm fine. What are you getting up to?"

"Would you believe me if I said I had plans? My drama group..."

"Right! How did that go? I can't believe I forgot. This morning we were all taking bets on whether or not you'd find a way out of it."

I don't have to ask who was betting in which direction, but since I had considered faking sick to avoid the presentation, I can't judge. Much. "I royally sucked, but some people from my group asked if I wanted to hang out after class, so that means I didn't turn myself into a total social reject with my performance. I figured I should just do it."

Riley squeals, clapping her hands together and drawing the attention of almost everybody left in the hallway. "Oh my God, that's so exciting! Will Kent be there?"

I shush my sister and step in closer, not wanting to be overheard. If someone mentions to Kent that I was talking about him in the hallway, I'd have to give up and leave town. "Yes. Not that I care." I emphasized the last line, hoping Reilly will take the hint.

"Sure. But as soon as you get home, I want to hear everything."

I shrug. I was probably going to tell her everything anyway, but if things go badly, I want to reserve the right to sulk about it on my own.

"So, where is Rhiannon then? Some study group?"

"She's..." I debate how much to share, but, in the end, I'm not willing to lie to Riley. Not about something like this, especially since Rhiannon hadn't said anything. "She skipped class. I don't know when she left, but she wasn't in math. When I texted her, she had already started walking home."

"No way." Riley stares at me, but when I don't contradict myself, she continues. "You're serious?"

"Yeah, apparently she didn't want to deal with math today. As if any of us ever want to deal with math."

"Rhiannon even likes math. As much as that's actually possible."

"Well, she should probably be home when you get there so maybe you can figure out what's going on. I thought she was starting to act more like herself again, but you never really know with her."

"Probably just having a bad day. It would've been weirder if she'd made it all the way through high school without skipping a class."

"Fair point. So you're sure you're okay walking home by yourself?"

"Yes, Mom. I can manage to walk home all by myself." She sticks out her tongue. "You'll have the best time. If you need anything, just call. You can do this."

"I hope so," I say as the two of us walk toward the front of the school. "If not, then you'll be stuck with me as your weird, spinster sister forever. I hope you're planning to buy a house with enough space for me and my books because if I screw this up, I'll probably die alone, friendless."

"Don't even talk like that! You put way too much pressure on yourself. You're way overthinking all of this. These people asked you to hang out. They want you to be there."

That's the second time today I've been accused of overthinking things. "You're not about to tell me to be myself, are you?" I ask as we push open the door from the main lobby. Immediately, I spot the green in Kent's hair close to the parking lot. Everyone is already waiting for me.

"Do whatever you want, just don't worry so much. You're great and everyone will see that."

I resist the urge to give my sister a hug. If only everyone else was as nice as she is, I'd have no trouble meeting people. Neither she nor any of my other sisters are going where I am now, so I will have to figure this out all on my own.

CHAPTER 9

THE WALK from school into town is a short one, as the high school sits not far off Main Street. In fact, everything in this town seems like it's just off main street. Just as we left the school parking lot, we'd been joined by another girl, Rosie. She has black hair and freckles spattered across her nose. Apparently, she has been friends with the other three since elementary school, but she committed blasphemy last year taking art class instead of drama.

"Lizzie's?" Jen asks once the school is out of sight.

"We always go there," Frank says, but the complaint seems halfhearted like this is a conversation they've had a million times before.

"I'm sorry. What's your issue with free food?" Rosie asks as she kicks a stone out of her path.

I'm following behind the four of them, trying to blend like I'm part of the group and not just some tagalong. However, I haven't been able to jump into the conversation yet. At least I know the place they're talking about since it was our hideaway on our first day in town.

Our destination is impossible to miss, a big sign reading

'Lizzie's Diner' hangs over an older-looking brick building. Rosie pushes the door open and holds it while everyone else pushes inside. A few other people from school already beat us there and sit clustered around tables, talking and doing homework.

While mostly the interior looks like a classic diner, the walls are decorated with hand-painted caricatures. It takes me a minute to recognize the pattern, but it's all women. Every single person who's included up there is named Elizabeth. There are a couple of queens, Elizabeth Banks as Effie Trinket. Elizabeth Taylor. Also, that girl from Bewitched and tons of others I don't recognize. They're all painted in the same style.

"Well, this place is... cool" I'm sure I sound like an idiot as soon as I open my mouth, but the need to say something was too much to ignore.

Even though the sign says to wait to be seated, Rosie leads us to a table in the back. I cast an uncomfortable glance at the sign as we go by, not liking to be the one to break a rule that's going to get us chased down at any second.

We take our seats, Rosie deposits her backpack on a chair before disappearing out of sight. She returns a minute later with a stack of glasses and a pitcher, which looks like it's full of cola.

The others are already chatting about some English teacher, Rosie turns to me as she settles the glasses on the table. "I wasn't sure what you liked. If you want something different I'll go grab it for you."

I'm about to ask if she works here, but a second later a gray-haired woman who looks to be about my mom's age, wearing a pink polka-dotted apron appears by our table. "Hey kids. Good day at school?" The woman leans down and plants a kiss on Rosie's head. She definitely has an in here. The two of them share the same oval face and small chin, plus the older woman even has a few freckles. Rosie's mom, I guess.

Everyone answers at once, filling the woman in on the latest gossip from school before her eyes find me. "Oh my goodness," she breathes. "We have a new addition today." She looks over at Rosie. "You didn't tell me you knew one of the Donovan girls."

"I didn't until about ten minutes ago. She's in drama class with these guys." Rosie said, gesturing to the others at the table.

Kent opens his mouth as though to retort something about drama class, but the woman shoots him a warning glance before taking over the empty seat across from me.

"Drama, hmm? Bold choice." Before I can say anything back about how it wasn't a choice I should've made, she continues. The way she's watching me is unnerving, like she's studying everything about me. "Let me guess which one you are."

I force myself to smile and nod politely, expecting yet another Fairview Four fan since everyone my mom's age and older seems to have the same interest. "Reagan." She declares after a minute. "Or perhaps Reilly?"

"You got it the first time," I say, smiling. Just keep smiling, I remind myself. This woman doesn't seem to mean any harm, and as long as Rosie's mom is less pushy than Kent's, I can't complain.

"I thought so, partly because of the drama class, and partly because of the way you watch everyone around you. I remember when you were a baby, you were always the most eager for attention. You could do much more than toddle around and babble the last time I saw you, but you would do anything you could to draw attention away from your sisters and back to you."

That puts a stop to all of the assumptions floating around in my head. "You knew me when I was a baby?"

"Oh yes, your mother and I grew up on the same street. When she had you girls, I had just had Rosie here. So, tag teaming five babies between all of us lightened the load a bit. They always appreciated the extra pair of hands." She looks down at Rosie and I, as though remembering how much work we had once been. "I still remember those first weeks after you girls had come home from the hospital, your mother was treating the whole thing like some science experiment, creating formulas and systems to keep you all fed and happy. Meanwhile, your dad was all over the place. He meant well, but he didn't understand the first thing about babies. You girls were a crash course like no other, and before you could say quadruplets, your dad was a pro."

Looking over at Rosie, I find it weird to think that this girl I thought I'd met for the first time less than an hour ago, used to share a crib with my sisters and me long before my earliest memory.

"You figured out who I was because I was an attention hog as a baby?" I'm sure she has me confused with one of my sisters. "Because taking a drama class was kind of an accident for me. I'm the Donovan sister least likely to stand in a spotlight for any amount of time."

"Oh, I'm sure. It was like you realized you were the one who had arrived first and deserved to be treated as such." I blush, a little uncomfortable with the unexpected trip down memory lane. "You were adorable. Don't you worry about it," she says before standing back up. "So what can I get everyone today?" She glances back at me. "One perk of knowing my daughter, is that the French fries here at

Lizzie's are always free. But for you, since it's your first time back, and since you were always such a nice baby, anything you want is on the house."

After taking everyone's order, Rosie's mom disappears back to the kitchen. Everyone else at the table is watching me like a freak of nature. I shrug, trying to get their attention back off me. "It's weird because I don't remember ever living here before, but everyone who is older seems to remember."

"My mom's got an old picture of me sitting between you and your sisters, right in the middle. We were about nine or ten months old. Beyond that, I don't remember it at all."

"Random question," I say to Rosie. "What's your mom's name? Or what am I supposed to call her." It's kind of weird due to the fact that this woman knows me on sight, but I don't even know enough to report back to my mom about who I met.

"Call her Lizzie, everyone does. Technically, it's her middle name—Lizzie was her mom—but it's always just been easier this way."

Clearly bored with the conversation, Frankie digs through his backpack. A moment later, he produces a stack of a few different graphic novels, handing them over to Rosie. "Thanks. Let me know when you get the next ones in."

"Pshh, do you really think I'd let you go without them?" Rosie answers, already fishing something out of her own bag. She hands him another pile of books. "Rat Queens. Only two volumes so far, but it's good."

Frank stares down at the cover. "Are all the characters girls?"

"Yes. Which I'm sure will be no problem for an enlightened human such as yourself." Jen gives him a hard look.

Frank grumbles but immediately starts reading. It's not long before our food arrives and the conversation dies down, everyone piles into burgers and sandwiches into their mouths. The BLT I ordered tastes even better than it looks, I'm already planning on getting my family to come out here. I wonder if my parents reconnected with Lizzie already. They've gone out a few times since we moved here, but I never really asked for details.

Before my sisters and I were born, our parents whole lives were here. How many other friends did they have that they never mentioned? Had they been keeping in touch with anyone? My mom had lived here until she went away to school, and then had come back, my dad in tow after graduation.

"You seem lost in thought," Kent says, leaning toward me as I pop a French fry in my mouth. My pulse quickens a little, but I try to ignore it. He's just being nice, all I have to do is act normal.

"So many people around here knew me as a baby, or they knew my parents. This place is new for me, but we're old news for everyone else."

"I'm guessing it sucks to be news at all. Have I apologized yet on behalf of my mother? She definitely doesn't see you guys as old news."

Well, that doesn't sound promising. I narrow my eyes, trying to figure out if I should read something more into this conversation. "Is there something I should know? Because we did the baby pictures in the paper for our birthday thing, I'm sure there has got to be something more interesting going on around here. I figured she would be over us by now."

"You're clearly new," Rosie interrupts with a sympathetic smile. "Nothing is ever going on in Fairview."

"Ignore her. Fairview is fine. There is almost always something going on. The Rhubarb festival is coming up, and one of the craft fairs, I think. You just need a guide to show you what to avoid and what's worth getting involved in," Kent says, leaning back in his chair.

"Getting involved? I'm not really a joiner."

Kent's eyes stay locked on mine. "Well, you didn't think you could be an actor until today, so there you go." I want to point out to him that I still don't think I can be an actor, or that what I did in class today could be considered acting, but he carries on. "Unfortunately, getting involved is basically a must here."

Jen nods, knowingly. "There are all sorts of volunteering and community involvement requirements for graduation."

How has nobody mentioned this to us already? Or had Mom been waiting to drop the bombshell until we'd already settled in a bit more? I try to swallow back my panic, save it for later.

"How is everything?" Lizzie asks, coming back at the right moment to keep me from getting up and fleeing the table.

I mumble another 'great, thank you', swallowing a French fry for effect. The food here really is amazing, but I can't shake the idea of having to get involved in any way shape or form. Group assignments are already torture enough, and those are all with people my age who hate the idea as much as I do.

"Do you all have your costumes sorted out for next week?" Lizzie asks as she and Rosie started clearing away everyone's plates.

I look over at Kent, hoping for an explanation. The costumes part I understood, but Halloween is still a couple weeks away, and while my sisters all decided what they wanted to be a month ago, I hadn't given it much attention yet.

"Every year the week before Halloween, the town puts on a costume party. It's pretty much an excuse for everyone older than ten to eat candy and dress up too. The town square gets decked out in all sorts of Halloween gear, usually someone nearby offers up their house for a maze or spooky house. You should come!"

I mumble an answer, but I don't commit to anything. I'm pleased that they thought to invite me but not convinced this is the kind of thing I'd like... at all.

We spend another hour sitting around Lizzie's and eating free French fries, and since drink refills are also on the house. I take more than my fill, hopefully Dad wasn't planning anything good for dinner.

As we're leaving, all set to go our separate ways, Jen and Kent turn back toward me. "Are you usually in the library for lunch?" Jen asks.

I shrug, not eager to confess anything.

Kent takes a step back toward me. "We probably only have a couple weeks left of decent weather before we start eating inside, so if you wanted to come hang out with us during your lunch, you should. I promise, we are not all as insane as we seem."

Yes. "Umm, I..." I struggle to find my words. I want this so badly, but I don't want to accept in a way that makes them re-think inviting me. Jen has already seen me sitting alone and reading during lunch, so it's not like I can pretend I have better plans. But I also don't want to sound like I'm taking some sort of pity invite, if they don't actually want me around.

"No pressure," Kent adds. "You can find us around the side of the building by the portables if you're up for it.

Lizzie sometimes sends cookies, so there's that to consider."

"I'll definitely keep that in mind." I end the conversation with a wave. Did that come up too bitchy? Do I sound like I think I'm too good for them? They must've heard about the debacle with the note in science class, but they still offered to hang out with me anyway. I guess that something. It's not like they needed to invite me out after school. Our presentation today didn't even come up.

As I walk along Oakridge, I attempt to find the best way to tell my sisters I may have found a group of friends to hang out with, without sounding lame. As I approach the house, I see that my mom's car is already in the driveway. She's home from work early.

Before I even step inside, I can already hear raised voices coming from somewhere inside. The front door glides open as I lean against it, trying to sneak in without making too much noise. From the sounds of it, at least half my family is pissed off at one another. The last thing I want is to get involved.

I drop my bag in the front hall on top of Reese's and head for the kitchen. So far, there's no sign of anybody else down here, meaning they are all upstairs arguing about something or other. "You're such a hypocrite sometimes," someone shouts from upstairs, and I'm guessing it's Rhiannon.

Do not get involved. Do not get involved.

But I only manage to pour myself a glass of orange juice before my curiosity gets the better of me. If Rhiannon is the one yelling, this could go from bad to nuclear level family drama in a matter of minutes. I make my way upstairs and see Riley leaning against a wall at the top of the landing. She's silent and watchful, keeping an eye on something that's going on at the other end of the hall. Once I make it up, I realize what's happening. Mom and Rhiannon are going at it. Reece and Dad seem to hover on the periphery, ready to jump in or try to calm things down respectively.

"You knew I didn't even want to come here in the first place. You should give me a little of slack. I'm *adjusting*."

"Drop the attitude, I've already given you plenty of slack. Skipping classes is just unacceptable. It's completely unlike you."

"So what? Because it is *like* Reece that makes it okay? She's allowed to skip class and I'm not? How *fair* is that?"

I can see Reece deflate, stepping away from Rhiannon. "Don't bring me into this. I've gone to every single one of my classes so far this year."

"That's an accomplishment?" Dad asks. "We should take a breather here. Feelings are running hot. Rhiannon has been nothing but a model student, if she needs to blow off a little steam from time to time, it's not the worst thing."

"So much for our united front," Mom snaps. "Saying we're okay with this now sets a precedent for everyone. We are not okay with this," she finishes, looking over at all of us. I'm already wishing I'd stayed downstairs. No one ever mentioned my missing a class on the very first day of school, but since everyone knew what had happened, I guessed that they were taking pity on me.

"Why are you even here?" Rhiannon asks, not willing to back down. "Aren't you supposed to be at your stupid job? The one that was so damn crucial for you to take that you had to uproot your family."

"Rhiannon, don't. Don't go there. We've had this discussion so many times already."

"No, you had this discussion! You tell us what you think we need to know, you don't bother answering any of our questions! Then you just make declarations for our entire family. Newsflash, that's not a discussion!"

Before anyone can say anything else, Rhiannon backs into our bedroom and slams the door. The rest of us stare at one another for a long minute before Reece slips into her own room, leaving the door open, making it clear she's not looking to continue the conversation either.

As our parents start talking to one another, Reilly turns towards me. "So, how was it? Was everyone awesome?"

I take a second to realize what she's talking about. In all the chaos here, everything else has already been pushed aside. Kent, his friends, Lizzie having known us as babies, all of it. In less than five minutes, my family has ruined my mood, and I'm not even surprised.

CHAPTER 10

WE'RE HAVING roast beef for dinner, which is a family favorite for everyone but Reilly, who doesn't eat meat. Tonight however, everyone is only picking at their plates, barely speaking unless absolutely necessary. No one has forgotten the argument that happened a few hours earlier.

"He was gorgeous," Mom says, continuing to ramble on about the baby she got to help deliver that morning. "It's been so long since I've been this hands on with my patients, getting to know my them and being involved in their lives."

Beside me, Rhiannon mumbles, "Well, hopefully they'll put that kid's picture in the paper instead next time."

Everyone pretends they didn't hear her. No one has the energy to get into it all over again.

"I've only met a fraction of the people from Doctor William's practice so far, I know some people have their own doctors elsewhere, but this role has made me feel like I'm part of a community again."

I'm happy for my mom, in a way. I'm not sure why she chose this moment to announce just how thrilled she is with her life in Fairview, it's like she doesn't get when to relax.

The room falls silent all over again, and I shovel a spoonful of mashed potatoes into my mouth. French fries and now this. It's been a fantastic day for me and potatoes in all their forms.

Nobody says anything, and we're all probably counting down the seconds until dinner is finished so we can go to our own corners of the house to get a break from one another.

"Well, I have an announcement," Reece says putting down her fork, clinking it against her plate. "Since I can't do the soccer thing this year, I'm going to start volunteering. Some people at school were telling me that there's a small animal shelter in town. Fairview isn't really big enough to have one, but some millionaire or something founded it like twenty years ago, now it serves a bunch of the towns in the surrounding areas. They always have a few dogs and cats in there, all looking for homes. It's something I might do after school." She casts a quick glance to each of my parents. "If that's okay, I mean." I don't think anyone of us expects my parents to argue with Reece volunteering since it wasn't something any of us could ever expected to happen. It's not that she's selfish, it's just that Reese's world exists in a tiny bubble around her. The fact that she asked permission at all hints at just how badly she wants this, even if she's playing it off like it's not a big deal.

"That's great, sweetheart." Dad shoots a thumbs-up to her from across the table, I stifle a groan. "Do you need anything from us? Permission slip?"

"No idea. I'm going in tomorrow to see if they even need any help. Who would say no to extra volunteers though, right?"

"Wait. You already knew about the volunteering thing?" I ask. "Or are you just doing this to get out of the house?"

Reece shrugs. "Why not both?"

"What's this?" Reilly asks.

"Apparently to graduate high school here, there are volunteering requirements, also some community involvement stuff. I didn't get the details, but nobody mentioned it to us when we enrolled."

"I forgot about that," Mom says, a glint of nostalgia in her eyes. "They did that when I was a teenager here too. By the time you graduated, you needed to have at least forty hours of community service, as well as volunteering for at least two town festivals."

"Wait, there are festivals?" Reilly asks, looking weirdly excited by the whole idea.

"I'm not sure how many festivals are still around," Mom answers. "But the town does a lot of events through the year. A lot of fundraising too. I'm sure you can each find something you're interested in. It's all part of the sense of community."

"I'm really not sure how anyone can call it volunteering, especially when it's mandatory," I say, still not in love with any of this, but also not sure why it bugs me. As if moving to a new town and having to deal with classes isn't enough, now I'm going to have to volunteer somewhere? The idea alone stresses me out. What kind of volunteering would involve the least amount of interacting with people? Reading to old people? Sorting donations somewhere?

"Why didn't anyone tell us but this earlier?" Rhiannon asks. She's already back on her phone, I can only imagine that she was looking for the most prestigious volunteer opportunities available. Or complaining to Derrick about how terrible her life here apparently is.

"I'm sure they're going to make allowances for the fact you girls came in late. At the very least, cutting down your community service hours by ten seems fair. One of you should talk to a guidance counselor at school to see what you can learn. If cutting back hours is an issue, I'll give the school call and see what we can figure out."

"So is it ten hours a year, or just forty hours before we graduate?" Reilly asks. She was always the one getting involved in causes back in Virginia, even when she didn't have to. Somehow, she's excited about this. She'll probably do more like sixty hours, if she can.

I have no intention about worry about it this year. At the earliest, Junior year will be fine.

The very earliest.

This year is already spoken for on every level, and while I try to convince myself that I'll be putting this off, because I want to better tailor my volunteer experiences to whatever field I decided I want to end up in, it has nothing to do with that. It probably makes me a terrible person, but, for now, I'm going to avoid this issue and hope it goes away.

———

Reece and Rhiannon retreat to the attic after dinner, probably complaining about our parents while they finish some of the tidying up they have insisted on before we can start moving our stuff up there this weekend. At least that gives me my bedroom to myself.

I crawl into bed, halfheartedly promising myself that I won't fall asleep and pull out my phone, already feeling a nap coming on. Today ended up being a way more exciting day than I would've guessed, I want to tell Nadine about all of it. Everything from my presentation, going out to Lizzie's, to my family being insane. This is the kind of stuff that only she will ever understand.

Reagan: Hey. Want to play a CoA? Had a crazy day.

Nadine: Can't get to my computer right now. What's up?

So much for that idea. How is it she never has time to be at her computer anymore?

Reagan: Nevermind. I'll fill you in later.

I frown down at my phone, disappointed. Feeling the call of my pillow more and more. If Nadine's not going to be around, there's really no reason not to sleep. I lay down, but my phone buzzes again.

Nadine: No, come on. Tell me.

Part of me isn't all that convinced she cares at all, but before I let my eyes drift shut, trusting Rhiannon to wake me up in the next little while, I type out everything. It ends up being a solid wall of text and there are still things that get left out.

I tuck my phone under my pillow and drift off. Sleep takes me quickly and lasts until I hear two sets of footsteps shuffling down the attic stairs, announcing my sisters return.

I glance at my phone. Looks like I was only able to get a half-hour sleep, but as I'll be back to sleep soon enough, I force myself to sit up. I swear, teenagers definitely need way more than eight hours of sleep, but the rest of the world seems to disagree.

A notification of the top my phone tells me there's a new text message. It's from an unknown number, not Nadine. I double back to the last message I sent, making sure it went through. It did. It's been read. She hasn't said anything back. It hasn't really been all that long, but usually I can count on Nadine to at least offer a sympathetic ear and to rant right along with me about my family. Since both of our families are equally dysfunctional, we both always act as a sounding board for the other when we need someone on our side.

It's getting harder and harder to squash that voice that's telling me I'm not a priority for her anymore, so I flip over to the new text message.

Unknown number: Hey, Reagan. It's Kent. Jen had your number from our group contact sheet. Just wanted to make sure you had mine in case you try to find us tomorrow at lunch. I mean... no pressure.

No way.

I read it again. Yup. Kent just messaged me, completely out of the blue! As if this day hasn't been up and down enough already. My stomach does a little flip-flop. There's still a very good chance Kent is only being nice to me as a charity case. But even though part of my brain is still trying to convince me this is all a pity thing, I don't believe it.

He's just that nice. And I do like his friends. The fact that they all seem to like me to is a bonus.

"What's up?" Rhiannon asks as she comes into the room, and sits down at her desk.

"Nothing," I say, shoving my phone back out of sight. "How are things going upstairs?"

"It's so close to done. I swear we're finding dust every-where. There's a lot of room up there, and it looks like no one who has ever lived in this house has used it for anything. I don't even think it would take that much work to turn it into two new bedrooms, potentially even adding a bathroom."

I sit up straighter. One of the first things I considered when the move to Fairview was announced was the possi-bility of each of us getting our own bedrooms. I would love not having to always share my space with one of my sisters, especially not having to share a bathroom with all of them.

That would be a freaking dream come true. But no, this house, which is twice as big as our old one, still only has three bedrooms. It has an extra room downstairs, but Dad claimed that for his office.

And Rhiannon's right, the attic is huge, almost as big as the entire second floor. There would be more than enough room to fit some extra bedrooms up there. "Have you mentioned it to Mom and Dad? Maybe we can get one last favor out of their residual guilt." I don't point out that Rhiannon may have killed any chance of that today.

"No point. The town owns the house, not Mom and Dad. So we probably can't do any major changes to the property while we live here. Even if we live here for twenty years, you know Mom's never going to do anything to risk pissing off her precious town council. She would just come up with some sort of bullshit excuse about how sharing bedrooms builds character. As if. Sharing two bedrooms between four people just builds insanity and claustrophobia."

I slump back down but only long enough to shimmy out of the jeans I fell asleep in before changing into pajama pants. I've long since gotten used to changing in front of my sisters; modesty isn't a thing when you're already stuck with identical bodies.

I can't shake the idea of having my own room. After this, it'll be off to college where we'll all be stuck sharing bedrooms with strangers in dorms. Then, we'll probably have roommates for years until we can afford to get our own places. Some of us might move in with significant others even before then. This could be our only chance to get our own rooms. Seeing as we literally started out sharing a womb, this is something that should have happened a long time ago.

I do my best to shrug the whole thing off, not wanting to antagonize Rhiannon farther, but I'm not letting the idea go. We finally live somewhere that has enough space for our bizarre, big family. If making the most of that is how the universe pays us back for having to leave our old house and our friends behind, I'm determined to make it happen. How? I have absolutely no idea, but thankfully I know three equally motivated people who will probably be game to help me figure it out.

First things first though. I grab my phone and open the message from Kent, reading it a few times to make sure there's no way I misinteretted the message.

Reagan: You talked me into it ;) I'll see you tomorrow at lunch!

Tonight, I'm feeling brave. Tomorrow, there's a very good chance I would have tried to back out. At least now I've made not showing up an even more awkward option than just ignoring the offer.

I have to do this. And even better, I actually want to.

CHAPTER 11

I DON'T REMEMBER it ever being this cold in October back home. The second after I get out of the van in front of Lizzie's, I regret not at least throwing a sweater in my bag.

Dad drives away once I'm free of the curb going home for a while since most of my family isn't arriving until after dark. Once I decided to go with Kent and his friends—I'm still struggling to think of them as my friends. It actually took very little work to get the rest of my family on board for the town's Halloween event in the square, the curiosity around Fairview's festivities was too much to resist.

With my costume still shoved in my bag, I walk across the square to where I promised to meet everyone. There aren't many people out yet, but intricate jack-o-lanterns sit every few spaces, portraying everything from typical geometric faces to intricate character designs. Booths line the north edge of the square selling everything from carnival food, to handmade jewelry to snacks made in the shapes of ghosts and vampires.

Every time I make eye contact with someone, I can practically sense their gaze following me as I make my way by. Nearly two months into living in Fairview and I still hate being this recognizable.

I spot Kent's hair first, but I quickly see Rosie and Frankie talking nearby, and Jen is making her way toward them from the opposite direction. I double my speed, doing my best to keep my head down. I spent the last week hanging out with all of them during our lunch periods, I still get nervous every time I see them, like having a crush on an entire group of people at once. And I'm still half convinced that it's almost inevitable that I'm going to screw this all up.

"You're not wearing a costume," Kent says, throwing his hands up as soon as I reach the group. "You promised you would. It's the whole point of tonight!" He was already fully decked out in a homemade Captain America outfit, it fits perfectly with Rosie's Black Widow and Frank's incredibly intricate Vision costume. Jen didn't seem to be dressed up either, until I took a closer look. She's wearing a button up plaid shirt and a 'Hello my name is sticker' that declares her Joss Whedon.

"I've got something," I promise. "But I need to find a place to change here. It's a thing with my sisters. I couldn't let them see what I was going as."

"Is your costume that bad?" Rosie said, looking up from her phone. She was smirking a little, but the expression didn't look unkind, only teasing.

"The costume party idea was half the reason my sisters decided to come. Not being recognized during a big down event has its plus sides. But then we somehow also decided to try and get one over on one another as well. So we're all dressing up in a way that cover's our faces."

"So, then what?" Jen asks. "You try to figure out if you still recognize each other without just looking for your own face?"

"Something like that. I'm not sure if there was really a point, but I'm curious to see how long it will take me to do it." There was never a doubt in my mind that I'd be able to track down each of my sisters eventually. I know them by so much more than what they look like.

After changing into my costume, I stepped out of the women's bathroom at Lizzie's dressed head to toe in a dinosaur onesie I'd picked up a few days before. I'd always been terrible at costumes, so having to come up with something last minute hadn't exactly led to my rising to the occasion. I popped on a facemask of a T-rex that didn't at all match with the stegosaurus I thought the onesie had been modeled after. At least I wouldn't have to worry about a sweater anymore.

"Umm, nice costume," Rosie said as I made my big entrance, clearly not meaning a word of it.

"What are you even dressed as?" Frank asked.

"Frankenstein's dinosaur?" I answered, feeling pathetic. "I may have been a little more focused on keeping my identity a secret than winning the costume contest. Besides, my family would have never guessed I'd be able to go out in public dressed up in something this sad looking." On the other hand, they had all seen me go to school last year dressed up as a book with cardboard stuck to each of my arms, and paper glued all over my clothes. Their expectations for my costume this year couldn't be all that high.

And now I feel like a moron.

"Well, if you're sure you want to go out in public like that..." Jen trails off, her eyes giving me the once over. For a second, I really consider scrapping the whole idea. If I just ditch the mask, at least I'll look somewhat passable.

"Don't listen to her," Rosie interrupts. "No one is going to know it's you anyway, right? Isn't that the whole point?

It's just a costume, and it sounds like things are starting to pick up out there."

Someone has turned on the music, the square is quickly filling with people. There's even a station to bob for apples, like this town is trying to hit every Halloween cliché all in one night. Back home, no one would have ever gone along with something like that, they'd be too worried about all the things that could go wrong or how someone with bad intentions might have tried to pull something. But here, a line is already forming to participate.

"So, where's this candy I was promised?" I ask. A few minutes later, for only five dollars, we each have a goody bag filled to overflowing with some of my favorite treats. It's been a few years since I've been out trick-or-treating, so this is my best haul in a while, I make a note to go back for seconds before I leave. I've only brought a twenty to spend, but I'm already sure I'll eat through my entire bag by the time I leave. I want to have some to snack on at school next week.

Already I'm on full alert, scanning the crowd for anyone who might be related to me. No one immediately grabs my attention, but the night is still young, and I'm determined to come away from it holding the crown of most observant Donovan.

"Boo!" A voice calls from directly behind me, making me jump straight into the air.

I turn to find Kent, he's holding out some cotton candy to me. "Sorry. Didn't realize that would actually scare you." He hands me the snack as a peace offering.

"Let's just say that Halloween isn't exactly my ideal holiday. I can't even watch scary movies, so the terrifying the crap out of people part of the holiday isn't my thing." I take a mouthful of pink cotton candy, humming with happiness as it melts in my mouth. "The candy part though, that I can get behind."

"Wait, no scary stuff? Does that mean you're not going to do the haunted house with us? It's the best part of the whole night. Every year, a ton of people sign up, hoping to get on the committee to do the Halloween House. They pull half of the volunteers from the high school for the community service requirement, and the other half are just super enthusiastic adults. Every year gets better and better as everyone tries to outdo the people that went before them. Last year, they made everyone take off their shoes before going in the house, saying that Mrs. Sangiti made that a rule of using her house. Then they covered an entire room in spaghetti noodles."

I blink at him. "How is that scary?"

"No idea. But it was gross so people loved it."

I squirm a little at the idea of getting spaghetti stuck between my toes. No thank you. "Sounds like something I would be happy to miss."

"Boo," he calls again, but this time sounds like a jeering crowd. "That's no fun."

We rejoin our group, not saying anything else about the haunted house, but it's already taking over my every thought. The idea of people jumping out at me with chainsaws and fake fangs doesn't sound like any kind of fun I'm interested in, I can already feel my willpower crumbling. I don't want to be left behind.

The sound of familiar laughter nearby grabs my attention. I look around, scanning the crowd until my eyes find the face I already knew I was looking for. Reece is standing in a big group of people, mostly guys, but also a couple of girls I don't recognize, howling with laughter and almost doubled over. She's dressed as what I can only guess is some kind of fairy princess, judging by the crown and the wings, the rest of her clothes is the same stuff she usually wore to parties back home—jeans and a tight t-shirt. A small mask, which was probably just supposed to cover her eyes to begin with, has already been moved up to sit atop her hair. So much for trying to hide her identity. She's clearly enjoying the attention.

Frowning, I turn away and try to jump into a conversation about the latest episode of some show I've never heard of. I make a mental note to check if it's on Netflix so I can try to get caught up before the second person within ten minutes sneaks up behind me.

"Reagan, I know that's you. I could practically feel you staring at me through that stupid dino mask of yours."

I turn around to stick out my tongue before remembering she can't see my face through the mask anyway, and find Reece making a face at me.

"Like you were so hard to figure out," I counter. "You didn't even try."

"The mask was itchy," she says with a shrug.

"Is everyone else here?" I ask.

"No idea. Rachel's brother drove us over. Reilly, Mom and Dad were still at home when I left."

I want to ask where Rhiannon went, but Reece has already left to go back to her friends. I realize how little I know about the people my sisters are making friends with since we moved here. Before, I knew all of their friends almost as well as I knew my own since everything from birthday parties to movie nights to school dances usually ended up combining multiple groups of friends into one big one. Now, I don't know who any of these people are. At least Reece would have had to have seen me here, standing around with a group of my own. If only I'd managed to have her turn up at a moment where everyone was laughing hysterically at one of my jokes. Not that I'd had one of those moments yet, but it could happen.

Too soon, Kent is leading everyone over to the Mclusky house where this year's Halloween House has taken over the otherwise colonial looking home. A graveyard marks the front lawn, lights flash in each of the windows, occasionally revealing the silhouette of a knife-wielding man. My heart starts racing all over again as I scan the area for anything that might want to jump out at me. Yes, nothing in there would really hurt me, but I won't know what's coming for me either. There's bound to be something in there that will give me nightmares beyond the initial heart attack it will give me.

"Who's ready to go?" Kent says, wiggling his shoulders like an overexcited flight attendant. Frank lets out a groan in response, but everyone else claps and hoots excitedly. I have a brief shimmer of hope where I think maybe Frank will stay out with me, but he steps forward to follow the group.

As the house looms over me, I'm resigned to going in, not sure if I'll be able to live down chickening out. No one has even looked back to make sure I was going with them, and as sad as it is, I don't want them to go through without me, creating more memories I wouldn't be a part of.

"Only four at a time," the man at the door says, moving his scythe down to block my way before I can enter through the front door.

Relief and disappointment both collide in my gut. At least I don't have to go in right away. Everyone inside stops to look at me. "No worries then. I'm too much of a pansy for this anyway." That's it, the universe has decided for me, I'm totally okay with not going in.

"No way! You got so close" Kent says, ducking under the scythe to rejoin me. "We'll go in the next group."

"Thanks," I chirp out. I'm still getting used to being around Kent with his friends as a buffer. Now I'm going to stand out here with Kent, and I'm going to try and not make an idiot of myself, all before having to deal with strangers jumping out at me in a haunted house. The nightmares just keep coming.

Kent is standing right beside me, his arm inches from mine, I try to remind myself to breathe normally.

Neither of us say anything as we wait for our turn to go inside the house. I try to follow every shriek, yell, and howl that comes from inside. I'll take any clue I can get about what's coming next. The anticipation is only making things worse, my brain can't decide what I should obsess over more right now, the house or Kent.

Kent. Kent. Kent.

I wish my stupid brain hadn't even let me think about him. Wasn't it in hardcore survival mode? Thinking about boys should have been its lowest priority.

I glance behind me to find no one else waiting to go inside the house yet, which means it will probably be just Kent and I, alone. It also means there will be only two targets for anyone inside the house intent on scaring incoming guests. If I shriek, pass out, or something, there's no way Kent won't notice. We're already failing at small talk. It's hard to see this situation getting any better once a little mayhem and fake murder gets thrown in.

As we wait outside for two more people, the undeniable sound of Rosie's laugh comes from above us and I almost jump right out of my skin and go running in the opposite direction, but instinct and terror keep me glued to the spot. She's laughing, not screaming out in pain. Relax.

A couple in their early twenties begins to make their way to join the line behind us, blocking my escape route. At least I don't have to worry about being alone with Kent yet. It's something I want eventually, but maybe when the stakes are a little lower.

This is not how I imagined any part of tonight going.

I kind of wish my sisters were here with me. Maybe not Reilly since she's as big of a baby about this stuff as I am, but Rhiannon and Reece would be way better at standing their ground, probably scaring off anyone before they got close enough to touch me, or laughing at the ridiculousness of it all and making the whole thing seem like less of a big deal.

"Hey, are you okay?" Kent asks, glancing down at me. For the first time, I really notice how tall he is, and, for half a second, it's enough to distract me from what's coming next.

I shrug, trying to seem uninterested in everything going on around me. At least my mask hides just how sweaty my hairline is getting. "I'm fine. This will all be over soon, right?"

"You make it sound like we're about to die. This is supposed to be fun. If you really hate the idea, I promise I won't give you a hard time if you don't come in. I'll just make Rosie go again with me. Sounds like she's having fun."

I seriously consider taking him up on his offer, but the couple has arrived behind us and already started making out. I know that there really is nothing inside that house that can hurt me, even if my nerves don't quite believe my head on that one. All I have to do is go through the house, then it's over.

I resolve that I should take advantage of this situation. After all, this is my chance to get one-on-one time with Kent, which is what I want. Over the past few weeks, I've come up with so many ways the two of us could get some time together and the fear part of my brain is trying to ruin everything. I can't let my brain mess this up for me.

"You're up," the doorman says, raising his scythe ominously, an effect ruined by the gum he's smacking.

"Are we doing this? It's your call." Kent smiles, I really do believe him that he won't give me a hard time if I decide not to go through with this. But it's that very same smile that has me wanting to follow him into the haunted house or right across the state if he asks me to.

I should probably start with the haunted house and see how that goes.

Taking off my mask, I scrunch it up in my fists to give me something to hold on to. I'm going to do this, but I'm going to do it with a clear field of vision. "Okay." I nod. "I'm in."

Kent grins, and after each handing over a five-dollar bill, together we head inside.

My can-do attitude shoots right out the window by the time the first plastic skeleton is flung from its hiding place to swoop over my head. I dig my nails into my hand to keep myself from yelling out but find I'm actually okay. I knew something like that was coming, the effect isn't nearly as scary as I'd been preparing myself for.

"Do skeletons even fly?" Kent asks as our group moves on from the first room to the next.

I'm too busy looking for clues about what to expect to answer, the people behind us have already started mocking the flying skeleton.

The next room is covered in toilet paper, making it harder to see too far inside of what is clearly the kitchen. But not hard enough to see that I can't make out the black clad body of the person standing maybe five feet ahead of me. I shift back, pretending to get distracted so that Kent will be the one in the lead.

There's no way he doesn't see the person reaching toward him, even in the gloom of the poorly lit room. Kent pretends not to, pointedly looking everywhere but straight ahead.

Right as we're about to pass the kitchen island, the sound of pots and pans clattering fills the room. It's just enough to pull our focus away from what's coming in order to look behind us. I turn back right as a hand reaches out to touch Kent's shoulder.

The blood drains from my face, even though this whole moment has been less than scary. I never considered that people here would actually touch me. Most places, it would be a law suit waiting to happen. Here, anything seems to go though.

Kent's laughing just in front of me, talking to whoever had just tried to scare him like they're old friends.

The couple behind us has given up on any sort of pretense and are just full on making out now.

Nothing about this is scary, I'm almost disappointed.

I start to relax in earnest almost as soon as we start our way up the stairs through to the second level of the house. I don't understand what the people who tried to organize this place was going for, but so far everything has been far more cheesy than scary. Kent is constantly looking from side to side, inspecting every element of the house for something that might genuinely scare him, he comes away disappointed.

"Okay, I can take this. This really isn't so bad."

"I swear, last year it was so scary. The effects were really well done. They put a lot of thought into it. I've heard multiple people swear that Jamie Daniels wet himself when one of the actors jumped out at him. This is... Well, this is not that."

I'm not sure how, but somewhere along the way we lose sight of the other duo in our group. It's possible they've decided to call it a day and gone back out the way we came, or they've slipped away into a closet to continue what they started in the kitchen. Either way, that only leaves Kent and me.

"And then there were two," I whisper, trying to sound ominous.

The second last stair near the top of the landing creeks as I put my weight on it, sending a shiver running up my spine. So far, that's proved far scarier than anything I've seen until this moment. The blacklight arrows lead us into an empty bedroom cloaked in fog. Before going in, my eyes scan the walls, but there is literally nowhere in this room that anyone or anything can be lying in wait for us.

"Do we go in?" I ask, looking over at Kent. He looks behind us and then back in toward the room where the black light arrow on the floor clearly points us deeper into the bedroom.

"I guess so. Maybe we're supposed to be contemplating the horror of solitude."

"You're starting to sound like Mr. Sullen," I say, making Kent roll his eyes. Together we step inside the room, taking each foot slowly and stopping in place before taking the next. Something is bound to happen. If this is an exercise in anticipation, I want my money back.

Nothing downstairs managed to scare me, and now I can't help but wonder if they were trying to lure us into a false sense of security. I should have just waited outside, at least then I wouldn't have to worry about any of this.

We make it all the way to the far wall of the room where

the windows look down on the happy crowds below. Nothing happens.

"Why do I feel like those people down there are about to get a great view of the two of us being murdered?" I ask.

Kent doesn't say anything in response, he's still on the lookout for what might be coming for us next. Again nothing happens. We stand there, barely breathing for as long as my nerves will allow. "Do we just go back out then? Could the person who was supposed to be in this room have wandered off?"

Kent shrugs, looking even less confident than I feel. We turned to head back towards the door, but once we take a step, something drops from the ceiling. I cover my mouth before I can let out a shriek, eyes going wide as I try to figure out what's happening. There's a huge part of me convinced that this is the end, not just of the house but of my entire life. My reaction is nothing compared to Kent's. As soon as the swish from above comes at us, he jumps back a solid foot, his hand wrapping around my wrist as though to tug me back with him, away from danger.

I make myself look up to see a hundred plastic bats tethered to the ceiling, hanging down only inches above my head. After a second, they're all completely stationary.

That was it? That was the big moment. As one, Kent and I exhale but only a second, before the two of us burst out laughing.

CHAPTER 12

EVEN AS WE leave the house five minutes later, I can still feel the impression of Kent's fingers against my wrist. We spent the rest of our trip giggling at the cheesy scares that had been prepared for us, but we were always ready in case something managed to break through and have us running from the house. All in all, it was the least scary haunted house I'd ever been in, but I don't have much to go on. I'm never going to forget Kent's mini freak out with the bats. Ever.

We see everyone else waiting for us nearby. Rosie waves us over and still seems to be laughing at whatever it was we missed. "Well, that was hilarious."

Grinning at her, I admit, "I'm not sure what I was expecting, but I was tough enough to take that particular house on." I side-eye Kent, who gives me a pleading stare. At that, a laugh bubbles out of me. "But this guy here is not quite as brave as I thought. I think he might've jumped from that second story window if he had the chance, just to get out."

"The empty room?" Jen asks. "Yeah, that was the scariest bit for me too. I was sure they were leading up to something really big and then the end result was so anticlimactic, all of my nerves just came tumbling out anyway."

Kent and Rosie start in on a play-by-play of each room of the house, even though there really isn't that much to reminisce about. As they talk, I spot someone I think I recognize standing at the edge of the square. Whoever it is, she's wearing a black costume that covers up most of her face, distorting the shape of her body slightly. In the way she's standing and watching everyone around her, I think it has to be Rhiannon.

"Be right back," I say before disappearing into the crowd. I quickly cross the distance between me and my suspected target. I wasn't sure if Rhiannon was going to come with anyone, but seeing her standing by herself—if it is her—almost makes me regret that I suggested we all come. I'd hate to be the reason she has a miserable time tonight, whoever this girl is, it doesn't seem like she's having fun.

But there's a chance it's not even her. The girl I'm watching has her hair tied up into a messy bun at the top of her head, in the dark it looked close in color to ours, but I can't say much more than that. The way she's standing is so very Rhiannon, I don't know if that's enough to go on. I'm not about to go up to someone who might be a stranger and accuse them of being related to me, because that's one guaranteed way to get the town talking about me all over again.

I'm less than ten feet away now and trying not to stare too obviously, as I wait for the girl to do something that would tip me off one way or the other. She's watching the crowd, if it's Rhiannon, I wouldn't be surprised if she's looking for the rest of us, either so she can win our little game or have someone to hang out with until it's time to go home.

Has she not met anybody in the two months we've been here yet? Was I supposed to invite her to come with me? I've been so busy worrying about how she's been acting at home, and I never noticed her at school, so I don't even have a guess. In math class, she focuses on the lessons more often than not. But that's her to a tee. Though she talks to me about her day after class, there's so much I don't see.

The girl I'm watching pulls out her phone, at once I know it's my sister. Not only is the phone the same one I see every day on Rhiannon's nightstand, white with navy blue stripes, but the way she's holding it I would recognize anywhere.

"Hey, Rhiannon," I say, coming up behind her and tapping on the shoulder.

She turns towards me and takes off her mask, looking bored. "Hey." I'm not even sure what her costume is.

I take in everything around me, nervous about being spotted by Reece or Reilly, though I doubt either of them are as interested in finding us as they are in hanging out with their new friends. "How's it going?" I ask. She looks entirely disinterested in everything going on around her. I want to ask if she came here with anyone, hoping I'm wrong, but the evidence seems to speak for itself.

"Kind of thinking I might go home. This is lame."

I study the square, trying to see what she's seeing. It looks like the whole town has come out tonight, everyone from toddlers to seniors are decked out in costumes, talking to their neighbors and eating homemade snacks.

I don't know how I do it, but I convince Rhiannon to come at least meet the people who I'm starting to think of as my friends here in Fairview. I don't think she's interested in meeting anyone at all, but the walk home by herself in the cold can't be all that appealing either.

"Hey," I say reinserting myself into the group. "I tracked down one of my sisters, I wanted to introduce you guys. This is Rhiannon." I wave my hands around in a flourish and pull my sister out from behind me.

"Hey." Is all Rhiannon says, not all that enthusiastically.

At once everyone is on her, introducing themselves. Apparently, she has two classes with Jen, I can already see the two of them having a bunch of things in common. If only I can get Rhiannon to open up a little.

We work our way around the square, checking out various stalls or stopping to eat. Rhiannon and I frequently end up hovering around in the back of the crowd as Jen, Rosie and Kent run into other people they know. Inevitably, were always introduced with great enthusiasm, and I do my best to seem friendly. I'm sure I come off as awkward more often than not, but Rhiannon makes no effort at all. She clearly doesn't want to be here and is taking it out on everybody.

Eventually, I pull her side. "Okay, what's wrong with you?" She's not a people person on a good day, but she's always been good at the political face and making small talk when necessary. Better than me, if nothing else. Today she's just being rude. She hasn't said anything outright, but she's making it abundantly clear she's not impressed with every-thing going on around her. She's barely speaking at all. I already regret inviting her to come hang out with us but can't exactly banish her. "You clearly don't want to be here. Why don't you just go home?" I try to make the suggestion sound as though I'm worried about her and not about me, but Rhiannon is not even listening.

"Mom and Dad won't let you stay out that much later

anyway, the younger kids have mostly already left. I may as well wait it out until I can get a ride back to the hellhole we call a house."

I don't have it in me to argue, so I leave her struggling behind us. It takes me a few long strides and catch up with Rosie, I'm praying that no one else attempts to talk to Rhiannon tonight.

"Well, your sister's a lot of fun," Rosie whispered as soon as I caught up to her.

"She's really not herself tonight. I'm sorry she's being so miserable." Rosie and I glance back toward Rhiannon, right away I wish we hadn't. When Rhiannon is wearing her resting bitch face, she looks just like me. Everyone's going to see her acting this way and think that I'm the same. Why does she have to ruin this for me? "She's been miserable ever since she moved here. I'm trying to make it better for her, but she just wants to be awful."

Rosie frowns but looks sympathetic. "Well, your other sister seemed nice. Reilly and I take art together. There hasn't really been any chances for me to talk to her yet, but she seems super friendly."

Well, at least half of the Donovan sisters can be trusted to make a good first impression.

Thanks to her eagerness to get away from anything that might be considered fun, Rhiannon and I are the first to arrive back in the parking lot where our mom's car sits beside Dad's new van—not his first choice in vehicle, by the way. I can spot both of my parents nearby, still huddled in a group of adults talking excitedly and pointing out people in the crowd.

By the time Reece joins us, she's ditched her costume entirely. Someone will probably find her wings and crown piled on a bench somewhere tomorrow, having no idea that they belonged to a fifteen-year-old girl instead of a ten-year-old one.

"Did anyone see Reilly tonight?" I ask. "Did she even come?"

My sister picks that same moment to show up from behind the van, toward us from the other direction. "I was there," Reilly says with a smile. "You just didn't spot me."

She's not wearing any kind of costume at this point either. "What were you wearing?"

"I don't know," she says. "You tell me, because I saw you hanging out with your drama friends, by the haunted house. You found Rhiannon for me, but unless either of you or our fairy princess over here can tell me what my costume was, I think I win."

No one has any answer for her, so I stick out my tongue. "I didn't even think you'd be playing." Reilly rarely has an ounce of competitive spirit, preferring to leave everyone happy rather than someone victorious over the others, but that doesn't always apply to her sisters. If there's one thing she takes pride in, it's knowing us better than we know ourselves.

For me, I feel like I'm usually wrong when I make guesses about my sisters, especially if I'm trying to base anything on what I would do. They always turn around and do something different, probably because they know it drives me crazy.

"Wow," Mom says, turning to Dad as the two of them approach us, "We didn't need to round them up tonight. I'm impressed and a little shocked."

I half expect Mom to follow that up with something

about Fairview bringing out the best in us, but instead she opens the car door and throws her purse inside, "Everyone have fun?"

We all mumble vague answers before climbing into various cars. I end up sprawled over the back bench in the van, twisted around my seatbelt so that if my dad yells back here to ask if I'm buckled in, I don't have to lie to him.

I grab my phone out of my bag for the first time in hours to find eight texts and two missed calls from Nadine.

Nadine: Hey, what are you up to tonight?

MISSED CALL FROM NADINE

Nadine: Big news! Call me right when you get this.

Nadine: Or wait, are you at that town thing?

Nadine: Dying to talk to you!

It goes on like that a bit longer before culminating in another phone call twenty minutes ago.

The drive back home seems to move perilously slow as everyone tries to leave the center of town at the same time, I hate talking on the phone while other people are in the room. For basically anyone other than Nadine and my family, I hate talking on the phone at all.

Reagan: On my way home now. I'll call you in ten.

Nadine: Finally!

A minute later...

Nadine: Nope. Can't wait. Telling you now.

I have all of a few seconds to brace myself, not sure if I should prepare for good or bad news before she spills it.

Nadine: I'm coming to visit! My mom talked to your mom yesterday and I'm going to spend Thanksgiving with you guys.

I scramble upright, trying to untangle myself before the next text comes in.

Nadine: You can't tell though. It's a surprise.

Reagan: What?! You were going to last all the way until Thanksgiving without telling me this? Yeah right. My mom knows that would never happen.

Nadine: Just for a few days until they told all of you. Your parents have invited people for your sisters too. One big reunion.

A little of my excitement fades at the idea of having a bunch of my sister's friends around at the same time as Nadine, taking away from the first time we've had to hang out in forever. But to be fair, they won't want anything to do with us either.

Reagan: I'm surprised your mom agreed.

Nadine: Right?! But your mom must have convinced her somehow. She'd already sorted out the details before she'd even told me. This is happening!

I head straight for my room as soon as we're home, hoping for a little time to ease my excitement before I have to talk to any of my family. If they see me right now they would definitely know something is up. Nadine has a bit of a reputation for not being able to keep a secret to save her life—she once told my sisters and me about our surprise party literally the day after she'd been invited—so my mom would immediately know what was up. I have to guess that Mrs. Nng wasn't supposed to even tell Nadine yet. I know it's going to be hard to pretend I don't know about this.

There's still a month to go before Thanksgiving, which is going to be slow and torturous to get through. Hopefully by the time Nadine gets here, I'll still have people I can introduce her to. People who hopefully help prove that not everyone who lives in a small town is as boring as we thought they'd be. I don't want her to think I've made some new life without her, but it would be nice to be able to show her that I've managed to make a few friends all on my own.

CHAPTER 13

WHEN WE GET home from school the next day, Dad is already in the kitchen working on dinner. A thick gravy sits in a pan on the stove, it smells like there might be roast chicken in our future. Thank God someone in this house knows how to cook.

My sisters and I will end up with high expectations for any partners we end up with because in our house, Mom is well known as a terrible cook, Dad has been preparing lunches and dinners for us for as long as I can remember. So far, not one of us has taken any time to learn how to cook for ourselves, something he is always threatening to get us involved in.

The four of us all collapse around the kitchen table, each taking our usual seats. "How was school?" Dad asks right on cue. We all say something along the lines of fine, but for once he doesn't pick a target to hone in on to ask for specifics. Even as he stirs something on the stove, he is using his other hand to type on his phone.

The front door slams shut and we all jump at once, Dad

almost dropping his phone. "Sorry!" Mom calls. "Hit the door too hard."

Everyone settles back down and a moment later Mom has joined us in the kitchen, one big happy and hungry family.

"I'm starving," Mom says before leaning over to give our dad a quick kiss. "When's dinner?"

"Not for a while. Anyone who's hungry can grab an apple or a granola bar. We are not eating until about six."

A few of us grumble as I reach for the fruit bowl. If it was up to the rest of us, we would always end up eating dinner by like 4 o'clock, always starving after school. We tried it for a while, but we end up hungry again by bedtime, looking for extra sandwiches or lunch food to fill our stomachs again.

Mom tilts her head back in despair, but when she looks back over at us she's smiling. "So, I've got big news."

"We're moving back!" I kick Rhiannon under the table.

Mom is unfazed. "No, but I suspect even you will like this news." Rhiannon looks unconvinced, Mom carries on. Even Dad is paying attention now. Convinced I know it's coming, I do my best to keep my expression neutral. "So, I've talked to your friend's parents and..." She pauses dramatically, watching all of us. My mouth twitches is the tiniest bit when her eyes lock on mine, but I'm not sure she notices. "We invited at least one of each of your friends to come spend Thanksgiving with us this year! Everyone will stay for two nights, we're are so excited to get to see everyone again."

"Everyone?" Reece asks. "Who's coming?"

From there, my parents go on to list off who they've won over to let their kids to spend the Thanksgiving holiday with us instead of with family. One of Reilly's best friend's is coming, but not the other because his parents didn't think it was appropriate that he spend a weekend in a big slumber party with a house full of girls. Two of Reece's friends will be here too. I'm surprised to learn that my parents asked Elise to come as well as Nadine, but her family had already made plans to spend Thanksgiving out-of-state with her grandparents, so that was a no go. Rhiannon's best friend from middle school, Marybeth, is also coming. I didn't realize they still talked, but with how much Rhiannon is keeping to herself now, or even before we moved, I'm not sure who she was hanging out with before we left. But the news even gets my most stubborn sister smiling.

My sisters are all talking excitedly over one another while Dad's goes back to cooking. Once again, Mom catches my eye, raising her eyebrows in an obvious question. I shrug guiltily. Mom rolls her eyes but doesn't seem mad. Even though she told Nadine's mom not to say anything to her, she had to have known this was a possibility.

"I may be pushing my luck here," Reece says, grabbing everyone's attention. "But how would you guys feel about us having a party on the Friday or Saturday night after Thanksgiving? Nothing big," she adds, although my parents already know all too well that anything involving having all of our friends in one place is automatically big. When you start with four kids, inviting anyone else in can add up. "But I'd love to introduce Aditi and Aly to a couple of people I hang out with here now."

My parents look at each other, I'm surprised when they don't immediately say no. "We'll think about it," Dad says, only temporarily ending discussion.

I'm not sure if it would be weird having Nadine meet Kent, Jen, Frank and Rosie in a big group setting. She'd probably like them, but either way, having five whole people over to one of my sibling's parties would be a new record for me.

"Fine," Reece says, not knowing when to take the absence of a no for an answer. "But remember that we did nothing for our birthday this year, so that should be taken into consideration."

"Noted." Mom nods, and that's that.

I pull out my phone and start texting Nadine to make plans. We still have a few more weeks of school to get through, but I'm determined to make the most of the time she'll be here.

Would it be too much work to have her mom drive her computer up here with her?

I take almost two hours to talk myself into what I want to do next, but in the end, I text Kent.

Reagan: Hey. What are your plans for Thanksgiving weekend? Also, I'm going to need everyone else's number :P

Even though a few weeks have passed heading out of class each day to track down my newfound lunch buddies feels weird. Now that it's colder, they've given up on doing much outside anymore. Every day seems to bring a new spot to sit down and wait out the lunch period together, after eating in the cafeteria.

Today, we all ate the lunches that our parents packed for us, then we disappeared into one of the stairwells where we've all hunkered down on the floor, hoping not to be discovered by any teachers. Another group of kids is sitting on the stairs above us, but their voices aren't much more than murmurs.

So far, no one has brought up my text asking who would

be around on Thanksgiving weekend to maybe come over. My parents haven't even approved the idea of a party yet, but I'm already sure that Reece will win this round. If she does, I want to be ready with people of my own to invite.

As everyone's talking about some gossip surrounding people I haven't met yet, I flip through my math textbook, preparing myself for a quiz at the end of the day. I should have taken Rhiannon up on her offer to help me study because I'm sure she's already got this in the bag.

"Oh, hey, Reagan. Totally meant to tell you, I will be around on the night of Black Friday, if you're having people over still." Rosie comes to my rescue without even meaning to, mentioning my party so I don't have to.

I perk up right away, closing the book in front of me with no concern for saving my place. Who was I kidding? I wasn't absorbing any new information anyway. "Oh yeah? That's awesome." I try not to look too conspicuously at everyone else group, hoping someone else will volunteer the same information without things getting uncomfortable.

Instead, Frank, Jen, and Kent all share looks with one another, my heart sinks. If only Rosie will be able to come, this whole party thing just got a lot more awkward. I probably shouldn't have risked inviting any of them.

"I'm with my dad that weekend," Kent explains. "Nothing for sure yet. I'm going to see if I can get back in time, but he lives a couple hours away."

"No big deal," I say. "Seriously, no stress. I figured I'd throw the idea out there. I get that everyone's usually busy for Thanksgiving."

"No, no. I want to come. It would be cool to meet your friends from home or even more of your sisters." He gives me a conflicted smile. "When I brought it up to my mom, you know she was all over the idea of my going into the

Donovan house. Like I would act as an undercover reporter or something. I have no idea why she's so excited."

"Well, let me know. Not a big deal either way." I shrug, trying to convince myself as much as him.

Frank mumbles something about his parents being weird on holidays, Jen says she isn't sure yet. I look down at my lap, wishing I'd still had my textbook open so I could have something to pull me away from this discussion. I'm betting Rosie wishes she hadn't spoken up because going to one of my parties without any of her friends probably isn't her idea of a good time.

Lunchtime passes in stilted conversation. When the bell rings, I'd love to just disappear for the rest of the day, but, of course, now most of us have drama class together. So I'm stuck, continuing to hang on to the edges of their conversations as we make our way to class. Then I have to sit with them, like I usually do now, on the floor of the classroom as Mr. Sullen starts his lesson.

Today, our drama teacher has decided that he wants to do an in-depth exploration of emotion that involves the entire class acting as a group. We all fake cry, fake laugh, and fake fall in love as one blob of students. It's a little easier to get out of my head when I know everyone else in the class is worried about their own performance and not looking at mine.

After acting out a dramatic death scene, I open my eyes to find Kent watching me. Instead of feeling self-conscious, I can't help but laugh out loud. This class isn't as bad as I thought it would be. I'm still definitely going to fail—despite the eighty-three percent we got on our first group performance—due to a complete lack of acting ability, there is now a small chance I won't humiliate myself before that happens.

Drama class ends in a flurry as the bell rings. Mr. Sullen announced that he had run out of things to talk about, almost ten minutes before and had left the class to their own devices as he started in on grading people's papers, making dramatic eye contact each time he turned to a new one, silently announcing to the whole room whose class test he was grading at any given time.

I slide my backpack up over my shoulder and try to go back and put my shoes on, which we all had to take off coming into the room today. Kent is hovering by the classroom door, looking at me but trying to act like he's not. My heart flutters, curious what it is he's waiting for. I look behind me but none of our other friends are still in the room, I know Ken's next class is on the other side of the building, so he should get going. But I could swear he's waiting for me

I take a step toward him, when Mr. Sullen calls out. "Reagan, do you have a minute?"

My breath leaves me in a huff. So much for getting one-on-one time with Kent. He looks over at both me and the teacher and leaves the room without saying a word.

"Yes?" I ask, looking down at my feet as I approach my teacher. Mr. Sullen has easily been my favorite teacher so far in Fairview, but sometimes his friendliness can be intimidating. I never know how I'm supposed to treat him, but always default to respectful student mode even though I'd love to be one of the students who can joke and laugh with him like some of the others.

Even now, when he's smiling at me, I worry I've done something wrong. There has never been a good reason to be called to stay after class, at least until drama. In the couple months I've been at the school, Mr. Sullen has called on nearly everyone else to talk to him for a few minutes after class at least once, a couple of the kids multiple times. I do not understand what the rhyme or reason to any of this is, so when I asked Jen or Frank why they stayed to chat, they both shrug it off like it's no big deal.

"You can relax," he says with a soft chuckle. "Although, I'm guessing that telling you to relax usually has the opposite effect. I'd have loved to talk to you sooner since I've known mostly everyone else since last year, but I got the impression you wouldn't be comfortable." I look up but am not sure what to say. He's dead on. "I don't mind." I say. Okay, I mind a little, but I'm not about to confess that. I'm just desperate to know what it is he wants to talk about. If anyone had told me what this chat is supposed to be, I could've prepared myself somehow.

"So, how are you liking Fairview so far? There was a lot of attention when your family first moved back, it seems like things have calmed down now."

If I'm being honest with myself, I hadn't thought about it in at least a couple weeks, maybe longer. While going to things like the Halloween festival, or even just walking around in town can sometimes lead to more staring than I'm used to, especially if I'm with any of my family. No one has said anything about the Fairview Four in a while, even the newspaper has even backed off. Something I like to think Kent is at least a little bit responsible for.

"It's been good," I say at last because it has been. I realize that's a boring answer. And for some reason, this is a teacher I don't want to think I'm boring. Even though I kind of am. "The attention hasn't been that bad, I guess. And my mom loves it here. I know I'm pretty lucky that I have three sisters in the same grade, built in friends in a new school."

Mr. Sullen nods appreciatively. "Gratitude. I can appreciate that." He waits, I know he's expecting me to say something else, but I have no idea what.

"Did you live here before?" I ask. "Back when we were born." I'm not sure why that's the question that tumbles out of my mouth, but more and more I've been wondering about when we first lived here in addition to my mom living here before that. It's something I barely thought about growing up. We watched the documentaries and new segments, which always featured a bit about the town. But it never seemed like a place that was part of my history--not until I moved here.

"Yes, actually. Fairview High was my first and only teaching job. So I believe I was teaching English back when your mom went to the school though I don't think I ever taught her myself. When her pregnancy was announced, it was all anyone around here could talk about. It's safe to say quadruplets were the most exciting thing that had happened to us in a while. When you all came out looking exactly the same, it was big news. Though, from your perspective I can see why maybe, that's not so much the case. From a lot of other people's perspectives as well."

"Yup. I never understood what the big deal was. We're basically double twins. No one gets this excited about twins."

"I have some theories. But, that's not why I wanted to talk to you today. I'm sure you've talked about the anomaly of your birth more than enough to last a lifetime. I just like to occasionally make a point of getting to know my students, now that includes you." He must see me glancing at the clock because he adds, "Don't worry, I don't have a class fifth period, I can write you a note if you need one. The people I work with are pretty used to me doing this. Of course, this is entirely optional."

Staying to talk to a teacher sounds a lot more appealing if it means I get out of math class. "I should text my sister to let her know I'll be a few minutes," I say.

"You're close with your family then."

"Hard not to be." I give a small laugh.

"Fair enough. I never know where to start these conversations if I don't have a jumping off point. I'll be honest, I don't know much about you beyond your family. You've been quiet so far."

I blush, feeling weird that he's noticed me at all. I'm used to being the least recognized Donovan sister at school. If someone's not busy mistaking me for one of my sisters, they've definitely noticed them more than they've noticed me. Rhiannon is always the one who gets the best grades, Reece is the one who makes the most noise, and people tend to flock to Reilly without her even trying. I'm usually just so-and-so's sister. Which I'm fine with. "Not much to know about me, anyway."

"Well, I'm sure that's not true. What made you opt into take drama class?"

I give him a long look, trying to figure out if he's teasing me. He has to have heard what happened, but he's still smiling politely and waiting for me to respond.

"Wasn't working out in biology class," I say and know immediately that it sounds like a stupid answer. "I knew I needed an art credit." Probably not the most artistically driven reason he's ever heard.

"Can't draw or play an instrument, I take it?"

"Zero talent whatsoever." Fairview requires that each of its students graduate with at least one art credit, drama is the only one that doesn't require any actual ability to begin with. I had planned to take art next semester and suffer through a few months of terrible drawings and crafts, but now I'd need to switch that out anyway in order to make back my missing science credit. "Not that acting is really my strong suit either."

"Want to know a secret?" Mr. Sullen asks.

"Always."

"Your actual acting ability counts for literally none of your grade. It's all right there in the syllabus, but we don't advertise that part. For many people, the acting is the fun bit, but it's not what we're grading you on." Mr. Sullen holds a finger up to his lips to emphasize our little secret, I grin.

"That makes me feel a little better."

"Happy to help. Well, I've kept you long enough for now. But let's do this again sometime, shall we?"

I nod and head for the door shortly after, note in hand to explain my tardiness for math class. I'm not sure what to make of what just happened, but it's hard not to feel like if Mr. Sullen was trying to get to know something interesting about me, then he was probably left feeling pretty underwhelmed.

CHAPTER 14

IT LOOKS like today is my turn to walk home by myself. Over the course of the last hour, I've gotten messages from all three of my sisters telling me they won't be around to walk together after school. Rhiannon, once again, is already at home. Reece and Reilly apparently have better things to do than just go home and start their homework.

I take my time gathering all my stuff into my locker. The weather is starting to go beyond the level of cold that I'm okay with, I'm in no rush to get outside. Hopefully, once December rolls around, Dad will take pity on us and start swinging by after last period to pick us up. At least those of us who want a ride would have the option. Dad swears that the middle of the afternoon is his most productive time of day, and, to be fair, we usually find him locked in his office when we get back from school, if he hasn't started cooking dinner yet.

A lot of other people seem to be hanging around after classes today though I can't guess why. If there's something going on that my sisters are involved in, I'm already a little bummed that they didn't decide to tell me. But no one seems to be doing anything in particular, I know Fairview has a lot of after-school activities. I just don't choose to get involved in any of them. Not my thing.

The gym is the loudest spot in the whole school, with the basketball team practicing on one end of the gym, and a few girls playing volleyball on the other. The bleachers are about a quarter full of people hanging around and watching the athletes. It's only by chance I catch sight of a familiar face during my cursory glance of the room. Reilly is sitting by herself near the top of the bleachers, watching the volleyball game. She's not even on her phone. Instead, she actually seems to be enjoying volleyball, but it seems weird that she would stay after school just for that. Since I have nowhere better to be, I step inside the gym, sticking to the wall so I don't get in anyone's way before I reach the bleachers and climb up.

Reilly spots me as I'm maneuvering up the steps and immediately blushes. It's something I don't see her do often. Why would she feel weird about my finding her here?

I almost wish I hadn't stopped to say hi.

"Hey," Reilly says, giving me a big smile that I don't quite believe.

"Hey." I sit down beside her. I'm already here, and it would be weird to leave now. "Did not expect to find you here." I say, tilting my head toward the game. Reece is the only one of my sisters who has any interest at all in sports. If anything, I'm surprised she's not here too, potentially even playing volleyball. Though she'd probably have the same issues getting on that team as she did with soccer. Reilly doesn't say anything right away, and pointedly looks away from me. "You're not avoiding me are you? Did I do something?"

Right away, Reilly looks back at me, concern in her eyes.

"No, no. Not at all. This will sound so stupid, I don't even know why I didn't just tell you. I'm just hanging out with someone after-school, and she's on the volleyball team, so I had to wait."

It takes me a second to figure out why she would feel weird about having plans after classes, something that happens a lot. I look over at the volleyball game and try to figure out who it is she's talking about, but don't have any ideas. Reilly's mentioned some of her new friends already, but I haven't been able to put any names to faces yet. An idea dawns on me. "Oh. Do you have a date?"

Now Reilly's face is beet red, and she seems to be trying not to stammer out a response. "No. No dates."

"Okay, so why are you being so weird?"

"I'm not being weird," Reilly says though there's no denying her behavior at this point.

I grin, finally getting it. Reilly hasn't dated much, but when she likes someone she turns into a flustered, stammering romantic. "You like someone then." I don't even bother to ask. She definitely likes someone.

"Shut up." She's smiling but there's more to her expression than merely being excited about meeting someone new. "I haven't *told* anyone here yet," she explains.

Oh. She likes someone and is clearly loving being around them. If no one here knows she's gay, then there's a good chance that the girl she likes might not feel the same way. But it seems like there's an obvious solution. "Why not tell? You were out back home and seemed happy with the decision. You've been out for like two years."

Reilly's smile disappears, replaced with worry. "At first, I didn't want to be known as the gay one, or to deal with any questions about it. This isn't a big city. I wish I knew how people here would respond, you know?"

I nod, understanding on my own level even if we don't quite share the same experience here. I want to say who cares what people think, but I know if I were in her position, I would absolutely care. Any more attention drawn to me would be entirely unwelcome. Being the subject of rumors and scrutiny would be Reilly's worst nightmare. She's already making friends here, and I can see why she wouldn't want to risk that.

"At least you know if people in Fairview get weird about anything, Mom would be all over them in a heartbeat."

Reilly laughs, probably remembering the same day back in eighth grade that I am. One moronic kid, Kimberly Greystone, gave Reilly a hard time, accusing her of having crushes on all the girls in their change room. My sister came home in tears. And then my mother shook the world, getting a written apology from the kid and the school. The only reason she didn't force the principal to do an entire assembly on acceptance was because Reilly would have been mortified.

Some kids back home were occasionally ass holes, but for the most part, it was not an issue. At least for the people who mattered. "So, you're hanging out with this girl and just trying to get an idea of if it might go anywhere?"

Reilly throws her hands up in the air. "I don't even know what I'm doing. I just like being around her. Sasha. It probably won't go anywhere, I worry I'm going to end up as that lesbian girl who has a crush on her friend who ends up being straight. When she asked if I wanted to study together after classes, I couldn't say no."

"Will there be other people there?" I ask, really hoping that this ends well for my sister. She shakes her head in response.

Even if Fairview ends up being the most progressive

small town ever, there's already a shortage of people our age to choose from, Reilly will have a harder time of it than any of us. Except maybe me, since I can't seem to ask out a guy even if I do like him and know he's single.

Now that I think of it, I don't know that he is straight, I should know better than to make assumptions.

Shit. One more thing to worry about.

Just then a loud whistle sounds from the floor, ending the volleyball practice. Girls standing on both sides clap enthusiastically before departing. "I guess that means I should go," I say, knowing I'm about to become an unwelcome distraction in a situation where Reilly is already stressing. I stand up and get ready to go.

"You can stay," she says. I can't tell whether she wants me to stay or go, but I remember how I felt back at the haunted house when I had a chance to be alone with Kent, and how it felt having him touch me. Even mostly by accident. There's a chance of that happening for my sister, I don't want to be the one to get in the way.

"Next time," I say already stepping down to the next level of the bleacher. "And there will be a next time. You're a Donovan. You're irresistible."

"Something you should remember some time," she says before sticking out her tongue.

"Good luck."

I take off as fast as I can without tumbling down the steps and drawing attention to myself. In less than a minute, I'm back outside the gym doors. I can't help but pause, pretending to check my phone so I can wait to see the girl that has my sister swooning. It's almost a full minute before someone strides up the bleachers towards her. The girl is tall and black, with curly hair tied back in a tight ponytail. I can't tell much more from her without getting closer, but all I really need to understand is the way that my sister is smiling as she approaches. I force myself to go, but silently continue to wish Reilly luck as I make my way out of the school.

CHAPTER 15

NADINE AND EVERYONE else had taken an early train together from Richmond that morning so no one's parents had to drive them here, missing their own Thanksgiving festivities. Before my sisters and I had even woken up, Mom took Dad's van to go get our friends. Just after breakfast, as I am putting my cereal bowl into the dishwasher, we hear the van pull into the driveway.

"They're here!" Reilly squeals, jumping up and down a little in place, in the middle of the living room.

I can't help but run for the front hallway along with everyone else. I've been waiting forever for this. I feel like I'm getting a piece of my life back, bringing it here with me to Fairview from home. The four of us clamber around a window and watch everyone pile out of the van. One, two, three, four, five. Everyone made it. I'm not sure why I was worried they wouldn't, like someone would just skip coming and not have told us or gotten lost along the way. But they're here.

Mom opens the front door and leads the group inside,

there's only a moment of silence before chaos erupts in a group huddle of hugs and high-pitched voices.

I dodge around my sisters before I can get to Nadine, as soon as she is within arm's reach, I pull her toward me in a massive hug. It's a little out of character for both of us, who tend to hold back from big dramatic displays of affection, usually mocking the girls in our class who have to hug their friends every time they see them like it's a ten-year reunion—Reece—but even we get swept up in the moment. She is really here!

I'm dying to ask a million questions even though I can already guess at all the answers, but it's been so long since the two of us could spend any real time together.

I'm not sure when my parents slip away from our group, but as soon as I calm down, I follow suit and drag Nadine to the living room. I don't want to share her today, but we only get a few hours before all things Thanksgiving commence. Dad isn't letting all the extra company deter him from cooking for his favorite holiday. As always, he's made it clear that sooner or later we will be expected to help. Especially now that he's being called on to make twice as much food as usual. A ridiculous amount of food, really. As if the amount of groceries that is stockpiled in our kitchen is any indicator.

"So, this is where I live now," I say, closing the living-room door behind us and hoping that everyone else takes the hint.

Nadine laughs. "I got the cellphone grand tour when you moved in." But she still ends up wondering the edges of the room as though reconciling everything I showed her when we moved in with the reality. More than once, she gives me a strange look and then opens her mouth as though to say something, but changes her mind at the last moment.

It's not long before she has settled in on the couch.

Mimicking her action, I flop out on an armchair before the two of us are chatting like nothing has changed.

I wish.

At least two hours pass before Dad calls through the dining room, looking for some extra pairs of hands, I'm bummed that our first few hours are already over. It's time we won't get back.

We take way too long to pull ourselves back into the real world and make it to the kitchen, entering a realm of vegetables, desserts and fresh bread. The kitchen smells amazing but looks like a war zone.

Dad gives me a long look as we slip into the kitchen, probably attempting to point out that we should have volunteered our services a while ago. Reilly and Lily have already set about making up the dining room table while Reece and her friends chop vegetables.

Nadine and I set to work on tidying up behind everyone else, doing our best to keep things organized as my dad directs his troops toward a successful Thanksgiving dinner, if not a hectic one. We will be using both the dining room and kitchen for our Thanksgiving meal. Despite the two designated eating areas, we still need a few more chairs to make room for everyone. If nothing else, we're well versed in chaos in the Donovan house, so things will work out.

———

By the end of dinner, my body is ready for a small coma because I had at least a few bites of everything. I ended up eating half of my dinner in the dining room, somehow losing my chair as soon as I got up to grab more mashed potatoes. I ate my seconds in the kitchen with Reece and her friends. For dessert, I ate standing in the doorway between the two rooms. Even Reilly's plate was stacked high with food, despite the fact that she's been a vegetarian for more than a year now and had less Thanksgiving options than everyone else. At first, Nadine mostly sticks close to me, but as she gets more comfortable back in the world of Donovan insanity, I can see her start to relax, easily falling into conversations with everyone else.

Eventually, almost everyone settles in to watch football. Those of us who care least about the sport volunteer to take on the dishes to keep busy until we're forced to join everyone else. Not long after, I fall asleep, unable to ignore my body any longer, I'm squished on the couch in between Riley and Marybeth. Nadine is already asleep on the floor near my feet.

I wake up as the game is ending, panicked that I've missed some of my time with Nadine. We only have two full days left, and I'm aware of every hour that goes by. It won't be long now before everyone heads upstairs to sleep, and we lose even more time.

I poke Nadine with my foot and find she's already awake. It looks like she's texting her mom to check in, probably not for the first time that night. Mrs. Nng is not the type of person who has ever been described as easy going. "Want to go back upstairs?" I ask Nadine.

She nods, we excuse ourselves quietly to go upstairs before Rhiannon can claim the space.

"It looks good in here," Nadine says, thumbing her way through my bookcase.

"I already sent you pictures of pretty much every room in the house," I point out.

"Looks better in person." She picks up a small superhero figurine displayed on my shelf, but puts the book down a moment later. "I'm glad I got to come see you." I'm about to say I'm happy she got to come to, but she barrels on. "So much has changed since you guys moved. We talk all the time, but it seemed like you and I were losing touch. We've both seen people move away before, and in the end, people always stop talking. It's just easier to be friends with the people close by."

I frown but don't respond. What am I supposed to say to that? Yes it's been hard, but I put in a real effort to make sure I was telling Nadine about everything that was going on in Fairview, while also making sure to ask her what was new in Richmond. What she would tell me didn't sound like anything was ever new. So what else had changed?

"Anyway, you're here now. I didn't think I'd get to see you again this soon after moving... You'll get to meet some people I've met at school tomorrow." I quickly change the subject, not wanting to dwell on whatever it is she thinks is going on here. All things considered, we're doing fine. The idea that when people move away they always lose touch has always been at the back of my mind but talking to people who don't live near you is easier now. Some of my closest friends are people I only talk to on the Internet, so why shouldn't I be able to stay close with Nadine?

"Out." Rhiannon marches into the room, glaring at me.

"We were here first. You can stay, but I'm not leaving," I answer, hoping she'll choose not to stay at all.

"Marybeth and I are sleeping up here and I want to go to bed, so you guys need to leave."

"We're all sleeping upstairs in the attic," I point out, getting defensive.

"Not me. They're all going to stay up late talking, I will

end up getting frustrated and leaving after an hour or two anyway. So, we're sleeping here. In beds. Including your bed," she adds, as if that point wasn't obvious.

"Whatever." Part of me wants to argue, but I'll only make things awkward. If this is how Rhiannon is going to be tonight, I don't want her included in the upstairs sleepover anyway. She always has make things so difficult. If nothing else, tomorrow morning everyone but Rhiannon will sleep in late, so this will be the first time since we moved in that my sister waking up early isn't going to be my problem.

As usual, Marybeth has nothing to add and goes along with whatever Rhiannon says, which is something she's done ever since they were kids. There was a while there where we all referred to Marybeth just as Rhiannon's shadow. It must be nice for her to have her sidekick back.

Eventually, everyone but Rhiannon and Marybeth end up in the attic. We only have one couch, so everyone has agreed to sleep on blankets and sleeping bags on the floor. We are all kind of bunched together in small groups, but everyone is close enough to chat with whoever.

My eyes are struggling to stay open as I hope that Reece's friends will stop talking and go to sleep sometime soon, but I must have dozed off at one point because I awake to Nadine poking me from her own sleeping bag.

"I can't sleep," she says in a whisper.

I want to point out that I was already asleep, so it's clearly possible, but I doubt that's what she wants to hear. "Okay..."

Nadine shifts around as though making a point. "I didn't realize we'd be sleeping on the floor."

"Okay." Is still all I can think to say. She knew we were having five extra people sleep over. Where did she think we would sleep? Marybeth is probably still fast asleep in my bed, so it's not like that's an option. "You can sleep on the couch. Everyone else is already asleep." That's assuming we haven't woken them up with the stupid conversation. "They won't mind."

"Can't we sleep in Reece and Reilly's room? There are two perfectly good beds in there."

I'm tempted to groan but keep my mouth shut. She came all this way to see me, so I don't want to piss her off. If she knew where she wanted sleep, why didn't she point this out hours ago? There is still such a big part of me that just wants to tell her to be quiet and go back to sleep. Still, it's the least I can do to try to make her comfortable. It's only for two nights.

Trying to get my eyes to readjust to sitting in the dark, I rub them and sit up. Neither of us bothers gathering up our sleeping bags before we make our way back downstairs as silently as possible.

Within seconds of getting to the bedroom, I crawl in to Reece's bed and pull her blanket up over my chin. I feel a little bad for bailing on the slumber party, but this is way more comfortable than the floor of the attic. I look over at Nadine and find her still sitting up on the edge of Reilly's bed. All I want to do is sleep, but she's looking around and there's no denying she has something on her mind.

Today was perfect. Why can't whatever this is be something that can wait until morning?

I'm about to give in and ask what's on her mind, but Nadine finally lays down. I figure this is my chance to get back to sleep, but it's less than ten seconds before she starts talking.

"Your life here seems great," she says, no longer bothering to whisper. "I love this house. And the town doesn't seem to be as bad as we thought it was."

"It's okay," I concede. "You know I'd rather be back home with you and everyone, right?"

"Yeah," she says but there's a note of disappointment in her voice. Suddenly, I'm wide awake. There's more going on here than I realized, I still have no clue what she's trying to say. Was this the reason Nadine didn't want to sleep in the attic? It had nothing to do with how uncomfortable the floor was and everything to do with wanting a chance to talk to me where we couldn't be overheard.

I'm trying to figure out what she could have done that she feels so uncomfortable telling me about, when she speaks again. "Elise and I both miss you a lot. Everything from going to classes, to hanging out after school is so different because you're not there. But other stuff has been changing to."

Part of me wants to say something just to get her to stop talking and hold off whatever is coming, but I can't figure out what to say, so I keep quiet and hope I'm overreacting. There is now an unspoken *we need to talk* hanging in the air.

"Laney is my best friend now. Or, we are best friends now, I guess." Wait, what? "It's just that I needed to have someone around once you weren't there anymore, and she's being really cool. You know how it is."

I really don't. I can barely figure out what it was she just told me.

Nadine has a new best friend now.

After all these years... I'm not Nadine's best friend anymore.

I moved away, and she's found someone new. The pit in my stomach grows to the size of a black hole. I don't know what to think or do, but Nadine seems to be waiting for me to say something. The silence is becoming suffocating.

I don't want her to see how much she hurt me-- is hurting me. It's now all too clear, she doesn't care all that much about my feelings. I've been replaced in a matter of months by some girl Nadine had only met two weeks before I moved. Laney had been the new girl in the neighborhood, one of many. For some reason, even before I'd gone away, Nadine made a point of hanging out with her. Like she was trying to replace me before I left. I saw it happening then, I tried not to think about it since.

Was this inevitable? Or could I have changed things if I'd just seen this coming?

I'm not Nadine's best friend. She found someone she likes better.

What I want to do is tell Nadine that it feels like I've just been dumped, but that's what I would say to my best friend—someone who I could rely on to have my back when it feels like the world is against me. Instead, I try and hide how much this hurts. "I guess we knew this would happen," I say. I consider telling her I had a new best friend too, but as much as I need to bury the sting of this, I also don't want her to be able to justify away what she's doing right now. After all, I don't have someone new. Nothing even close. I met new people, but I've *always* thought of her as my best friend.

Is she still my best friend if I'm not hers? It's not like there's anyone else I'd list instead.

I try so hard to keep my tears at bay. At this point, crying is only going to make things uncomfortable. Or maybe that's exactly what I should do. Maybe if she sees how upset I am she'll change her mind, but as soon as the thought crosses my mind, I know that it's a bad idea. It's an impossible idea.

We both wait almost indefinitely for the other person to

say something else. No one speaks. Eventually Nadine turns over in bed, pointing herself away from me. She's making it clear that there's nothing I can say that will change this.

Nadine has a new best friend.

I wipe my damp cheeks on Reese's pillow and try to sleep. Instead, I spend at least an hour replaying the conversation we just had and trying to figure out what the hell happened.

CHAPTER 16

I COULDN'T HAVE GOTTEN MUCH SLEEP last night, but I don't wake up for good until Reece shows up and storms around the bedroom as she gets dressed.

"Sorry," I groan. "We took over your room." Right. We ended up leaving the attic for a little one-on-one time. I got hard-core friend dumped last night. Okay, not dumped in the literal sense, but broken up with. And it's hard to imagine going through this with a boyfriend feeling much worse.

Nadine and I are no longer best friends.

I didn't realize how much being Nadine's best friend had been part of my identity. I'd seen my sisters go through several best friends for as long as I can remember. They'd announce new ones, rank their friends from best to worst, and meet new people faster than I could eat lunch. But my best friend had always been Nadine, and she'd come all this way to tell me that everything had changed.

God, had she only come out here because she didn't want to dump me through a text? Why was it necessary to even tell me this at all? Okay, I would have been pissed if she hadn't told me or if I found out some other way. This would have crushed me no matter how it played out.

Nadine is still asleep or at least pretending to be. She has always been a ridiculously deep sleeper, her mom is constantly banging around the house doing renovations. Still, I can't be sure whether she can hear everything going on around her right now. I signal to Reece to be quiet before disappearing through the bathroom to my own room. Unsurprisingly, Rhiannon and Marybeth are already up and gone, which begs the question of what time it is. Also, where is my phone?

Mornings are really not my thing.

I give up on accomplishing anything more than changing into jeans and a shirt and make my way downstairs. Years ago, my dad would put together a big post-Thanksgiving breakfast. This time, it looks like he's simply stacked a variety of cereal in the middle of the table, put out nine bowls, clearly having gone back to bed. It's kind of sweet he thought to do anything at all.

We all owe both our parents so many thank yous once this weekend is over.

Reilly and Lily are still sitting at the table eating breakfast a couple of the bowls are already in the sink. I fill up the one closest to me with Rice Krispies, eating them as fast as I can before I take off, not saying more than a few words to anybody. I don't want to deal with anyone right now, there's still nowhere I can go to get a little privacy. Going on a walk might've been an option if it wasn't already around freezing outside.

I plant myself in front of the TV, turning on some cartoons, hoping everyone will get the message that I'm not awake yet and not willing to deal with people.

I only move when Nadine comes downstairs to eat.

Okay, it was kind of lame of me not to wait for her or woken her up, especially because I knew she wouldn't be comfortable coming downstairs on her own. Instead of heading to the kitchen to keep Nadine company—I still don't know what to say to her—I move around the house at a frantic pace, cleaning up anything left behind from last night's dinner. As much as everyone wants to take the morning to finish digesting, we are still having people over tonight, it'll be the first chance anyone here has to see the house.

Too weird.

Any other day, I'd be annoyed that absolutely no one moved to help me, but we hadn't made that much of a mess last night. The less people working to tidy up, the longer it would take me. The longer I could avoid talking to Nadine.

So much for hiding how much she hurt me, but it's not like she has tried to talk to me yet either. She probably thinks I'm avoiding her. Which I am. I still need more time to process.

The hours pass and I eventually crack, talking to Nadine, but only when there are other people in the room. I don't want to be petty, I can tell I'm making things weird for everyone, but I'm also not ready to talk about what happened.

This wasn't how this weekend was supposed to go.

T-minus-three hours left until everyone else should arrive, and my parents force us into a board game day. It's something we did almost weekly in Richmond but haven't gotten back into since moving to Fairview. The joy of kicking Rhiannon's butt at Ticket to Ride is almost enough to take my mind off everything else.

When Nadine and I end up at the same table to play Scrabble, we somehow manage to talk like nothing has changed. I guess for her, nothing has. She's known about this for a while now, I guess. How long has she been thinking of ways to let me in on the news?

I'm basically an idiot, but I force the thought away. If I dwell on this enough, I'll start crying again. I need her to think I'm okay. It doesn't need to be true, but she needs to think it is anyway.

For a second, I search the seven letters in front of me to find some passive-aggressive way to get my frustration out, but the best word I can come up with is 'fork', that hardly seems appropriate. Though, if I play it right, it may get me at least a few points.

"Nadine, I can't wait for you to meet Rosie. I think you guys will get along." I keep my voice light, Nadine watches me like I've gone completely insane. My dad and Reilly both nod long, looking excited and having no idea what's going on between my ex-best friend and me.

Now I'm imagining how I will tell my sisters that Nadine has declared me not good enough to be her best friend.

Nope, nope, nope. This is not what we're doing today. I only managed to get *one* of my new friends to come over tonight, and that's what I need to focus on because my friends in Fairview are the people I need to learn to count on.

I chatter on about my new friends here for a bit longer before realizing Nadine can probably see right through all of this. When it comes down to it, she still knows me better than anyone I'm not related to. She'll get exactly what I'm doing, and that I can't stop obsessing about all of this in my head.

It's not my job to make this okay for her! Frustration keeps hitting me in fresh waves, all I want to do is rant to her, to anyone. To get all of this off my chest!

Couldn't she at least wait until her last night here before dumping this on me? She had to know how crazy this would make me. Otherwise, she wouldn't have felt the need to tell me anything at all.

It's only when the doorbell rings that I finally force myself to push all of this aside, at least for now.

A bunch of people I don't recognize arrive first. I assume they're friends with Reece, a moment later the black girl I'd seen talking to Reilly that day after the volleyball game follows in behind everyone else, talking with Jen.

Wait, Jen's here?

I rush towards the door, eager to greet my first guest, even if it's one I wasn't expecting. I never heard anything from Jen or Frank after they'd first told me they weren't sure whether or not they'd be able to come tonight. I assumed that was their way of politely blowing me off, but here she is.

"Hey, you're here!" Okay, not the way most people would welcome friends to their house. I should try sounding less surprised when people want to hang out with me.

"There is literally nothing going on in my house, so my mom couldn't come up with a good reason to keep me there. Besides, the holiday was yesterday. Today everyone was just sitting around and digesting or listening to my aunt's Black Friday horror stories."

People pile into the house, introducing themselves to my parents before finding a place in the living room to sit. I hope my parents will realize that they need to get out of here soon or things will only get more awkward. By the time the doorbell rings again, they've already gone. They're probably still hovering in the kitchen, listening to everything's happening. At least they are not right here making things weird.

Although, things may end up being all kinds of weird all on their own. Parties are not my natural habitat. At least this time around both Reece and Reilly are there to help get things going, and, before long, Reece's old friends are talking to her new friends like they've all known each other forever.

Jen is still hanging around with Reilly's friends, which means Nadine is the only one left for me to talk to. If I don't want to keep standing in the hallway looking like it's the last place in the world I want to be, then I *have* to talk to her.

"I suck at parties," I say, more honestly than I intend, but it's not like this is news to her.

"Don't think of it as a party," she suggests. "It's you and your sisters having people over. Like you did at home. This is a lot of the same people, it's still your house. This is your comfort zone, own that."

It's hard not to give an appreciative smile. I'm not sure if I think of this new house or these new people as my comfort zone yet, but I still welcome the advice. A big part of me understands there's no reason not to be comfortable here. Her advice doesn't help that much, but it's a start.

Just when I'm starting to wish I'd found a way to get out of this party thing all together, Rosie appears in the front hall, jacket in hand. After everything else, I'm more than a little worried she'll head over to Jen and join that group too, making it perfectly clear to Nadine how on the outside I still am with my new group of *friends*. Within seconds of taking off her shoes, she's walking toward the couch whereas Nadine and I are doing our best to look engaged in conversation rather than left out.

Yup. I'm the life of the party.

"Hey," Rosie says with a wave. "This house is amazing. I've always wondered about it but never got the chance to see inside. It's like this icon of the town, it's weird to think that people actually live here."

"Thanks," I mumble before introducing Rosie to Nadine. "This is the part where I should jump in with some fantastic icebreaker, but as usual, I got nothing. "

"Actually," Nadine says, "Reagan was just offering to give me the grand tour."

I blink at Nadine. She's been here for more than a day and has seen much every corner of the house already. She stares back at me expectantly, like she's trying to tell me something.

Oh.

I pop up out of my seat. "Yeah. I mean, there's not that much to it but if you wanted to check it out, you should come with us."

Rosie looks around and quickly seems to make up her mind, instead of simply taking me up on the offer she turns toward the other side of the room and calls out. "Jen! Reagan's going to show me the house. Want to come?"

Within a minute, five different people are up and ready to check out one of Fairview's oldest homes. Most of our friends from Richmond stay back with my sisters. As I look over the living room, Reilly mouths at me, "Want me to come?" I shrug helplessly, but in the end, she stays put. I'm on my own.

For the first time today, I'm glad Nadine is there with me.

"You guys saw the living room and dining room," I start as we move into the kitchen, trying to figure out something to say beyond the name of each room. "This is where we eat. It's a kitchen. Really not that much to see." To my surprise, the group behind me laughs like I've said something funny.

"Let me guess," one of Reese's friends says. "You guys

redecorated? There's no way Doctor Halbertz's kitchen looked this good. I swear his entire office was covered in wood paneling."

As easy as that, everyone is chatting as we make our way through a quick rundown of the backyard and the laundry room, which we can barely see in the dark. Soon, we're upstairs. The next stop is in front of our bedrooms, I explain who shares with who, popping the doors open but not stepping inside. I hope people will take hint, but instead they are soon sticking their heads inside our bedrooms and having a look around. I really wish I had thought this through and tidied up a little more, but thanks to Rhiannon, our room is never really that bad. Reece and Reilly's on the other hand, is a disaster. No one says anything about all the laundry that's everywhere, but I can't help but notice that our room gets a few more compliments than theirs does, despite the fact that no one would ever accuse Rhiannon and me of being the cooler duo in our family.

"That's my parents room," I say pointing to the end of the hall. "I'm guessing they're hiding in there and don't exactly want us going in. But it looks like a bedroom in all its bedroom glory. There's two bathrooms on the floor as well, I promise they are not all that exciting. That is the attic." I say, pointing up at the hallway ceiling.

I lead the crowd upstairs, looking over my shoulder to see Nadine and Rosie chatting at the back of the group. "This is the attic. We're still renovating it. The idea is it will be a bit more space for the four of us to spread out, since we can all drive each other kind of crazy if we're stuck in close quarters for too long."

"This is amazing," Rosie says. There isn't much here besides our desks that we've just moved up here and the couch. There's even still a fair-sized pile of blankets in the middle of the room from the slumber party the night before.

I can't help but grin. "This was totally my favorite part of the house before we moved here," I admit. "I love the idea of having a whole floor to ourselves."

"Not anymore?" This time it's Nadine who pipes up with the question. "This place seems so you."

I have to think about that. I barely think of this house as home and even then, the effect is incomplete. "Too early for favorites."

Just like that the tour is done, we all head back downstairs to see what everyone else has gotten up to. Now, there's both music playing, a TV on in the background playing a movie I don't recognize. At first, the party mostly breaks up into Fairview people hanging out together and Richmond people talking in the corner with my sisters and I flitting in between. Yes, even me. It looks nothing like the high school parties I've seen in movies, but we make it work. Though that one, brief night is the one where our two worlds collide, it's hard not to remember that one of those worlds is quickly slipping away from us. If we did this again in a year, what would the ratio be between people from our old lives and those from our new ones be?

If Nadine and I aren't best friends anymore a year from now, will we even be friends at all?

The weight of betrayal hits me all over again but only for a second. I'm already kind of looking forward to Nadine going back home so that we can sort all this out from the safety of our computer screens and cell phones. There's no way I'll be ready to talk about this in person. I don't even want to talk about it at all.

Around eleven, the Fairview parents start arriving to bring their kids back home. Looking back on the night, I'm happy enough with how things went. I managed not to make an idiot of myself, which is more than I manage at most of the parties my sisters drag me to.

Rhiannon and Marybeth quickly take over our bedroom once again, making it clear that who will be sleeping in our beds is not open for negotiation. When Nadine doesn't try to make a play for the other bedroom, I'm not at all surprised. Tonight, I think we're both happier sleeping in a crowd of people where we don't need to face one another or our thoughts.

CHAPTER 17

EVERYONE LEAVES on the train early the next morning, so they'll have time to get back home before the weekend is completely over. Tomorrow, life goes back to normal. Our new normal. Back to school, back to homework and routine. The only 'back to' being not back to being best friends with Nadine.

Nadine officially crossing me off the list as her best friend makes me want to do the same. Do I need an official best friend? Will I be able to confide in her the same way I had before, knowing she doesn't care about me like she used to?

This sucks.

I end up in the attic with my sisters, cleaning up after the weekend and trying to get the floor that belongs to us into some sort of final configuration that makes sense. There is a ton of room up here, and we try to make the most of it. It is just one big space, so breaking it up into different parts looks awkward and forced. I'm still dreaming about the day when we're able to add an extra bathroom to this floor assuming that's even an option. There has to be a way to pull this off.

We ended up aligning our desks along the far wall and putting a room divider in between each so we can pretend we each have a separate office space. All anyone has to do is roll her chair back to see the people beside them, but if nothing else, it means that our desks are finally out of our bedrooms. Besides, we have a little more room to move around, and to avoid the sister we're stuck rooming with.

"So, that was equal parts fun and weird, right?" Reilly asks as she piles up folded blankets in the corner of the room beside the couch.

I'm doing my best to organize some of the stuff on the shelving units Dad put up last weekend. It's mostly random textbooks and unreturned library books, they look like a mess no matter how I arrange my stuff.

"For sure," Reece says. "I think everyone got along though, not that it matters."

It's hard not to agree. The party was actually fun, but the weekend as a whole was more weird than anything. Probably weirder for me than it was for them.

"Nadine told me I'm not her best friend anymore," I say, talking quickly so can get the words out before I can stop myself. There's a big part of me who would be happy never to have to bring this up again. But I have to tell my sisters. "Pretty much out of nowhere she announced that the Laney girl from back home is her best friend now. Not me. Not anymore."

Even though my back is to the rest of the room, I can sense everyone else stop what they're doing and hone in on me. I turn to find Rhiannon staring right at me, head tilted slightly to the side. "Wait, what?" She asks. "You guys have been best friends for almost our whole lives."

"Yeah, are you sure you didn't misread this somehow?" Reilly asks.

"How? She made it pretty clear. I'm sure. That first night, when she didn't want to sleep up here. She said it was because the floor was uncomfortable, but really she just wanted to get me alone somewhere so she could friend dump me." I can hear the anger rising in my voice and attempt to keep calm, but I know no matter how I play this, my sisters will see right through me. Nothing about this doesn't suck.

The more I say aloud, the more humiliating all of this sounds. There's no taking it back. It's out there now, and my sisters are looking at me with a mix of sadness, worry and anger.

My sisters take care of the rest.

Somehow, we end up crowded around the small shared TV my dad let us have up here. Reece and I are on the couch with my legs spread out over hers, Reilly and Rhiannon are squished into the loveseat opposite us. Without meaning to, I'm crying. I'm still trying to fumble out what happened, but I can tell I'm not making much sense-- none of this makes much sense to me.

"I'm kind of glad you didn't tell us earlier," Reece says, seething. "I definitely would've said something to her. This weekend was not the time to bring up any of her overdramatic crap. This was supposed to be a good time."

"I still had a good time, I think. Last night was fun. But yeah, when I remember this weekend, this is what I'm going to think about." For some reason, the idea of my sisters being angry on my behalf makes me feel the tiniest bit better.

"Your new friends seem really cool," Reilly adds. "Rosie seems like a lot of fun." I note that she doesn't seem to think the same about Jen, but I'll take what I can get when it comes to the seal of approval on the new people I hang out with.

Nobody mentions that no one from Fairview turned up for Rhiannon last night. Thankfully, she at least managed to be more friendly than usual and made an effort to talk to everyone else, so maybe this would be the introduction she needed to start making friends here as well. That is if we could pry her away from her textbooks, long enough for her to get to know anyone.

"What I want to know is how you two...," I look at Reece and Reilly, "...managed to meet that many people already."

"I had three people here," Reilly says. "Only one more than you. But you shouldn't be keeping score. I just met some decent people in my classes so far."

Reece on the other hand, had five people show up and all of them pretty and athletic. She keeps quiet during this discussion, still looking somewhat proud of herself. It's not like I actively want to be more popular, though I've always liked the idea of people secretly thinking I'm more interesting than I am. If I ever got stuck in a room with any of Reece's friends, old or new, we'd have absolutely nothing in common.

Back home, I would always watch her during lunch surrounded by this huge group of friends, guys and girls, who seemed to shift in and out of her group constantly. It made me wonder what that would be like.

Now, at least I have my own little group of my own, even if we usually hide out during lunch instead of parading around the cafeteria and making as much noise as possible.

Hours pass before we finish the attic. The final touches take the longest. The sloping ceiling that leads up after the stairwell has been covered in photographs. Among the four of us, we have a lot of pictures. We also now have a lot of abandoned, empty photo albums.

As a group, we decide we're giving up on any sort of formal memory storage. Everything's on Facebook now anyway. Our new plan is to have the photograph wall grow out from the first three feet or so (the part we put together today), and hopefully cover all of the attic's walls one day.

Looking at the pictures makes me conscious of my anger and hurt, how they haven't gone away. Nadine and I... Okay, it still sucks, but if she doesn't want to be my best friend anymore, then I don't want her in my life. Maybe I can convince myself of that. After all, I have something she'll never have. That most people will never have.

For me, Nadine's spot as my best friend was never the true top of the people I cared about. I have three sisters, who are just like me and also so different, for whom the term *best friend* pales compared to the reality of my sisters and I's relationship. There's no question that they will always have my back. In the end, it's Donovan sisters first. It's always been that way. And that's something that no one will ever be able to take away from me.

———

The rest of the night slogs on, as if our usual weekend routine had never been disturbed.

Of course, most of my teachers took advantage of the long Thanksgiving holiday to pile on even more homework than usual, none of which I'd done during the past few days, I had working on all of that to look forward to.

I was just finishing up taking all the dirty plates from the table so that Reilly and I could tackle the dishes, our usual Sunday night chore, when the doorbell rang.

For a second, all six of us stare at one another, not sure what to make of the disturbance.

"Is anyone expecting someone?" My mom asks, looking at us. "Because at least two of you still have papers to finish before bed."

Almost as one, we shrug.

"I'll get it then," Reece says, standing up. While this neighborhood seems to be big on getting to know the people who live around you and involving one another in your lives, I can't imagine any reason someone would be compelled to come bug us on a Sunday night, and at the end of a long weekend too. I feel way too tired for someone who just had extra time off, and the last thing I want to do was deal with company.

"It's for Reagan!" Reece's voice echoes through the house, snapping me back to reality. I look over my shoulder, convinced that my sister has misspoken. Reilly nudges me.

"Go," she whispers.

I put down the plate I'd been scrubbing while I rack my brain for who could have shown up, hoping to see me tonight.

Absolutely no one comes to mind.

Reece is standing in the hallway, grinning. Beside her is Kent.

Nothing about what I'm looking at makes any sense. Kent hadn't mentioned coming over tonight or ever.

"Reagan, there's someone here to see you." Reece waggles her eyebrows, looking ridiculous and probably trying hard to embarrass me, which I have to say is going pretty well.

"I can see that, thanks." She continues to stand there looking between Kent and me. "I've got this."

Reece takes the hint and goes back to the kitchen. I can

already imagine what she'll say to everybody else and the interrogation I'll have to sit through later, I can worry about that once I got through this.

I remind myself to exhale.

Kent stands, staring down sheepishly at his feet. "Sorry to just randomly show up like this," he says, looking up. "But my dad was on his way to drop me off back at home, and I wanted to stop by and apologize again for not being able to make it this weekend."

Oh. "You didn't have to do that. I knew it was a long shot with Thanksgiving." My heart thumps against my ribcage as my body tries to work out what's happening.

He came all this way just to apologize? It was just some stupid party, but I don't say that out loud. For some reason, he made the effort to come here tonight, I'm not sure how to respond. A smile is struggling to fight its way onto my face, I'm determined to play it cool.

"Did you want to come in?" I ask before remembering what he *just* told me. So much for cool.

"No can do. My dad has to drive back home, so I don't want to keep him waiting." He locks eyes with me. "So how was last night? I heard both Rosie and Jen came by. They loved seeing the house up close."

"I really can't figure out why people care about this house." If I'm being honest with myself, I can't figure out why most people in this town care about any of the things they did. Maybe complaining wasn't the best way to continue this conversation. "But yeah, it was fun. A little weird having those two different groups of people all here together, I think it went well though."

"Rosie said she had a great time, and Jen managed not to find anything to complain about. So that's a good sign."

"I promise you didn't miss much. If you want, I can do a

private tour just for you some other time." Did I actually just say that? "Although at this point, I feel like I should add some plastic bats falling from the ceiling just liven things up. People seem to have high expectations for this place."

"And low standards for haunted houses." He chuckles.

I laugh. "That too."

A dish clangs from behind me. I turn around in time to see someone's head popped back out of the doorway. Great, we have an audience. Everyone in my family is clearly going to read way more into this than they should. Kent is just being polite. Him coming is super sweet, and granted more polite than anyone would ever think was necessary. It's not like it means anything.

Right?

"Well, I'll let you go. I still have to finish pretty much every piece of homework I got for the weekend."

"I did most of it at my dad's place since there wasn't anything else to do. I'm still going to thank Mr. Sullen a thousand times for not adding on some ridiculous paper just because teachers seem to think they need to give us home-work whenever there's a chance we might be enjoying our free time instead."

I grin and say goodbye, wishing I could be the kind of person to spontaneously hug people. I stay and watch from the door as Kent made his way back to his dad's car. His dad had been sitting in the driveway and is now politely looking at his phone instead of at us. He has dark skin and hair a little curlier looking then Kent's. Even from here, I can see that Kent looks more like his dad then he does Mindy.

It's a surprising reminder that besides Rosie, I really don't know that much about my new friends outside of their school lives. Has everyone else met Kent's dad? What are Jen's parents like?

Is that why Nadine had decided that Laney would make a better best friend? Was I too self-involved? How often does everyone hang out outside of school without me?

No. Not now! This is not the time to let these stupid thoughts get the best of me. I've made an effort to get to know people outside of school now, and I'm not going to let Nadine ruin this part of the weekend for me too. Kent just showed up at my house, just to be nice!

As they drive off, I wave goodbye and close the door, leaning my head briefly against the door frame as I collect myself all over again. That had been the most unexpected dishes detour in a while, but I can't stop grinning.

Even if Kent had just stopped by to be polite, he'd done it all the same. He was thinking about me. I'd gotten to see him on a weekend, which was pretty much a first for me and any guy. Ever.

Thankfully, no one is watching me from the kitchen as I head back inside as I try to steady my breath. I brace myself for the onslaught of questions I'm sure is coming, already prepared us to downplay everything that had just happened. I want time to figure out what this means for myself first.

CHAPTER 18

TO MY SURPRISE, when I get back to the kitchen, no one says a word. My family's silence speaks louder than any pointed comments they could be making. I can practically hear the ripple of giggling underneath everything. They all act like this is business as usual, like I have guys coming over just to say hi all the time.

Actually, no guy has randomly showed up on the doorstep yet just to chat with Reece. I'm the first in Fairview.

I win?

I still wish my whole family hadn't been here to witness that. I don't know what they're thinking right now, but it's driving me crazy.

"He was just on his way home, he wanted to say sorry he couldn't come yesterday."

"Well, that's very nice of him. Whoever he is," my mom says, her tone ominous.

"You've met him before. Kent. He was here with his mom the reporter, the one from the day we moved in."

My dad nods, and thankfully no one else comments. As

nice as the silence is, it's unnerving. I almost wish they would. Almost, if only to break the tension. While it's nice in theory that they are all respecting my privacy, they'll be whispering about this behind my back. I would do that too if it had been any one of my sisters.

Maybe they don't think that any guy could possibly have come to see me for any sort of romantic reason, maybe that's why they're not saying anything. That could be the more realistic option.

Yeah, I have no idea what I'm doing with myself right now.

My family soon disperses, each retreating to their own corners to finish up the rest of the night. They're either reading way too much into this, or they're not.

I'm the last one in the kitchen, because I'm avoiding announcing anything at all about my plans for the evening. I'm just going to work on my homework in the attic, getting ready to face the world again tomorrow. I feel like anything I say will make me sound guilty, but I have absolutely nothing to feel guilty about.

Kent coming over was nothing.

Yeah, right.

———

I'm really desperate to make sense of all this. Instead of tracking someone down to ask, I decided that I need some time alone. When I see Rhiannon heading up to the attic, I detour to our room.

A second after I plant myself on my bed and haul my backpack up behind me, Reece appears through the bathroom door. She didn't bother to knock, but she closed the door behind her, as though to make sure we're not over-heard. This makes me want to run the other way.

"Hello," she says, dragging out the word. She's grinning at me. I have a sinking suspicion of what I'm in for. So much for being left to my own devices on this one.

"Hey," I say, trying to keep my voice casual. "What's up?" Yep, that will fool her. Absolutely nothing going on here.

"A boy came over to see you today." She announces, as if I somehow missed it completely.

"Oh, you don't say."

"Reagan, come on. Why was he here?"

"Oh, like you didn't hear every single word he said. It's exactly what I told you. He came over to apologize for not coming to the party. He was on his way home and what he did was a nice thing to do. Not a big deal."

Reece lets herself farther into the room before sitting down on Rhiannon's bed, staring at me like a hawk. "Like you're one to judge what's a big deal or not."

What's that even supposed to mean? I don't bother asking. I roll my eyes before pointedly looking down at the textbook in front of me, something I'm making a habit of. If these awkward situations keep up, I may actually absorb some real knowledge this semester. Not likely, but it's possi-ble. "Whatever."

Finally when she says nothing for nearly a full minute, I shift my eyes back up toward her, finding her gaze has soft-ened somewhat. It's almost as though she's studying me, so I find myself observing her right back. Reece has always been the sister that I've felt I had the least in common with. If there wasn't already evidence to the contrary, it would be hard to believe we shared any DNA at all, let alone all of it. She's athletic, extroverted, and genuinely good at knowing what to do around other people. There are times I feel like we couldn't be more opposite.

"You know..." she says, "...you're doing pretty well here in Fairview so far. Like really, your life here doesn't look anything like your life back in Richmond. That's weird, right?"

"That's kind of by design." I confess. "Things back in Richmond were good, but this was a fresh start for all of us. I tried to make the most of it, but maybe if I hadn't made an ass of myself on the first day of school, things would've gone even better."

"Nobody cares about that anymore, so you're clearly doing something right. It's possible that if you stayed in biology class, you wouldn't have met your drama friends. That'd be the only difference." Reece his mouth twists into a frown. "You're doing good."

"Easy for you to say," I counter. "You have tons of friends here. You would do well anywhere we would to move to."

"That's what makes my opinion so worthwhile." The smile she forces on her face doesn't meet her eyes, and the frown returns. "I like the people I've met here, but I would still go back home in a heartbeat." For a second, I entertain the idea that Reece is trying to tell me that she's unhappy here too. But that's something you could honestly never tell by looking at her. No matter where she ends up, she always fits right in. Except when things are completely outside of her control.

"Well, you'll make the soccer team next year." I say, trying to sound reassuring. "Those coaches don't know what they were missing with you."

"You have no idea. Their team actually kind of sucks. I don't think anyone here really takes it that seriously."

"Whatever happened with that volunteer gig you wanted? That sounded perfect."

Reece shrugs. "That was a no-go too. The owner doesn't take volunteers or something, or she handpicks them from people she knows. So because I'm new, again, I don't have a shot. I could take up dog-walking or something instead." Her response is impossibly casual, there's no question she's forcing her attitude.

I shouldn't have brought it up. If there had been good news, she probably would have shared it already. It's just too easy to assume that things would just go Reece's way no matter what, the sheer force of her willpower always seemed to bend the universe into doing what she wants it to.

"Sorry." It's all I can think to say, but I'm sure it doesn't help at all. "I'm just trying to think of this year as our readjustment. We're meeting new people and figuring things out here. Next year, things will make more sense. Fairview will feel like a place we belong."

"I don't want to waste a full year of my life waiting for things to figure themselves out. I'm not myself here. It sucks."

I'm just making this worse. "Anything I can do to help?"

"Now that you asked, you can stop dodging the topic of that guy today. Even if he meant nothing by coming to the house just to say sorry, anytime he comes up you get super weird. He obviously means something to you, and you haven't told us about it. I'm crying sister foul on that one."

I blush as guilt swells in my chest. I have had a crush on Kent pretty much since we moved here over three months now. I haven't told anyone, mostly because I've known it's not going anywhere. As much as my sisters are happy to talk about every single person they are interested in, I've never really done the same. Actually, now that I think of it, it's only Reece that really shouts from the rooftops every time she thinks someone is cute.

"Fine, I like him. Doesn't matter anyway." I find saying the words out loud stirs something deep within me. I *like* him. This might be the first time I'd liked a guy I was even a little close with. Before, I'd always developed crushes on random guys in my class I'd never really spoken to, or just happened to see in passing a few times. But, I like Kent because he's ridiculously nice; he was kind to me when there was nothing in it for him at all. Also, that green streak in his hair, oh my.

I like Kent. Yeah, that's something I could get used to saying. At least within the safety of my own house, or maybe just in my own head.

"I knew it!" Reece cries out. Now she's grinning for real, wiggling in place with excitement. "Reagan's going to get her first boyfriend!" she continues in a singsong voice.

"Okay, getting ahead of ourselves here. Just because I like someone doesn't mean they have any interest me. I'm not you. It's harder than that for most of us."

"He obviously likes you! He came to your house on the Sunday night of Thanksgiving weekend, after driving from wherever, when he probably just wants to go home and sleep. All to see you! That really has to count for something."

"You're crazy." But is she? For the first time in a long time, I'm mildly optimistic about my own dating prospects. The idea seems so absurd that I push the feeling away, trying to make myself be more realistic, but now Reece's voice has worked its way into my mind.

"That's not enough to go on." I point out. "I'm open to the idea. How would you, being the relationship expert you are, figure out if someone likes you or not?"

"No, no, no. I'm not giving you some list of how to tell if your crush is into you. It's something you have to do by yourself. It's like a sense. The best way to figure it out is just going to be to ask. I've asked out more guys on dates than guys have ever asked me."

I'm well aware because she points that out to us every time it happens, like a point of pride. Neither Rhiannon or I have ever asked out anyone at all, or been asked out ourselves--or at least my sister hadn't been until Derrick came along. I'm never going to have the nerve to ask someone out, blindly hoping they'll say yes and risking that they say no. Saying no means I'll have to avoid them for the rest of my life. Not a chance.

"That's not going to happen. You and I both know there is no way that's going to happen. What's Plan B?"

"I'd say spend more time with him and report back. Let me know if he says anything, or if he's paying a lot of attention to you. You've already been hanging out with him for a while, have there been any clues?"

I think back to classes and lunches spent with Kent and his friends, but everything seems like a blur. "He offered to do the haunted house with me last month. It was just the two of us. It's not like he made a move or anything."

The more I think about it, the more convinced I am that Reece is way off the mark. Kent hasn't done anything that would suggest he likes me as anything more than a friend. I should feel lucky he likes me even that much.

"Has it never occurred to you that he's playing the same game you are? Holding back and hoping for some kind of sign from the universe." Reece sighs like I'm the most exasperating person on the planet. "Tell you what. Tomorrow at school, just pay more attention. Consider the possibility and see how he's acting. No commitment for you to do anything, just wait and see. Don't be so busy hiding from the possibility, you might miss it entirely." With one big flop, I'm lying down on my bed, groaning in despair. "Now I wish you hadn't said anything. I'm sure he doesn't like me. Now I'm going to take any possible thing he does as a sign or something."

"*That* does not sound like you're taking my advice and keeping an open mind." I look over to find that Reece's expression has taken on one that looks frighteningly similar to that of our mother. I groan again to make a point, but I don't argue.

As Reece stands up to leave, I pull myself up as well and latch onto her in a big cheesy hug. "Thank you for being the only one of us who is remotely competent at this kind of thing." I don't know why I say it, it's not even really what I want to thank her for, but it's something. I truly mean it.

After a second, Reece pulls away and looks at me, giving a helpless shrug. "I have no idea what you guys would do without me."

I let out a dramatic sigh before conceding. "Same. Maybe if you aren't feeling like yourself here yet, find a way to change things. Do something big, something totally Reece to make you feel like you're owning Fairview just as much as you were Richmond. We both know that sooner or later you're going to be running this town in no time, so stop waiting around for it to give you permission."

Reece sticks out her tongue, but just maybe she's considering what I've said. I may have opened a giant bag of worms on that one, or maybe she'll go to sleep in a couple of hours and forget that we ever had this conversation.

Reece gives me a quick wink and then disappears back through the bathroom.

For now, I'll let Reece worry about herself and I'll worry

about getting this homework done or I'll worry about Kent. Okay, I'll be worrying about Kent because tomorrow I'm going to see him again. As of now, it feels like everything has changed.

I want to do as Reece says and believe. I want to be open to the possibility, but it's so far away from everything my life has ever been. Having a guy like me like that just doesn't feel like who I am, and I know that's ridiculous. Reece's voice is still whispering in my mind that this could really be happening. Not wanting to screw it up, I open my phone. I promise myself that this will only be a five-minute detour from homework, searching some lists of ways to tell if your crush likes you.

CHAPTER 19

BY THE END of second period the next day, I've freaked myself out at the mere thought of seeing Kent again.

So far, all my teachers are interpreting the end of Thanksgiving break as an excuse to move full throttle into preparing for exams. I can barely focus on the influx of new assignments, all I'm thinking about is Kent. At least half of my brain has been on the lookout for him at all times, since arriving at school this morning. So far, nothing. His absence should have given me more time to figure out a plan, but I'm more confused than ever.

Right before the last bell, I got a text from Rosie saying that the plan for lunch today is to meet in the cafeteria, eat fast then go to the library. She and Jen need to study for a test tomorrow, meaning we'll be on our own in terms of entertainment. I'm probably going to have to figure out something to say to Kent. Before today, that had never seemed like a particularly daunting task, now it seems like the hardest thing in the universe. Frank will be there to act as a non-studying buffer, but odds are that right after we get to the library he will open a book and we won't hear from him again until it's time to head to class. Something I'm kind of wishing I could attempt too.

With this whole Kent situation on my mind, it took less than an hour to imagine five different ways I can screw this all up in a matter of minutes. Despite these thoughts, a big part of me wants to see how this plays out. Reece will expect some sort of report after school, I want to have something to tell her. I want to know is if maybe she's right. Could he like me too? The fact that I'm even considering it as a possibility seems insane, but I so desperately want her to have this all figured out since I definitely don't.

Why does this all have to be so difficult?

I'm the first one to arrive in the cafeteria, so I sit myself down in my usual spot and make a point of looking busy, which is not so hard to do since I never finished my math homework last night. I start in on the massive pile of problems I'm supposed to have finished already, trying to work through them when my brain struggles to remember what we're studying in class. If only Rhiannon didn't get so annoyed every time I asked her to share her own homework with me.

"Hey," Rosie's voice interrupts me. I look up as she and Kent sit down at the table beside me. Soon after, Jen and Frank arrive as well, already in the middle of a conversation about some old movie. Everyone else keeps quiet as their conversation turns into a heated debate, causing us to do our best to stay out of the crossfire.

After a minute, I risk a sidelong glance at Kent, glad to have Rosie as a buffer between us. I'm not sure I'm ready to face him head-on yet, so time and space are good right now.

Reece was right. All the lists I found online were completely useless. Sure there are dozens of signs I could watch for, but any one of them could be interpreted a million different ways. My best bet will be waiting to see what Kent does, and if I can read anything into it. I'll probably end up just reporting back to Reece and letting her sort it all out.

"Fine!" Jen says, placing her hands down on the table. "You win. I will watch the original Buffy movie and tell you what I think, but I think this is all a huge waste of time." Frank looks triumphant, but he doesn't get a chance to respond before Jen continues. "Which brings us back to the real world. New presentation assignment today in drama. The last one before we start in on Alice in Wonderland as a class. Groups of three."

Crap! I should have had the syllabus memorized weeks ago so I'd be able to brace myself when these things are coming. Not only will I have to perform in front of the class again, but there will be only two other people up there with me to share the spotlight. Since there are four of us in class together, it means I will be doing this with people I barely know.

I've been lucky that Jen has taken pity on me every time we needed to work with other people during class. It's always worked out so that me and the three of them either formed our own group, or became part of a bigger one. This time, I'm not so lucky. Groups of three means someone is getting left out, and it's going to be me.

No one says anything at first, so I prepare to volunteer as tribute before anyone has to tell me I'm out of luck.

"Okay, so two and two," Frank says.

But before I can wrap my head around the fact that the world isn't ending after all, Kent chimes in. "Me and Reagan, you and Jen." My heart stops. "Makes sense to mix up the genders so we have the most versatile groups possible." he quickly adds, before shooting me a glance.

I still don't say anything. Kent wants to be in a group with me. He could ditch me altogether and work with both Jen and Frank, but he wants to work with me!

Is this one of those signs I'm supposed be looking for? Or is this just Kent continuing to be insanely nice? Like everything else, there are too many ways I can interpret this. No matter what it is, I'm screaming inside.

Jen and Frank agree like it's the most natural thing in the world, they then dig into their food as if they don't notice what just happened.

Kent picked me. Me!

Maybe they aren't acting like it's a big deal because it really isn't. I pop a carrot stick into my mouth and chew slowly, trying to buy myself more time to pull myself together. I shift to look over at Kent but find Rosie staring right at me and looking at me, much in the same way that Reece did last night.

Why is everyone treating me like some social anomaly fit for study?

I give her a questioning look back and make myself focus on food instead of Kent. Later, I'll replay all of this for Reece and hopefully she'll be able to help me sort it out.

I mean, it's possible that this doesn't mean anything at all. Maybe this along with the apology yesterday, as well as everything else since we moved here, has just been Kent being Kent. He's a nice guy. I have to think there are guys out there who are nice even to girls they aren't interested in dating.

No, I won't say anything to Reece yet. This is a good sign, but it isn't definitive. I can't let her talk me into believing otherwise, not without real proof. All I can do is wait and see, keeping note of everything else for the next few days. I won't write this off, but I won't start imagining me and Kent going on our first date together either.

That's a lie. I definitely will.

———

The next few days pass almost normally. Except that I'm hyper aware of Kent and everything he does. Every time he says hello to me in the hall or at lunch, I note his expression and tone before stumbling a greeting back. When he grabs my bag for me after drama, I can't help but wonder if he's doing it as a way to get my attention. As an afterthought, I remember to thank him. I'm pretty sure that trying to pay more attention to what Kent's doing is making me act like an idiot around him. If he did somehow like me before all of this, there's a great chance he's not going to by the time he actually gets to know me.

The thing is, I'm starting to suspect that possibly, there is the slightest chance that he does actually like me. Or is it just wishful thinking?

The way he acts around me isn't quite like how he is with Jen and Rosie. I catch him looking at me in the same moments when I'm already trying to subtly look at him. While it's harder to tell with his darker complexion, I'm pretty sure he's blushing nearly as often as I am.

Is this really my life? Did I moved to a new town, promptly make an ass of myself, and then somehow still manage to come out at the other end with the new group of friends, with the guy I have a crush on liking me back?

Maybe. Maybe not.

I'm probably overthinking this.

By Friday, I've given into the reality that I will need a second opinion. It's time to bust out the big guns and ask

Reece what she thinks. Will she tell me what I'm supposed to do next? Or am I just going to need her to talk me down and convince me that all of what I've been seeing is in my head? By the time we get home from school, I'm ready for either possibility.

When I try to take my first chance to get Reece alone, she practically sprints for her bedroom and shuts the door. I try to use my own room to come at her from another angle, but I find the door locked. When I circle back to the hall-way, the door to her bedroom won't open either.

Reilly comes up behind me. "Reece said she needed the room to herself for like an hour after school." She shrugs, heading up for the attic with her backpack still on. Typical Reilly. I'm guessing she's planning to get a jumpstart on her homework tonight, so she doesn't have to think about it for the rest of the weekend. Odds are, Rhiannon is already up there.

Everyone is doing something, leaving me to my usual routine of City of Ages. Playing for a bit couldn't hurt, right?

As I make my way upstairs to the attic, I try to figure out what I'm going to say to Reece the second she gets out of the bedroom. I have no clue what she could be up to in there, part of me suspects I don't want to know. Either way, she couldn't have picked a worse moment.

Before going to my computer, I make sure to leave the attic door open, so I can hear when Reece makes her reap-pearance. As I suspected, both of my sisters are already hunched over their desk and working. If I were smart I'd do the same, but taking on a quest or a boss in the game might be the only thing that can distract me right now.

I log in to find Nadine already in game, and I almost log off immediately.

All week, I've been avoiding thinking about Nadine. She hasn't exactly reached out either, leaving me to wonder if this wasn't just a best friend break up, but her telling me she didn't want me in her life at all. I mean, she's the one who did this, so she should be the one to make it less weird.

But, I'm also not going to let her scare me away from my favorite game.

A minute later, she messages me a simple hello, I mentally exhale. She's not trying to avoid me completely, but that also means I have to deal with this now.

Kinsey: Hey, I didn't think you'd be online.

Niddles22: Sorry about the disappearing act. Just had a busy week.

Just like that, we decide to take on one of our favorite daily quest lines together, teaming up to help the Allied army storm the castle on Mount Flaimver. We both throw ourselves into it, staying as a group of two while we work with others to take on the horde of trolls. While I'm sure we're both thinking about it, neither one of us brings up the last weekend or any of the things that happened. I almost feel bad for not reaching out sooner. Almost.

Just when it seems like things could be normal again, I stick my foot in my mouth, asking her what she's getting up to for the weekend.

Niddles22: Laney's mom is taking us to this craft show in the suburbs. She has a table there, she's selling a bunch of crochet stuff. We're going to help out for the morning, she'll pay us a little money. Which we'll probably use pretty much right away to buy jewelry at the fair. Laney has all this great stuff from going last year, there's already a bunch of things I want to get.

Right, *Laney*. Nadine's new best friend. Of course,

Laney's mom has a cool job and will pay Nadine to help out. I'm not even surprised that she has this awesome style and great jewelry that Nadine wants too. She probably even likes Laney's mom more than she likes me.

All the bitterness I've been trying to push back over the last week comes right back up, but the game keeps moving. I'm forced to push back the response I'm already trying to craft in my head, somehow getting in a subtle dig. It's just enough time for me to take a breath and decide not to be an idiot after all, because if I say something harsh now, there's not going to be any coming back from it later. This is the first time I've hung out with my oldest friend in a week, simply because things have been so weird. If I make it weirder, then there will be no one to blame but myself. Well, I'm sure I could still blame her a little.

I can't help but pretend that I have more interesting weekend plans than I actually do, claiming I'm going out with Rosie and Jen to do some shopping for Christmas presents. Hopefully she won't ask me about it again later.

The quest eventually ends, and our side is victorious. Just as a message from Nadine pops up on screen, asking me if I want to go again. I hear a door shut down stairs. I type a message quickly.

Kinsey: BRB, first. Have to go check something.

I should log off completely, but I'm already busy going back over all the things to ask Reece as I charge down the stairs. She's not in the hallway, but the door to her bedroom is now wide open. I peek my head inside. Still no Reece.

I find her in the bathroom, staring at herself in the mirror. She can't be looking at herself half as hard as I am, because something is very, very different. It takes my brain a second to catch up, to figure out what part of this picture doesn't belong.

Reece turns and looks at me, and for the first time I don't see someone who looks like a near identical variation of me. Still mostly identical... The face is all the same, but Reece's hair is blond. Gone is the light brown color that looks just like mine, Rhiannon's and Reilly's.

Her hair is blond. How is that possible?

My gaze finds the box of product still sitting on the counter and I piece together what she's done.

"Do you like it?"

"Uhh..." I've forgotten how to form words.

"I thought a lot about what you said to me the other day and realized I needed to make a change. This is a new town, so why not throw a new Reece into the mix? Please tell me it isn't awful."

"Mom and Dad are going to kill you." It's not the compliment she was looking for, but it's all I can come up with. Whether or not it looks good is way beyond what I am capable of in this particular moment.

Reece frowns but then squares her shoulders. "You're right. The first thing is going to be dealing with them. Do you think I should just come out and tell them, or do I wait for them to notice on their own?"

"Well, they're going to notice the second they see you. You can't exactly hide this."

"Okay, I'll face this head on. This is happening. No going back." She claps her hands together like she's breaking up a huddle. The slightest quiver in her voice is the only thing to betray that she's not quite as confident as she's acting.

With that, Reece sidesteps around me and makes her way toward the stairs heading to the first floor. I sprint up the stairwell in the other direction. First things first, I tell Nadine that I need to log out for a few minutes.

Kinsey: Gotta go. Donovan apocalypse is incoming.

I shutdown my computer and turn to my sisters. "You guys are going to want to give the homework a break. There's about to be a showdown of epic proportions." I don't bother explaining to them what Reece has done, because I don't want to miss whatever's coming next. My parents gave up on trying to get us to dress similarly years ago, but they've never once budged on our dying our hair until we got older. Sure, it would have given us a quick and easy way to differentiate ourselves, but they didn't care.

A second later, I hear the sound of both Reilly and Rhiannon following after me.

CHAPTER 20

WE CROWD TOGETHER at the bottom of the stairs. The main floor of our house consists of a fair-sized hallway leading from a foyer at the front of the house. If you go straight down the hall, it leads to the kitchen or you can hang a right and go to the living room which connects to the back of the house by the dining room. From the sound of it, my dad and Reece are in the living room. I didn't hear my mom come home yet, but it's possible I missed it. I'm not sure what to expect when I take a breath and step through the hallway to the living room.

It looks like my dad had been watching TV, but he's now standing up in front of the couch with Reece ten feet away from him. She's also standing, with her hands in her back pockets and her newly colored blond hair hanging down loose over her shoulders. I wish I knew what she'd said when she'd walked in the room, probably whatever she thought would make the biggest impact. But the aftermath is impossible to miss.

My dad inhales a sharp breath fueling himself to start

yelling at Reece, it's a stance I know well. Instead, his eyes lock on me. "Reagan, not now."

Reece turns around to look at me, I can see plainly on her face she has regrets about the last few moments. If she'd taken even a second to think things through, she wouldn't have announced it like this. Or, maybe she knows she shouldn't have done it at all without talking to all of us, because this affects *all of us*.

I'm about to back out of the room and retreat to Reilly and Rhiannon, who still don't even really know what's going on, when we all hear the rumbling of the garage door being opened from outside.

Mom's home.

"Do you want to tell her what you've done or shall I?" My dad asks pointedly.

"Pretty sure she will figure it out on her own." I mutter.

I move back toward the hallway and find my sisters waiting for me. I cock my head toward the kitchen and the three of us make our retreat. It would be just as easy to watch what's going on from the other side of the room, but none of us wants to be anywhere between Mom and Dad for whatever happens next.

Rhiannon spots Reece for the first time from the kitchen. "She actually did it? Her hair is blond!" She stammers out, eyes wide. I nudge her to get her to be quiet.

"Yup." I whisper. "There was a highlighting kit in our bathroom. That's why she wouldn't let any of us in."

"That is a lot of highlights." Reilly points out. She's right. Looking closer at Reece, who can see us staring at her, I can tell that her natural color is still the base of her hair, but the top is almost entirely streaked with a natural looking blond, even if the streaks themselves are a bit heavy handed.

"You guys would not believe the day I've had." my

mom's voice cuts through everything else, she enters through the front door and dumps her stuff in the hallway.

Usually I'd shout out a hello, but today I stay silent. I'm totally content to pretend I'm not here right now.

I don't know who will speak first, but it won't be me. It looks like Rhiannon and Reilly have the same idea.

"Hello?" The sound of her heels clicks down the hallway toward us, but my dad's voice stop them.

"In here." he yells out. "Brace yourself."

I groan internally, not sure why my dad is insisting on getting my mom's back up before she's even seen what happened. "You girls may as well come in here too since we're well aware that you're standing in the kitchen."

We come out of hiding as my mom enters the room from the front hall, looking confused and wary. Shortly after, she's perfectly observant and notices exactly what's going on.

"Reece. What did you do?" My sister turns around but not before casting the three of us a pleading glance.

It's not like there's anything we can do to help her now. The fact that she didn't even tell us what she had planned, doesn't make me all that sympathetic to her cause.

Around this time last year, all I wanted to do was put one streak of pink in my hair. My sisters and I had all come up with different things we wanted to do to alter our own styles just a little. Back then, not one of us wanted to do anything drastic, just something to stand out a little. We came up with this big PowerPoint presentation, we even showed it to our parents. We'd all been on the same team, even when we lost miserably.

Reece decided she was doing this one on her own, so she'd have to fight for it on her own too.

"I put in a few highlights." Reece says, stating the obvious. My mom doesn't respond, she simply collapses down into the armchair behind her.

"Did you know about this?" she asks my dad. "You'll let them talk you into anything."

"Wait, what? No! I did not know about this. She did this all on her own! When she came home from school today, she looked just like the rest of them. Now she's a blonde. I didn't even realize you could do this kind of thing at home by yourself."

Reece shrugs, but doesn't point out just how easily someone can die their own hair. The whole thing cost her ten bucks and an hour of her life. "She knows what our rule about this is. None of them would die their hair until they were at least sixteen, even then we would have to discuss it. There were no guarantees. They have beautiful hair and adding chemicals to it is just a bad idea." My dad stamps his foot a little to emphasize his point. I'm honestly surprised he's as upset as he is. "How easy do you think it will be to dye back to its natural color?"

Everyone looks over to Mom as one. She furrows her brow but doesn't speak.

"I'm not dying it back. It's my hair and I can do what I want with it. I needed a change, and this the best way I could think to do it."

Crap. I guiltily fix my eyes on the far window. I had wanted her to do something to mix things up, but I never considered that she would make such a permanent change. I can't even guess how long it would take for those highlights to grow all the way out again. Even dying over top of the highlights would still end up looking different from before.

Everyone stands still, waiting for my mom to place her verdict. There's no way Reece isn't at least getting grounded for this one, but I'm surprised that I can't see the smoke coming out of my mom's ears yet.

"One, you know you should've talk to us about this. We have rules, they aren't just there for your amusement." My mom's voice is steady, I can tell by the tone of it that her mind is racing with some idea or another. Which is kind of terrifying.

"But, Greg, I think she has a point. It is *her* hair. It wasn't too long ago that I didn't like the idea of them dying their hair, because most of our girls couldn't be trusted to stick to one decision from one day to the next, let alone for months at a time. We weren't about to make rules that applied to some and not all of them. But, what's done is done."

I can't read Reece's expression, she has to be sensing the triumph coming her way. "I think we should let her keep it."

"Our rules are there for a reason. What's this going to teach her?"

"I'm not sure this is as black and white as all that. You tell me that all the time!" How often are our parents talking about this kind of thing when we're not around? "We need to take the punches as they come." She turns toward Reece, "It's just us looking out for you girls. I, for one, don't think anyone else should make decisions about your bodies. Except for punching holes in them. That, I still hold the right to weigh in on. Only because I've seen just how wrong those things can go."

My dad stammers, but he doesn't formulate any real response. I don't think this was the moment he'd had in mind when he called my mom into the room. It's not at all what I thought as coming. If she'd waited just a little longer to come home, this could have gone very differently. "So much for a united front," he grumbles.

"You're right, I wish we'd had the chance to discuss this, but Reece has taken matters into her own hands. Since we're talking about this here and now, her vote needs to count for at least as much as ours. Reece, I assume you want to keep your hair like it is?"

"Hell yeah!"

Mom's expression tightens, not enjoying Reece's enthusiasm. "Fine. Give us a few minutes. Your dad and I will discuss this and then we can go from there."

Reece knows when to call it and heads back to the kitchen. We follow her in. I don't think anyone of us knows just how far we're supposed to go, or how much time to give them. They don't start talking until we leave the kitchen and trudge back up the stairs. We can only hear a faint whisper of voices. Rhiannon stops at the top of the stairs, and we plant ourselves down on the landing.

Reilly leans over and touches Reese's new hair, pulling a strand toward her. "It's blonde. That's weird."

"You guys like it though?"

"Yeah, it's great!" Reilly reassures her.

"I kind of wish I'd had one of you help me," she admits. "It was hard to do the streaks at the back on my own." She turns her head so we can see the back and sure enough, a couple of the highlights she's put in are a little blotchy near the top. I won't be the one to point that out to her. It's still too weird looking at my sister and seeing her hair that doesn't look like mine.

I'd never have thought this would upset me even a little, but something about it is sitting weird in my gut. Reece now looks different from the rest of us. Before this, we were a matching set.

"So why didn't you tell us?" I ask, trying to keep the hurt out of my voice. "Why did it have to be such a big secret?"

"I don't know. It was kind of spur of the moment."

"How spur of the moment could it have been?" Rhiannon asks. "You obviously took the time to go buy the hair dye. We all know you well enough that you wouldn't risk screwing up your hair without at least giving it some thought."

Reece has the decency to look at least a little ashamed. "Okay, so I've been thinking about it for a few days. I wanted to make the change and this seems like a good way to do it. I loved the idea of having blond hair. I would've done my whole head, but I know you're not supposed to do that much bleach at home on your own. I wanted to see how the highlights went before jumping into something more drastic."

"Well I think it worked. So, that's something," I say, the ords coming out harsh. This feels still like a betrayal. I was supposed to be coming home today to confide in my sister about something that I am super sensitive about. Instead, she pulls this. Deep down as far as Reece knows, everything is always about her.

"Relax, Reagan. Not everything has to be an identicals thing. Not everything is about you."

I blink.

Reilly slides down the wall she's leaning against slightly, until her head rests on Reese's shoulder. "I like it." she says. "It suits you."

"Then it would probably suit you too, if you wanted to do something like this. If I get away with this without permission, they're not going to hold the same thing back from you guys."

"I have some ideas." Rhiannon is grinning, looking way too excited. I'm not sure I even want to know what she has in mind.

"I wish we'd at least gotten one last picture with the four of us having our hair the same." I say, pouting a little. "Who knows if we'll all ever have the same hair again."

"Yeah" Reece says, sounding thoughtful. "I actually didn't think about that. Eventually we'll all get old and stop caring about our hair so much. We'll be identical little old ladies."

"Oh good." Rhiannon says. "Something to look forward to."

Just then, my mom calls up the stairs. "Girls come on down. We've made our decision."

———

Reece was right. My parents agreed that it was our hair and that we were old enough to decide what to do with it. They even mentioned the bright pink highlights I'd been imagining last year. The only caveat is that we'll only be allowed to do it every few months, no changing up the color whenever an idea pops into our head.

Which means while the rest of us would get haircuts and professional coloring done that same weekend if we want it. Reece is stuck with the amateur job she did in the bathroom. A bathroom she'll have to scrub thoroughly as part of her punishment. The bleach smell that has now permeated everything.

"That is so unfair. If I hadn't done mine, you never would have agreed to let us do dye our hair at all. There was no way for me to win that conversation."

"Oh, I don't know..." my mom says. "...you could've tried having a discussion with us."

"We tried that last time," she argues. "It didn't get us anywhere."

"Well this time, you got what you wanted. But you're going to have to wait and live with the hair you've got until early next year. Maybe you'll learn a thing or two about spontaneous, and potentially reckless decisions."

With that, Reece storms off, swearing under her breath. I'm still mostly just stunned. When I'd woken up this morning, we'd all had the same hair. Now I would be going to a salon soon to change mine, if I want to. After that, a chunk of what makes my sisters and I so similar will be gone forever.

On one hand, maybe we won't get mistaken for one another as often, but probably not. If I've learned anything from being an identical quadruplet, it's that people are not particularly observant about anything that doesn't directly involve them.

As for me, I'll see the difference every day when I see my sisters or look back on old pictures of us. Even when we first moved to Fairview, we made a point of doing our hair the same in order to give the newspaper what they wanted from us. Identical sisters. That wouldn't be an option anymore.

If this had happened on a different day or in a different way, maybe I would've felt more excited about it. As it is, I'm having trouble getting my head around any of it. This feels like way too big a decision to make this fast. I don't like change on a good day, and this change feels like it's stripping away part of my identity.

Yay.

CHAPTER 21

WE GO to the hair salon on Sunday morning—and by we, I mean all the women in my family who aren't Reece. I'm all set to achieve my year-long dream of adding just a little of pink to my hair. By the time I'm in the stylist's chair, I've chickened out. Why would I want that kind of extra attention? I do end up getting several inches taken off my hair and adding in layers. So that's something.

At least I still feel like myself.

———

Like me, Reilly mostly looks like she did when we left school on Friday. All she did was take a few extra inches off the bottom of her hair, so little you wouldn't consider it more than a trim. She added in a few layers around her face but not much. Her hair color, like mine, is exactly what it was before.

It's Rhiannon who gets the award for most dramatic difference. Her hair has gone from long to sitting at her shoulders. What once was the signature Donovan brown color is now a deep shade of red. I'm surprised at how well the color suits her. Suits us. She looks like a new person, older. She's even changed up her makeup today, shifting the products she used just a little so they better suit her new style. It's working for her.

By Monday *everything* feels different. Not the freaking out over the Kent thing. That's still the same. If anything I've talked myself even further down from pursuing this at all. But beyond that, a new hairstyle can change everything, even when it's not your hair that's different.

What I'm not ready for is all the refreshed staring from kids we go to school with. When we turn up, we're obviously looking a little less identical than we did before.

Standing outside the front doors of the school, Rhiannon is the Donovan sister that's attracting the most attention. Though as people go to approach her and complimented the new hair, it's obvious that she doesn't know what to do with it.

Reece gets a few of compliments on her changeup too, but doesn't seem like she's enjoying it as much as I thought she would. It's hard not to wonder if maybe the three of us accidentally stole a little of the thunder she was trying to create for herself with this makeover.

After the big shakeup on Friday night, I never did get up the nerve to confess to Reece all the signs about Kent I had noticed last week. I'm still on my own. When I turn up in the cafeteria for lunch, I'm starting to feel like I can handle this. I can't remember the last time I felt this confident about how I look at school. Having the new hairstyle, I made sure I put in a little extra effort today on all fronts, and I think it's paying off. I could be imagining it, but I'm pretty sure Kent is looking at me even more often than he was last week.

"I'm loving your haircut, by the way." Rosie snaps a cookie in her mouth while giving me a nod of approval.

"Thanks. I didn't do much but am feeling a little weird about the change. Well, not my haircut. It's not a big deal. It's that my sisters changed their hair at the same time. It's freaking me out a bit."

Honestly, I'm not sure why I admitted that to this particular table. If anything, it was the kind of thing I would usually tell Nadine. I had mentioned it to her, sort of in passing. Her response had been brief, and I didn't want to continue to obsess about my sisters' hair to her because I know it's something she would find kind of stupid.

I should probably stop obsessing about it at all.

"Not something you guys have done before?" Jen guesses.

"Nope. Totally new. Pretty sure this is the most dramatic thing we could have done to make ourselves look different from one another. It's great on some levels, and just strange on others."

"A couple of you could have gotten fat, if you wanted to go for something different." Frank looks up from his book, raising his eyebrows. When nobody answers, he goes back to reading.

"We'll call that Plan B," Rosie says with a laugh.

"Well, I like it." Kent says, looking at me again.

"Really?" I'm grinning before I can stop myself. Now I'm glad I didn't do anything else with my hair. This is perfect. "You don't think it's too short?" Not only did Kent actually compliment me a few seconds ago, but I'm already fishing for more. I don't know what's come over me, but I'm waiting, heart racing to see what he says next.

"No. It's great. It suits, err, your face." Kent glances

away, staring across the room like something endlessly fascinating is happening over by where the food is being served.

I smiled at him for another second before my eyes wander. I notice Rosie watching me all over again.

"What?" I ask her and immediately regret it. If she's caught the way I'm looking at Kent, then the last thing I want is for her to call it out in front of everyone else. In front of Kent. I may be acting a little braver, and there may be a lot of signs pointing toward Kent being interested, but it's not something I'm willing to put to a public test now or ever.

"Nothing." All of my newfound bravado retreats back inside me. It's like Rosie notices that moment too. Her eyebrows shoot up a second after I slump back into my chair. Rosie's eyes move to Kent, and I do my best to act normal. "Actually, I was wondering if any of you guys wanted to see a movie with me this weekend. I'm up for whatever, I just need to get out of the house."

I'm nodding yes before I can think about it. This is the first time these guys have asked me to hang out with them after school since Halloween. I don't care if Rosie just wants to see a stupid action movie, or one of those comedies that I never really find funny, I'm in either way.

We spend the rest of lunch making plans, Rosie taking the lead. I can't shake the feeling that there's something more going on here. Something I can't quite figure out.

Before I say much of anything, the details are set. The five of us will be going to a movie on Friday night. No one seems to have any real idea about which one we should see, but that doesn't seem to be the point.

By drama class, Friday is all I can think about. I'm not sure if I'm more excited about the idea of finally getting out of my house on a weekend, or if I'm just loving the idea of sitting in a darkened theatre with Kent for two hours, pretending like it's not him I'm paying attention to. I'm already imagining ways I can maneuver things so that we'll be sitting together for the movie.

"All right, team." Mr. Sullen stands up from his desk with an exaggerated stretch, waiting until everyone in the room has stopped talking before he starts his lesson. "The time has come. We still have smaller assignments to tackle this semester. From here on out, most of our focus will be going into our final performance of the year. I'm sure all of you have been diligently reading the *Alice in Wonderland* script I assigned you two months ago and are more than ready to face this challenge head on."

I look around the class and see everyone looked about as guilty as I feel. Note to self, read that script tonight. Due to the size of the class, Mr. Sullen breaks us up into three groups by drawing names from a top hat. I end up in the same chunk of the class as Frank, with Jen and Kent split up in the others. The last three days of the semester will be dedicated to our final performances, and while Mr. Sullen assures us it won't be as big a production as the school play he helps put on in the spring, he expects us to dedicate our time and energy to this.

While the eight or so of us in my group sits on one side of the classroom, hemming and hawing over different ideas and trying to figure out who will take on which areas of the production, it's hard not to notice that Jen has already taken control of her group, already issuing orders.

Leah, a black-haired girl that's also in my first period class, tries to do the same for our group, but she isn't nearly as effective. Instead of deciding anything at all, we opt to take the night to brainstorm so we can all come back to this tomorrow, hopefully with better results.

———

We're walking home from school later that day, when Rhiannon chimes in with a question. "Are you guys still getting many questions about the Fairview Four thing?"

I take a few quick steps so I'm caught up to her. "What do you mean?"

"Until today, I'd thought people had mostly gotten over it. But now they're all are suddenly asking me the most random stuff. I'm wondering if you've all been getting this crap the whole time?"

Reece turns around so she's walking backward and facing us. "People are still interested, yeah. But it's died down from the first couple weeks of school."

"I haven't been getting any questions at all, but that probably has a lot to do with me avoiding people. Not with them or the things they are curious about," I add.

"Or, it has everything to do with that note on the first day of school."

"Shut up." I stick out my tongue out at Reece, glad that at least no one else had brought that up in a while.

Once people realize that Rhiannon isn't super interested in engaging, I suspect that the newfound interest in her might fade a little. I hope that somehow this could be the open door she needed to start getting to know people a little better. Except... how many times do I need to hope for that before it actually happens? "Guess what I'm doing on Friday?" I say, changing the subject.

I don't bother waiting for anyone to respond before I continue. "I'm going to the movies with a couple of people from drama class. Rosie and Jen are going too."

My sisters mostly mumble something about that being cool, but Reece gives me a knowing look. I give her a small nod in return. Yep, Kent will be there. I'm well aware that this might be my opportunity. I might find out for sure if he likes me or not. During a big hangout with friends isn't the most straightforward way of going about things, but if it works, it works. I make a note to myself to pester Reece for ideas later in the week when we won't have an audience. If this goes badly, and I somehow embarrass myself or have been reading way too much into all of it, the less people know about my secret humiliation, the better.

When we get back home, Rhiannon and I both end up in our bedroom. My homework tonight is thankfully minimal, and I was kind of hoping to get in and nap before dinner. Rhiannon has other ideas. She's searching through her drawers and the bookcase beside her window.

"What's wrong?" I ask, a little annoyed.

"The same stuff that's always wrong, Reagan. You may have gotten used to this stupid little town, but I haven't."

I sit up, eyes still heavy with the need to sleep. "Where's this coming from? What are you even looking for?" On the way home, she didn't seem annoyed exactly, but once again, her mood has turned on a dime.

I wonder, not for the first time in the last few months, if she's still talking to Derrick. Are they still together? I know she would never tell us, one way or the other. She still doesn't seem a hundred percent herself, no matter how many of her old friends come to visit or how many new haircuts she gets or even how much time passes, she's still unhappy. Today seems to be one of those days where her feelings are seeping through the cracks.

"Did something happen today? You seem extra pissed all of a sudden."

Rhiannon then leaves the room without saying anything else, slamming the door unnecessarily behind her. I'm still sitting on my bed slightly stunned, when Riley pops into the bathroom. "What was that?"

"Rhiannon. Obviously."

"Should I go talk to her?" Reilly looks over at the door, I can tell she's being pulled toward Rhiannon, just a little.

I shake my head. "No point. I'm sure she needs to work things out for herself."

"That's been our strategy for a while now, it's still not getting us anywhere. Rhiannon has never been one for big mood swings in any direction, but I swear, I've seen her smile no more than five times since she got here. This is a long time to hold a grudge, even for her."

"Leave her alone!" Reece calls from the other room. I so wish I had some space to myself. Instead, I wriggle down into my bed and put my blanket up over my eyes so Reilly will take the hint. I don't hear her leave, but when I peek back up over the blanket, she's gone.

Now with the bathroom door closed again and Rhiannon gone, the space feels emptier than it should.

Even though I do my best to ignore it most of the time, there's always a part of me that is hyperaware that of the four Donovan sisters, I'm technically the oldest sister. It was luck of the draw I was plucked out of our mom's uterus first, but there's no denying birth order. In a lot of ways, it's always felt like Rhiannon should've been the first born instead of the last. She's always been more of an adult than I will ever be. Especially if being an adult means having to give up video games and comic books.

I promise myself, two more weeks. Rhiannon can have two more weeks of sulking, moping and mood swings. After that, I'm going to have to talk to her. Even though I'm not even sure what I'd say or how to bring it up, if she's been this upset for this long, it's my job as part of her family to make it better. Right? Even if that means having to go to our parents, something I'm sure she wouldn't thank me for.

Two more weeks brings us right up to Christmas vacation, the extended break could be exactly what she needs to start acting like herself again. There's already been a bit of discussion about some of us going back to Richmond for the week between Christmas and New Year's, but nothing is set in stone yet and Mom is pushing against the idea.

Once we have our plans figured out, Rhiannon might come around on her own.

If not, then I'm going to need to figure out how to pull off a Donovan sister intervention.

CHAPTER 22

HAVING my dad be the one to drop me off at the mall is the most uncomfortable thing I've ever experienced. Before Fairview, he would drive Nadine and me around all the time, but he always knew the places I was going to and the people I was going with. Fairview doesn't even have a movie theatre, so he's driving me all the way to Meadow Green, which is still only a slightly bigger town than Fairview. At least it has a movie theatre.

Rosie took charge of planning tonight, one hundred percent. All I know is when and where to meet everyone, even where to park so I can find them inside a mall I've never been too before.

I'm texting with everyone else the whole ride there, but as we pull into the mall, it seems like absolutely everyone is running late.

"So you're sure you have a ride home?" My dad asks, keeping the car in neutral as he stares me down again.

"I should be fine. I'm sure someone else will drive me back so you don't have to go both ways."

"Well either way, I'm just going to pop over to the hardware store across the street for about half an hour. If for some reason, you want to go home in the next little while, just give me a call. Even if you want to go home midway through the night, let me know and I'll be here."

I give him a look, trying to reassure him that he's overreacting. I still appreciate the gesture. "Thanks, Dad. I'll keep that in mind."

I hop out of the car and try to keep my head tilted down, away from the falling snowflakes until I slipped inside the building. The movie theatre is the central point of this small mall, but we're meeting at the food court first to grab something to eat and buy cheaper candy to smuggle inside our purses.

Reagan: I'm here. Anyone else?

Kent: Five minutes.

No one else answers, which probably means they've already been distracted by shopping. Either that, or they're just rushing out the door, meaning Kent and I will be the first ones here.

I find the burger joint where we said we'd meet and sit down to wait, wishing someone else had already been there waiting for me. Still, Kent and I might get a few minutes alone together... and I'm not as nervous as I should be. A few minutes at a time, I can do. My phone rings, startling me a little. "Hello?"

"Hey Reagan, it's Rosie. So, bad news. Kind of. I'm not going to be able to make it, and since my mom was Jen and Frank's ride, they're out to."

"Sorry what?"

"Things just kind of fell apart. I'm really sorry." Something in the tone of her voice makes it sound like she doesn't feel bad about any of this. How had they not mentioned they were all carpooling before this?

"So, it's just you and Kent tonight. Totally didn't do this on purpose or anything. Good luck." She hangs up the phone before I have any chance to respond.

Oh.

It becomes perfectly obvious just what this is. Kent and I have been set up. Now it's just the two of us, alone in a different town going to the movies together. My heart thuds against my ribcage, but I don't have time to panic because I see Kent coming from the opposite end of the food court. I wave him over pathetically as butterflies assault my gut.

"Where's everyone else?" he asks.

I'm guessing he didn't get that same fortuitous phone call I did. Now I get to wait and see what his reaction is, hoping it's not sheer panic because this is about to get either all kinds of exciting or mortifying very quickly. "They're not coming. Rosie just called, none of them can make it."

Kent's mouth drops in surprise but soon the expression turns into a grimace. I don't know how much to tell him. I'm sure that Rosie did this on purpose so Kent and I would be alone together. I don't know if she did this because of anything she'd seen from him. She caught me looking at Kent more than once. Would she have pulled something like this based on that alone, or does she know something about Kent's feelings that I don't?

Or she's telling the truth. And I'm officially in way over my head.

God, this is terrifying. Also, kind of wonderful.

I'm desperate to text my sisters and let them know the situation I've fallen into, but now Kent is here, he's looking at me and we're the only ones here to keep this conversation going.

"Well we're here, so I guess we should see the movie?" My eyes search his for any sign that he's uncomfortable. But

I'm too nervous to make sense of anything right now. At least Rosie picked the latest fantasy blockbuster for all of us to go see, so it's something I'm interested in either way. Not that I'll be able to focus all that hard on it with Kent sitting right beside me.

"Sounds good. But I'm starving. If you're okay with it, I'll go grab us some burgers. My treat." Kent smiles shyly and my heart just about explodes. All I can do is nod along and put in a request for no pickles.

As soon as Kent leaves the table, I whip out my phone and start a new text to Reece.

Reagan: Help! This whole going to the movies thing was just a set up. Everyone else bailed, so now it's just Kent and me. What am I supposed to do or say? I don't know if he feels okay about this whole thing. I'm not even sure he realizes what this whole thing is supposed to be and I'm not about to tell him. I literally have no idea what to do next. He's getting food, then we're going to see the movie.

I stare at my phone, willing my sister to respond for the entire time Kent stands in line, gives and gets our order, and then makes his way back to the table. Nothing. Apparently, today's the day that Reece decides she doesn't need to be on her phone at all times. Meaning, she's absolutely no help to me.

I pocket my cell as Kent slides the tray across our table. "Fries okay?" he asks.

"You can never go wrong with French fries." I grab one and take a bite, not sure what if anything I'm doing could be construed as flirting. I want to be flirting, but I'm pretty sure I'm not. More likely, I'm seconds away from doing something embarrassing that'll have Kent screaming and running from the building.

We eat in silence for a few minutes, Kent looks up at me

from his food every few seconds but never speaking. Since I haven't come up with anything all that great to say either, I can't fault him for not talking. This is my chance, and I'm in the process of blowing it.

I open my mouth to ask him something about drama class, trying to find common ground, but Kent speaks first. "I'm really sorry about this."

"You're sorry? About what?" I try to read his face to guess what he is about to say, but I can't think over the sound of my pulse in my ears.

"About Rosie. I should have seen this coming. She's tried this stuff before, it never ends well but she keeps going, determined to be some kind of matchmaker or something."

I stop chewing. I stop eating. So he *does* know what this is. "You got nothing to apologize for. You didn't do it."

"I guess." Kent takes a long breath and then locks his eyes on mine. "I'm pretty sure she did it for me though, thinking she was doing me some kind of favor."

I can feel a smile tugging at the corner of my mouth, but I refuse to let it loose. What does that mean, Kent? Be specific! "Oh. Well, don't worry about it. I wanted to see this movie anyway." I do my best to brush the whole thing off, to hopefully make him feel less uncomfortable. I'm realizing that it's now or never. Either I can laugh this whole thing off like it's no big deal, or I can make even a tiny confession of my own. "I don't mind that it's just us."

Okay, so that was pathetic, but it was something. Now Kent is the one studying me, and I wish I could give him more to go on. I could have been less pathetic if I'd had some kind of warning I was about to go on my first date ever. I have absolutely no experience in any of this, the one dating expert in my life has probably forgotten her phone in the bathroom, and won't find it again for three hours.

So I guess I'm on my own. Except, I'm with Kent. *I'm on my own with Kent.* My brain is not processing this information right now. I consider slipping away, saying I have to go to the bathroom and either calling Reece or texting Nadine, but I'll save that plan for an actual emergency. So far, things are just a little awkward but not bad. When Reece went on her first date last year, though my parents refused to call it that, she said she and Andrew whatever his last name was, barely spoke the whole time. Apparently, it was super awkward, but she had so much fun anyway. I'm willing to ride out a bit of awkwardness to see where this goes. If nothing else, it's possible Kent just confessed that he likes me. Or at least that Rosie thinks he likes me.

I take a big bite out of my burger and chew to give myself time. What are we supposed to be talking about? As I'm eating, I feel a gentle nudge against the side of my foot. Every muscle in my body freezes in place as I try to piece together what just happened. I'm pretty sure that Kent's foot is now leaning against mine ever so slightly.

I look over at him but he's pointedly looking away, giving me a great chance to admire from up close, seeing just how cute he is. He's wearing a blue plaid, button down shirt. I don't think I've ever seen him wear at school. Did he dress up? His hair on the other hand, looks about the same as it always does, curly but controlled.

Kent looks over and catches me staring. At first, he looks away. But a moment later his eyes are back on mine, and we are both grinning like idiots. Very happy idiots.

I'm on a date with a guy I actually like. How is this my life? All at once, the whole idea of moving to Fairview feels like the best thing that ever happened to me.

"So where does your dad live?" I ask, because it's the only thing I can think of. My mind has gotten stuck on his quick visit to our house after Thanksgiving. In this moment, it's looking a lot more like there was a reason beyond just being polite for him to stop by that day.

"The absolute middle of nowhere. He and my step-mom have this kind of farm, a couple of hours from here. They don't actually farm anything. It's just all about growing their own food, keeping free range chickens and basically living in their own little bubble."

"Please tell me they have a stable Internet connection," I joke. "Because I don't care how much space they have, without being able to get online, I don't think I'd be able to manage."

"It's not good, but it's functional. It took forever for them to get any Internet at all, so I'm not willing to complain. Yet."

"How long your parents been divorced?" I'm not sure if that's too heavy a question to ask, but it seems like a natural lead-in from our conversation.

"Four years. Five now I guess. I was ten when it happened." He doesn't elaborate, and I don't ask any more questions. It's possible that failed relationships weren't the right conversation route to take, but I want to know everything about him. My instinct is to just ask every question that pops into my head even though they aren't remotely related. What is his favorite class at school? What's his favorite movie? Does he have any brothers or sisters? I want to know it all.

Before I can ask anything at all, my phone rings letting loose with the theme song to Doctor Who. "Oh, that's me. Sorry." I grab it from my pocket and stand up, taking a few steps away before I answer since I'm fully expecting to hear Reece's voice shrieking at me from the other end of the line as soon as I answer. Instead it's my dad.

"Reagan, honey. Are you there?"

"Yeah, Dad. I'm fine. You can go home. I promise." Has it been forty minutes already? Hard to believe how quickly all of this is flying by. Kent and I should probably make our way over to the movie theatre soon, since the showing we were aiming for starts at seven-thirty. Which means soon it will be just Kent and me alone in a movie theatre.

I wonder if he'll try to hold my hand.

"Any chance Rhiannon told you where she was going to be today? Your mom can't find her."

CHAPTER 23

THE QUESTION HANGS in the air between us as it registers in my brain.

"No idea. She barely said anything to me after school." I say, hoping that will be the end of the conversation. Hoping this isn't anything serious.

"I'm going to need you to meet me outside the mall where I dropped you off, in about five minutes." Only then can I acknowledge the tension in his voice, the anxiety. He has to be overreacting. I don't answer, so he prods me for a response. "Reagan. Just tell me you understand. I'll see you in five minutes."

"Do I need to come now?" I spit out the question without thinking. This is just starting to go so well. "I can find my own way home." Rhiannon should call any second now, but my night is already ruined.

"Reagan, we both have to get back to the house. Rhiannon could be missing. We're not sure, but no one can get a hold of her and she's not at home. She didn't tell she was going out and she's not answering her phone. Five minutes."

My dad has already hung up the phone, so there's nothing left to do but to pull mine away from my ear and stare at it as though that will make what he just said make sense. But it really doesn't help at all.

Rhiannon is missing? I take a breath. That has to be some kind of mistake. There's a difference between not knowing where someone is, and them being missing.

I open my phone again and search for my last text from Rhiannon. It was at lunchtime yesterday.

Rhiannon: No idea.

She'd been answering my question about what we were having for dinner. Before that, we'd been texting about plans to marathon Planet Earth a few days earlier. It was all business as usual.

"Everything okay?" Kent is standing behind me, his hand reaching out as though to touch my shoulder but hovering in midair between us.

Right, Kent. I look at my phone for a few seconds more, and then shake my head to try and clear my thoughts. "I have to go."

Kent's expression falls at once from worried to disappointment. He thinks I'm leaving because of him. He has to. So while family drama isn't usually something I'd want or need to broadcast to anyone, I tell him what my dad just told me, then wait for him to respond as though somehow, he'll be able to make sense of this where I can't.

He nods once. "Okay, let's go. I'll walk you out front and wait till your dad gets there. Everything is going to work out."

I gather my stuff and we start moving through the mall. I feel like I should be sprinting or something, but I'm in a daze. More than once, Kent gently nudges me when I go in the wrong direction. It's been less than an hour since I first walked through this mall, and already everything looks foreign and new.

"How are you going to get home?" I ask when the thought occurs to me. He probably just had someone drop him off too, someone who could be back home in Fairview by now.

"Don't worry about me. I'll figure it out. I'm sure my mom will come back and get me."

Sure. I nod like that makes perfect sense. A moment later, we're outside and the bite of the air is stinging my face. My dad's car is already waiting at the curb. I see him before he sees me, leaning against the steering wheel and tapping his hand impatiently.

I walk toward the car but then remember Kent behind me. "Thanks," I say. "I'll see you at school on Monday?" My voice has no tone at all. I sound like a robot, even to me. But I'm already walking toward the car before I can make it better.

"That's Kent, right?"

"Yeah." I answer, buckling myself in. There's so much I want to ask, I'll wait until we've at least pulled away and are heading back toward home.

"He's not on his own, is he?"

"What? Yeah. The rest of our friends bailed, so he's going to wait for a ride home."

"Don't be silly. Tell him to get in, I'll drive him back to Fairview so he's not stranded here by himself. His mom can come get him from our house."

On any other day, I'm sure that my dad would have been more suspicious of the fact I'd told him I was meeting with the big group of friends and then show up with only a guy for company. But the thought doesn't even seem to occur to him, which worries me more than anything he'd said earlier.

Kent is still standing huddled in the door, using the protection of its frame to shield him from the frigid weather. I'm sure he's watching and waiting for us to leave to be polite. He looks at me when I wave him over. Once he's standing beside the car, I roll down the window. "We can drive you back to Fairview. Could your mom come and get you from our house?"

"Don't worry about me." he says.

I do my best not to huff impatiently. This conversation is now holding us up from getting back to my sisters. "It's no trouble. Just get in. We've got to get going, but we're not going to leave you here either."

Kent doesn't argue. As soon as he's settled in the back seat, my dad pulls away from the mall. Only then do I realize that Kent is about to see the dark side of Gregory Donovan because even when there isn't a family crisis going on, his driving is less than ideal. My relaxed, goofy father becomes something of a demon when there are other drivers involved.

I sink into my seat as Dad yells something obscene at a little old lady who he doesn't think is going as fast as she should be. We haven't even left the mall's parking lot yet. It's just enough to pull me back into my own head, out of the fog that overtook me after my dad first called.

This all has to be a big misunderstanding. By the time we get home, someone will have already found Rhiannon and dragged her back home from some study session, or to the bookstore where we both have been known to lose track of time.

I gaze down at my phone but there are no new messages

or missed calls. No news yet, but that doesn't mean it's not coming.

The van swerves suddenly into the left lane. I look back and mouth a quick 'I'm sorry' to Kent who's gone a little pale in the back seat.

If nothing else, at this rate, we will be home in no time.

By the time we pull onto Oakridge, I'm having trouble sitting still in my seat. Dad invites Kent to come inside and wait for his mom to get him, but as we step through the front door, looking at Kent's expression, I'm guessing he would've rather waited outside than to get involved in our family drama. My mom and other sisters are already waiting in the living room, each of them on their phones. Reece does a double take when she sees Kent standing behind me but says nothing.

"Nothing new?" Dad asks, dumping his coat over a dining room chair rather than hanging it up, before he moves to go sit beside my mom.

She shakes her head. Dad leans over, putting his arm around her and giving her shoulders a quick squeeze. "She'll be okay. Something like this was always going to happen eventually. Kids act out. I'm sure this is all that is. I'm sure she's fine." Somehow, he almost manages to sound like he believes it.

"I wish she'd just call to tell us she's okay. What if this isn't her acting out? I've been trying not to overreact, trying to let this play out and hoping she'll just show up any minute."

My head spins as she talks. What if something's happened? What is she even considering? A kidnapping? Maybe Rhiannon's been hit by a car and is lying in a ditch somewhere.

I look helplessly over at my sisters and catch Reilly's eye. "What did we miss?"

It's Reece who answers. "Not much. We were calling earlier and her phone was ringing, but now we go straight to voicemail. She's turned it off. Like she's sick of us pestering her, and worrying about if she's okay. We've only gotten one text from her since we noticed she was gone, and it didn't say much of anything." Reece's voice is hard with anger, but I can hear the waiver of worry underneath what she's saying. What if it wasn't Rhiannon who turned off her phone?

"So, we call the cops," I say. As soon as thoughts of worst-case scenarios entered my mom's head, we should have called the police. One vague text doesn't mean she's safe.

"What if this is nothing? I'm worried it will only make things worse. Rhiannon's been so unhappy since we got here, and if she's just hiding out somewhere to get some space and we send the police after her, I'm sure she won't thank us."

"She doesn't need to thank us. If she's in enough trouble that the police are needed, then this is the only move. If not, then I'm guessing she's in a whole lot of trouble anyway and no one here cares what she thinks. What did the text say?"

Reilly looks down at her phone, shaking her head. "It was right before you guys got here. It was just 'I'm fine, leave me alone.' And that's around when she turned off her phone."

"I know." My mom looks up and locks eyes on Kent, who has as far as I know, has been hovering behind me since we got home, trying to stay in view of the driveway so he can sprint out of here at the first opportunity. My mind screeches to a halt, but as it starts working again, I just know

I'm worried about the same thing my mom is. He can leave our house, right to his mother's car. His mother the reporter who showed up at our house on moving day, completely uninvited who seems to think news about our family is the only way to sell papers.

I'd bet good money that no matter how this turns out, Mindy Harris would be very interested in the details on what's going on at the Donovan house tonight.

"You won't say anything will you?" I ask, turning on Kent. "I mean, I know she's your mom. but no one here thinks a fifteen-year-old girl being M.I.A. is news, right?" Unless, she really is missing. I don't say that out loud, I don't allow that to be a possibility.

For a brief moment, Kent looks hurt by what I'm suggesting. I have to assume he is a bigger fan of his mother than I am. I know if one of my friend's siblings didn't come home, I'd tell my parents in a heartbeat. It's not a judgment, but an unavoidable conflict of interest.

"What can I do to help?" is what Kent says instead. "If you guys need to call the police, you don't want this getting out more publicly, I can keep her distracted." Kent looks down at his feet, not loving having five sets of eyes boring into him. "Or, if you want the entire town on a looking for Rhiannon, I'm pretty sure I can do that too. I know my mom would want to help. She can be a bit much sometimes, but when it comes to rallying the troops, you really can't do better." He looks over at us helplessly, I turn to my parents. Whatever happens next is up to them.

"Do you know the chief of police here in Fairview?" Mom asks Kent. "If we wanted to keep this fairly quiet and just get more eyes on the street, could we do that?" It hasn't been that long yet, maybe forty minutes, but I'm still surprised that my mother is even considering holding off on the no holds barred attitude. She's not one to panic, but Rhiannon's safety could literally be at stake here.

I hate to think it, but it's very possible that my mom is still letting Rhiannon's grudge get the best of her. She's doing what she thinks will piss Rhiannon off the least. I do know my sister, and having her picture broadcasted on all the local TV stations, or having a radio announcer tell everyone that she's not at home would be her worst nightmare. If she is fine, and she hated living in Fairview before, I can't see her getting past something like that after. Is it possible I'm the one over-reacting here, rather than my mom under-reacting?

"Okay." I say. "So we call the police as a precaution. Say we know it's probably not an emergency but ask for help. That's what they're there for right?"

Kent nods. "Constable Williams is a good guy. His daughter is just a couple years younger than us. He might even have more ideas about how to help without blowing all of this up."

"We will go try to find her too. All of us." As I speak, an idea forms in my head. Because, in a town as small as this one, there are only so many places she could be. Sitting around here waiting for her to come home will not help us at all. "One of us will wait here, just in case she comes home or calls. The rest of us will look." I glance out the window and wish it wasn't quite so dark outside even though it's not that late at night yet.

Although, it's not like she's going to be hiding in the bushes or anything, so light or dark, it probably doesn't make a difference.

A set of headlights pulls up into our driveway.

"What do you want me to do?" Kent asks, already backing out of the living room towards the front door.

"Nothing. It's fine. I feel weird asking you to hide something from your mom."

Kent smiles so little, I almost miss it. "So you *do* want me to hide this from my mom then?"

I grimaced apologetically. "You said it, not me. Keep your phone on, I'll let you know if anything changes." From out of nowhere, I'm smiling. Kent has started to act like part of this team with absolutely no trouble at all. It's something I need to thank him for once I've thoroughly yelled at Rhiannon for causing all of this drama in the first place.

If she's okay. God, I hope she's okay. Even if she's safe, there has to be something big that caused her to do this. She's not one for random acts of defiance, at least not before we moved here. Lately, I never know what to expect from her anymore, which is probably what makes this so scary. I can't imagine what she's going through that had her acting like this was her only option.

Kent mumbles an uncomfortable goodbye before slipping out of our house and out into the night.

This was not how our night was supposed to go.

A minute later my parents, Reece and I change into our winter clothing as well. Reilly will stay at home and keep trying Rhiannon's cell phone. When it comes down to it, she's the one who's most likely going to get a response, she's the most unintimidating option. I can tell she wants to be out helping too, but we all agree that this is our best plan.

It's only once were outside and on the porch that we realize none of us have much of a game plan. If my parents are both taking their cars, that means Reece and I are limited to where we can walk to.

But odds are wherever Rhiannon has gone, it's somewhere she has to have been able to walk as well, unless she took the bus. She also has a head start.

Yeah, this whole thing is kind of a disaster. I try to stop myself from second guessing my every thought and to go with my gut. There are days I understand Rhiannon better than I do myself, that has to count for something.

"Mom, can you drive me to the town square? I'll start there so Reece and I are covering different ground."

CHAPTER 24

I COULD'VE WALKED to the square on my own, but as my mom drops me off with a distracted wave, I'm glad for the head start. I don't have details on where anyone else is headed, so I pick a direction and walk, using the time to wonder where Rhiannon could've gone, or what she might've been thinking.

Rhiannon hasn't told me much of anything at all about herself recently—I should have pushed, should have made her tell me everything. I get that she's angry. And that things here haven't exactly been the makings of a teen movie. But it's been months. Is Derrick still even in the picture?

I take out my phone, wishing I had time to charge it a little before leaving the house, and search Facebook for any sign of Derrick. If I can get in touch with him, he'll know how to get in touch with Rhiannon if he cares about her at all. I can't imagine he wouldn't try to hide her from her worried family. After searching, I find out that Rhiannon isn't friends with anyone named Derrick, no matter how I try to spell it.

On a whim, I try messaging Rhiannon over Facebook as

well, just in case she's somewhere with a computer even if she's avoiding her phone.

Reagan: Everyone is worried about you. Can you please just come home? I'm not even convinced you'll be in trouble, Mom and Dad will be so glad to see you.

I hit enter and wait, but the chat still shows Rhiannon as being off-line.

Reagan: Come on, Rhiannon. Whatever it is, we'll figure it out. I just really need to hear that you're not dead.

Rhiannon: Not dead.

The response comes right away, and, at first, I double check to make sure I didn't imagine it. She's answering, she's just been screening her messages. I exhale a long breath, lightheaded and relieved at once.

I can't just leave it there.

Reagan: Pretty sure that's what a murderer would say if he had your phone.

Rhiannon: A murderer wouldn't know you left your soggy towel on the floor of our bedroom this morning. Now, I'm fine. I'll be home, eventually.

Eventually? What kind of crap is that?

Reagan: Where are you?

I'm not surprised when I don't get an answer. Sending back one last message, I ask her to at least touch base with Mom and Dad. Just in case she doesn't, I send out a quick message with an update to everyone else.

Reagan: Just heard from her. She's okay, but still won't tell me where she is or why she's doing this.

I almost add in a quick note about good news; she's not dead. I doubt my parents will find that funny. Still, I'm glad she's not dead.

When I look back down at my phone in my hands, I'm

surprised to find I'm shaking a little, even though in theory, everything is more okay than it was a minute ago. Rhiannon's okay at least physically, and that counts for a lot.

It's only once I know she's fine that my mind truly comprehends that it was possible she wasn't.

This still hasn't had a happy ending, but it's hard to wrap my mind around all the things that could have happened.

I need to find my sister.

Already I'm getting texts back from my family, hoping for more information, I already told them literally everything that happened. Instead, I use my phone to call Rhiannon. Or at least attempt to. Just like I'd been told, her phone went straight to voicemail. So either it's off, or she has it set to block calls. If it's the latter, in theory her phone is trackable and I would think she would know that.

Assuming she truly doesn't want to us to find her, then she's using something else to get online. Even though I've lived in Fairview four months now, I really haven't done much exploring of what the town has to offer. I kind of assumed there wasn't much, at least not compared to Richmond. I have an idea, but I'm not sure who to ask. Kent seems like the obvious solution, but I've already asked so much. Instead, I search out Rosie's number from when she called me earlier.

Reagan: Quick question. Probably a long shot. Is there anywhere in town with public computer access?

Rosie: Fairview isn't some hick town with no amenities you know? Just because this isn't the big city doesn't mean we don't have a library. :P Why? Wait. Where's Kent?

Reagan: Explain later. Thanks!

Yup. I'm an idiot. Of course, Fairview has a library, and

a quick search online tells me it's open for another hour. It's about a ten-minute walk, and if she's somewhere else, I could be going in the wrong direction entirely but it's the best guess I have. Rhiannon would absolutely think of a library. She's probably been there for school stuff a million times already.

I find the building without too much trouble even though I spent most of the walk hunched over trying to keep my face protected from the wind, attempting to notice some town landmarks as I go so I can make my way back later. The convenience store, bus stop, a used clothing store, and then the library. It's a small building, about the size of my doctor's office in Richmond, but it's a library. The sign out front advertises everything from a book club to free Internet access.

The building is quiet as I slip inside, and the interior looks like I imagined it. The checkout desk is small and an older, bespectacled woman sits at the computer out front. Fairview obviously hasn't adopted self-checkout for library books yet. When I enter, the woman looks up then back down, but her head snaps back toward me for a second look.

While I am beyond tempted to search out the fantasy and young adult sections here, I'm on a mission. I'm just going to have to remember to come back later and give the library the time it deserves. I find the computers at the back of the building, and with them my sister.

Rhiannon's brand-new red hair is impossible to miss, hunched over the third computer. The one beside her has out of order sign stuck to its monitor. I sidestep so I'm hidden behind a shelf, giving myself time to regroup.

Now what? I never figured I would be the one to find her first. I'm not even sure what I'm supposed to do. It's easy to guess what my parents would say. But now that I see her, and it's not like she can make a daring escape from the building, there's time to be a little more cautious. There's no way all of this was all because Rhiannon wanted a little alone time at the library. There's more to what's going on. Until I know what it is, I can't risk bringing anyone else into risk of pissing her off more. They know she's safe, which is good enough for a few more minutes.

I try to walk quietly toward the computers, but my foot hits a creepy spot in the floor and Rhiannon's head jerks up.

"Reagan?" I can tell that she is surprised to see me, but her shocked expression doesn't last long.

"You didn't see me here. Just go." Rhiannon's expression is hard, so I'm not expecting any more jokes about would-be murderers. There's no question she did not want to be found. She didn't want us to worry she'd been horribly slaughtered either, her eyes flare with disappointment that I tracked her down.

I ignore her request and sit down at the broken computer. "Rhiannon. Everyone is freaking out. You just disappeared and no one knew where you were. How did you imagine everyone would take that?"

"They'll get over it. They get over everything else easily enough."

I don't even ask what she means. "You need to come home at some point. The library closes soon, and I don't think Fairview has a great nightlife."

"I'll be gone by then." Rhiannon stares pointedly at the computer screen in front of her, browsing some forum for nerds who actually enjoy school.

Gone? There is nothing I can say in response to that, so I wait, and stare at her intently.

"I'm going back to Richmond," Rhiannon says. "The bus leaves in about forty minutes."

Damn. If I'd taken even a little longer to get here, we wouldn't even be having this discussion. She'd be gone already.

She can't believe for a second that I can let her get on that bus without calling my parents in a panic to stop her. Now that I'm here, she has to see there's no way she'll be able to see this plan through.

"So, what? You're running away from home? That's what this is? You've decided it's too much work being part of this family so you're just going to... Hide in Marybeth's house until you graduate from high school?" Rhiannon must hear how ridiculous I think this all is. This isn't anything like her. Stupid plans are Reece's thing, sometimes mine, maybe Reilly's. Never Rhiannon.

"Don't be an idiot. I was just going for a visit, there was no way Mom and Dad would go for it. So I'm going to catch the bus, stay for the weekend and be back by Sunday night. What's the big deal?"

Yes, she's fine now, but that doesn't mean she'll stay fine if she takes a bus across state lines when no one knows where she is. I want to say that the big deal is that we are fifteen, and she's a crazy person, but I don't think that would go over well. The fact that I've made it this far without pissing her off is already a miracle, I'm not going to push my luck. Mostly, she seems tired.

I smack my head downward into the keyboard of the computer in front of me, trying not to think about all the germy fingers that must've used it in the past. "Seriously? How did you even get a ticket for the bus? You need to be eighteen."

"Derrick is eighteen."

I keep my head down and force myself not to groan out loud. All of this was so she could go see some guy she's never even bothered to introduce to us? And he was willing to just buy her a ticket so she could do it? Clearly this is Prince Charming we're dealing with.

After sitting up, I shake my head slowly. I've gone through so many emotions today that I can no longer put a name to whatever it is I'm feeling now.

I give the rolling chair Rhiannon is sitting in a nudge with my foot, forcing her to face me. Tears are forming in the corners of her eyes.

"You're not going to Virginia. I don't want to get you in any more trouble, and there's no way I'm letting you get on the bus. It's not safe and it's not worth it."

Rhiannon tilts her head back as though trying to hide her face from me. "I know." She looks back at me and tries to blink away tears, but instead one escapes and rolls down her face. "I screwed everything up."

"Text Derrick and tell him you're not coming. Otherwise, I'm stealing your phone and giving him a piece of my mind." As I give her instructions, I feel like Rhiannon's big sister again for the first time in a long time. I hate how defeated she looks, but I also don't want to fight anymore. Not now. I expect this weekend will be a bit of a nightmare in terms of screaming matches, hurt feelings, and crying sessions.

I was barely involved in any of this, and I need to hide in a corner somewhere and have a good cry. I'm not even sure Rhiannon will make it all the way home before she has hers.

When Rhiannon takes out her phone, I do the same. "Don't." Rhiannon moves her hand to cover my screen. "Please don't tell them to come pick us up. I don't want to be stuck in a car with either Mom or Dad right now. Not yet. I need time to sort all of this out."

"Okay," I agree. "Let's go home."

"That's what I was trying to do."

I know responding by telling her she is already home is not only super cheesy, but it also isn't going to fly. I haven't even really started to think of Fairview as home yet either but home is where my sisters are where my parents are. Even though Rhiannon is hurting more than I am, it still sucks a little to think she doesn't see it same way.

"Fine. I won't tell them where to come get us. But I have to tell them I've found you. You have to understand what this feels like for them, for all of us. I was imagining grisly murders, Rhi!"

Rhiannon doesn't apologize for everything she's put us through, but she does pull her hand back. She has to realize that she isn't in much of a position to bargain from anyway.

While Rhiannon crafts her own messages, I type out mine. It's less than a minute before I have five responses back, with everyone having been glued to their phone waiting for news. Mostly, they're just relieved. Reece seems to be the only one of us who has immediately shifted toward anger, but we'll deal with that when we get home.

I don't bother asking what Rhiannon has told Derrick. I doubt she'd tell me anyway. She's still crying, it both makes me uncomfortable and breaks my heart. I hate seeing other people sad and never knowing what I can do to make it better. If I hadn't decided to wait two weeks before talking to Rhiannon, would all of this have been avoidable? Okay, so giving her space had been the wrong move.

The two of us leave the library together, side by side. I wave to the bewildered librarian and brace myself for the incoming cold that whooshes in to surround us as we step out the door.

My mood shifts from confused and bewildered to miserable in five minutes flat as we walk home. I have to think even Rhiannon is regretting insisting we walk in this weather, but she doesn't say a word. We both notice a bus that passes us, heading out of town. She would've been on that. It's possible she would've simply come back a couple days later, but I can't be sure. I don't think I'm any more ready to talk to her about what is happening here than she is to talk to me.

More than once, I consider pulling out my phone and calling Dad for a ride home, but we've come this far but if Rhiannon needs time to clear her head this desperately, then I can do that. She will have to make it up to all of us later. She'd better.

When we turn onto our street, we're greeted with an array of colored Christmas lights up and down all the houses, making the scene appear less gloomy than it feels. I'm sure that at least someone will be watching for us from the window, so in just a few minutes Rhiannon's self-imposed solitude is going to come to an end.

"Get rid of the bus ticket. If you still have it." I say, not sure what made me think of it. "If there is any chance of avoiding Mom finding out about your big plan, you want to take it."

Rhiannon stops walking and looks at me, her fingers already fumbling around in her pockets. She takes out a small piece of paper and rips it into quarters before letting it go in the wind. I want to mumble something about not needing to litter, but that seems beside the point now. At this point, littering is the least of her sins today. It's hard to believe that when I remember my first ever date, this will be the overwhelming memory, not Kent and I alone in a theatre, inching toward one another, with the possibility of holding hands. Not a first, nerve-racking kiss in some quiet corner of the mall while we wait for our parents to come collect us. Nope, instead I get this.

My heart thuds at even the thought of Kent leaning in to press his lips to mine, sending electricity right to my toes. I don't even get to enjoy that thought for long.

"So what do we tell them?" Rhiannon asks. She's already ripped up the bus ticket, so I think we both know that lying to our parents is the best way to get out of this, though not all the way out. There's no getting around just how nervous she made all of us, or around the fact that my mom had to call the town police to report one of her kids missing. I don't think we need to tell them that Rhiannon was planning an unauthorized trip back to Richmond, to see her older boyfriend who our parents don't know about. No one needs that kind of headache.

"Tell them whatever you want." I say, I can't be bothered to make up a lie for her. I'll let her dig herself out. I'm not doing the heavy lifting. "But you need to tell Reilly and Reese the truth. Tonight. This will not be some little secret that we pretend never happened. You've been avoiding us for months, never really talking about anything anymore. If letting you do that is what led to this, then you know that it's not going to happen again."

Rhiannon groans but doesn't argue, she turns and she takes the first step up our driveway.

CHAPTER 25

WE DON'T EVEN GET to the front door before my mom's swings it open, immediately leaning over to embrace both Rhiannon and me at once, pulling us inside.

"Thank God. Rhiannon. We were so... I'm so glad you're home." Mom takes a shuddering breath before closing the front door.

Now that my body is faced with the heat of the house, I'm shaking more than ever. "Any chance bringing her home wins me some hot chocolate?" I ask, teeth chattering. My mom looks five years older than when I last saw her, I desperately want to get us back to normal. Also, I would really like to be warm again. I don't even remember what the sensation feels like. Dad has been hovering in the doorway to the living room but retreats toward the kitchen, hopefully to grant my request. No one else says anything yet, but words have to be coming.

"I'm glad you're home." Mom says before leaning over to plant a quick kiss on top of Rhiannon's head. She isn't much taller than we are now, so it looks a little awkward. I can tell how deeply she means it though. Soon after, Mom moves in for a second hug and whispers a thank you in my ear.

Neither Reese nor Reilly goes in for the big reunion embrace. Ultimately, Rhiannon wasn't even gone that long.

Somehow, Mom manages to wait until we're all seated around the dining room table nursing big mugs of hot chocolate, passing around a bag of marshmallows before she asks the inevitable question. "I don't want to yell, Rhiannon. But I need to know what happened, and you need to tell me it is never going to happen again." Everyone's watching Rhiannon, I can see her choosing her next words carefully. I never pressed her to figure out what she would say rather than the truth, I'm not actually sure she has any idea. I'm actually hoping she's not stupid enough to tell the truth, because right here, right now. Things are pretty okay. We're all here. Everyone is safe, and I need it to last.

"I wish I had some big, meaningful explanation to give you. It was stupid. I was just getting so cramped in this house, I needed to get out. This town can be a little suffocating sometimes." Rhiannon somehow manages a perfectly timed lip quiver before looking down at her mug. "I'm really, really sorry. I tried to at least tell you I was okay, but I wasn't ready to talk. Honestly, I'm still not ready to talk. But if that's what you guys need, I can do it. Whatever it takes to make this better, I'm in."

I can see Reese rolling her eyes from the other side of the table, I can't tell just how sincere Rhiannon is being right now. I have to think that her saying exactly what my parents want to hear, if there is such a thing in the situation, is something they could see right through. Neither of them respond, instead my mom reaches across the table and puts her hand on top of Rhiannon's, giving it a squeeze.

"You know what, we've all had a long night. I hope it

goes without saying that you will not be going anywhere this weekend, but we will discuss this further once we all get some rest and sort ourselves out a little." She looks over at my dad, who nods. The whole family meeting thing ends up lasting only a fraction of the time it took to get us here.

Our parents have never been strict, Mom has always believed in parenting by letting us make our own mistakes. Between Rhiannon running away and Reese dying her hair without permission, both of which seem to have almost no consequences whatsoever, I'm wondering if I should have made some sort of big change or declaration before this new version of my parents wears off. Guilt from moving us back to Fairview can only last so long. But thinking about this is a little ridiculous.

Now I feel like a jerk for being mad that Rhiannon didn't get in more trouble.

My phone sits in my lap, I use it to text both Reilly and Reese while my parents and Rhiannon are still distracted by one another. I'm not letting Rhiannon get off quite this easily. To be fair, my parents don't know what I did, but Rhiannon scared us all. I'm not sure they're driving that point home enough for my liking.

We agree to all meet in my bedroom in five minutes and promise not to let Rhiannon out of our sight when we get her there. This is happening, and it's happening now.

Rhiannon doesn't argue when I nudge her up the stairs and lead her into our room where the other half of our unit is already waiting. Our meeting is unlike our birthday, where we all crawl into bed, sharing space and covers to find comfort in one another. This time, everyone is sitting up and alert. Rhiannon sits up near the head of her bed, using her pillow as support against the headboard. Riley sits on the other end with her feet dangling over.

On my bed, Reece and I sit side-by-side, our bony hips digging into one another as we push our legs out over the bed. Our feet stretching exactly the same distance. I give her a quick nudge with my foot, just to say I'm here. She nudges me back and the tension on my chest eases just a little.

Once we're all settled, I'm faced with having no idea how to get the ball rolling. However, Rhiannon speaks first, saving me the trouble. "Yeah, I suck. But you guys don't understand how hard this is."

Three heads turned toward her as one. "Umm... what?" Reece hardens her expression. "If you mean the move to Fairview, we went through exactly the same thing. Except that we've all been trying to deal with it whereas you've been moping for months now. We all left people behind and if you think about it, you left... never mind."

"Hey, you don't understand anything about what I left behind." Even from across the room, I can feel Rhiannon getting defensive, something I can always trust Reece to lead the way on.

Reilly shifts uncomfortably beside her. "Well that could be because you haven't told us anything. I swear we've all started keeping so many more things from each other."

"Well to be fair..." I say, "...Rhiannon has been hiding this particular thing from us even before we moved."

"That's not fair. I told you." Rhiannon snaps.

"You didn't tell me when you were planning to hop on a bus back to Richmond today, just get away for the weekend. Oh I'm sure we would've all had a great time this weekend heading up the manhunt looking for you." I match Rhiannon's tone as my rising anger kicks its way out of me.

"What, seriously?" Reece sounds impressed. "You were going to take a bus back to Virginia all by yourself."

"To see a guy." I regret the words as soon as I say them. Not only was is not my secret to share, but it's also not going to do anything to win Reece back over to my way of seeing things. Taking a bus back to Richmond is probably something she wishes she would've thought of first. Though I don't think she would've ever actually gotten up the nerve to do it. Two hours ago, I wouldn't have thought any of us would have had the nerves to do something like that. Especially without telling one another first.

"I knew it!" Reece says, triumphant. "You were sneaking out back in Richmond. I totally knew it! But you wouldn't confess to anything." Somehow this revelation has sucked some of the venom out of Reece's tone. "Tell me more about the guy and your plans."

Rhiannon actually does. She doesn't sound quite as love-struck as she did when she first told me about Derrick, but she shares every detail anyway. She fills Riley and Reece in on everything that happened before we moved, and I can practically see the puzzle pieces falling into place inside their heads. Rhiannon's talk explains a lot about how she has been acting since we moved. As far as I'm concerned, it doesn't excuse it.

After Rhiannon finishes, the four of us fall into silence once more as this doesn't feel finished. Not yet.

"You haven't seen him since we moved, right?" Reece asks. Rhiannon shakes her head. "What did he say when you told him you weren't coming anymore?"

"Not much." Rhiannon shrugs. "I asked if I could call him to talk, but he said it was a bad time. Lately, it feels like it's always a bad time."

At first, I'm tempted to keep my mouth shut. I can tell my sister is already hurting and I don't exactly want to pile on. Maybe if I'd said something to her earlier, none of this would have happened.

"You have to know what that means, right?" I ask.

"What, what means?" Rhiannon's tone gets abrupt, distancing her from the rest of us.

"Derrick avoiding you. I mean... this clearly isn't the best relationship ever."

"What would you know about relationships?"

Nope. We're not doing that. Not tonight. "Enough. I think anyone can see this guy is hurting you. It shouldn't be like that." I'm running on instinct here. I'm definitely no expert, but this has got to stop. "Rhi..." I continue, my voice softer now, "...you're the smartest person I know, but maybe you can't see this whole thing properly from the inside. You deserve so much better. Trust me."

For a heartbeat, the silence sits heavily between my sisters and I.

"I'll think about it, okay?" Rhiannon says, finally. "I just need some time to think."

That's the closest I'm going to get to Rhi admitting that maybe I have a point. I'm willing to take it.

"So, what else?" Reilly asks when the silence fills the room for too long, no one knowing what to tell Rhiannon. "I have no idea what's going on with any of you anymore. So spill." When no one speaks, she continues instead. "Fine. I'll go. My life is actually super boring right now, there's basically nothing to tell. I like some of the people I've met here, but it's not the same. Mostly, I just miss my friends from home."

"Is it possible that your new friends don't know you because you aren't telling them about a huge part of yourself?" Reece asks. I guess she and Reilly had a similar conversation to the one we had on the bleachers.

"Do you feel like your straightness is a huge part of you?" Reilly responds, sounding uncharacteristically sassy.

"No comment. But mostly, yes. Thank you very much. No pressure from me one way or the other, you know that. Just discussing the possibilities."

"Noted."

I doubt any of us planned it this way, but things continue to unravel from there in the best possible way. It turns out we all had things to say to one another that we'd been keeping inside since the move to Fairview, for one reason or another.

Rhiannon even admits that she didn't hate absolutely everything about Fairview. She even thinks that coming from a small-town background could be more of an asset to her then coming from a city for college applications, if she can find a way to work herself into this town somehow. The biggest shocking confession of the night, at least for me, came from Reece.

She took a big breath. "Okay, here's mine. I have friends here already and all that, but I'm a little bit jealous of how well Reagan has done here. I mean, her life in Fairview is better than what it was back home. She took what she had already and built on it. That is kind of awesome."

Reilly and Rhiannon both nod in what I can only interpret as agreement, causing me to become even more confused than I was a minute before. Jealous of me? It's not like I have done anything special while here in Fairview. Yeah, I have friends and possibly even a guy who likes me. Okay, almost definitely a guy who likes me. But these were all things that Reece has had a million times before. When I point this out to her, it doesn't seem to sway her in the slightest.

"Those things are easy for me though, but they aren't for

you. You're taking a drama class for God's sake. You're doing all of these things and you have this big life I never would've guessed you would've had, if things had stayed the same back home."

I stop and think about that one because in a lot of ways, she's right. My life has changed a lot from what it had been a year ago and not just because I'm living in a different state. At this point, my sisters don't even have all the information on just how well I am doing. So I cave and tell them everything about Kent, right up to the almost date I might've had tonight. Everyone is excited and shocked all at once. While they are pumped that I might've had a date, they all seem to think it is so typically me that I was tricked into going on it rather than getting there on my own. I can't exactly argue.

"Not that it matters anymore. I'm here with you dorks instead of with him."

"It's eleven at night. You'd be stuck here with us anyway." Rhiannon points out like that will make this less her fault.

"You get what I mean. I could have had my first kiss tonight. But no. I mean, I'm not holding it against you." Yeah, right. "Okay, I sort of hold it against you." I stick out my tongue and hope that Rhiannon is already in a place where we can joke about tonight's events. She doesn't make a face back, but she doesn't snap at me either, so I'll take it.

I'm not sure how, because I'm not particularly comfortable, but somehow all four of us manage to find spots on the bed that work well enough for us to fall asleep. Reece spreads out over the course of the night, taking up more than her fair share of the bed, but I've always been comfortable sleeping curled up in a tiny ball near my pillow. When

I wake up the next morning, I feel better than I did the night before.

To my surprise, I'm the first one awake. Even Rhiannon is still fast asleep, snoring softly with one of her arms flopped over Reilly's head.

A quick look at my phone shows me it's only six o'clock in the morning, way too early for me to be getting out of bed on a Saturday, even if I'm already feeling like I had a good night's sleep. Adding to a good morning's sleep can only make this whole situation better, right? I drift back off eventually and don't stir again until everyone else wakes at the sound of our parents banging around in the kitchen downstairs.

We all get up without saying much of anything, but I feel more connected to all of my sisters than I have in a while. We needed this. Not Rhiannon running away, but some time together, just us.

Once were all seated in various parts of the kitchen, the magic is broken a little as we eat breakfast and go back to our phones. Rhiannon still has a long, uncomfortable conversation with our parents to get through, but at least this feels a little more like normal. Except, Reece keeps looking up at me every couple of minutes. I get the impression that my sisters are texting each other but not me, leaving me to wonder what they could be plotting. With the three of them, the options are pretty much endless.

It's only at lunch time that the three of them finally corner me in the attic and let me know what's been going on, despite the fact that they've been denying anything and everything all day.

"You might want to hop in the shower." Reece says. "That'll give your hair time to dry, maybe Reilly can do something with it."

"Why would I want to do anything with my hair?" I stand up and move away from my computer, mostly because I'm feeling like a cornered animal being watched by three hungry dogs. "What's wrong with my hair?"

"Your hair is fine, but we thought you might want to do something a little fancier for Kent tonight."

Um, what? I repeat the thought aloud.

"You're going on a date tonight" Reilly announces, clapping her hands together.

"We felt bad about last night." Rhiannon shifts uncomfortably. "Okay, I felt bad about last night. We all came up with the idea of making it up to you."

"So you decided to trick me into my second date in as many days?"

"This was a little more on the up and up." Reilly shrugged. "At least this time you both already know it's a date."

I glare at all three of them until I realize what they did. "Wait, you talked to Kent? How did you get his number?"

"Rosie. We take art together, remember? We've been talking a little," Reilly says with a twinkle in her eye. "So I got in touch and she was on board with this idea. She reached out to Kent, now the two of you are meeting up for dinner tonight."

My heart flutters as I accept that this might be happening. "Kent is okay with this?"

"Have you not checked your phone recently?" Reece asks.

I practically dive back at my computer desk and grab my phone. There's a text message waiting from more than fifteen minutes ago. From Kent.

Kent: Rosie just filled me in. Are you okay with this? Because if you are, I am completely on board.

I don't respond, I'm grinning too hard to think of any cohesive words to respond with. Instead, I flip my phone over and make my sisters read what he said.

Reilly is practically giggling with me equally. "Respond to him!"

I already know he's in for this insanity, so writing back seems like a pretty safe bet.

Reagan: It's a date.

As one, the four of us squeal together, I'm even jumping up and down a little right along with Reece. I've got a date tonight! I've got a date with a guy who actually knows he's going on a date with me!

I'm so not ready for this.

CHAPTER 26

DINNER AT LIZZIE'S probably isn't the most elegant first date that's ever happened but as far as I'm concerned, it's perfect. Kent and I sat at a small table in the back of the restaurant that had been set up with a couple of candles. We did our best to ignore that Lizzie was probably texting updates to Rosie the whole time we were there. We had a really nice time and the two of us talked about almost everything, with very few breaks in the conversation.

Unfortunately, my guess that Fairview doesn't have many places to go on a Saturday night, was dead on. The weather is a lot milder than yesterday, but wandering around still feels a little pointless when there is no destination in mind.

"Maybe we should have just gone back to the movies." Kent says apologetically. "At least we would have something to do."

At first, I was disappointed we weren't going to be doing the movie theatre thing again, because it meant I'd have to be functioning like a dateable person for an entire night, I'm glad we did had dinner instead.

"Don't worry about it. This has been fun." I look over at Kent to see if he agrees and find him already nodding.

"Yeah, this is definitely better than yesterday. And I'm really glad everything worked out with your sister."

I follow Ken's lead as we take a left turn into an empty park. The playground equipment and path around the grass are all covered with the latest layer of snow, there's no one else in sight. We end up on a bench near an old oak tree, and I huddle into my coat for warmth. I'm not even trying to hint at anything, but a minute later Kent hesitantly puts his arm around me and pulls me closer. "Is this okay?"

I nod, too nervous to speak. I don't think the two of us have ever been this close together, and even in this cold open air, I can almost sense the heat coming off of him and smell the faintest hint of cologne.

When I get up the nerve to look over at Kent, our faces are only inches from one another. He's already looking at me.

"Are you okay?" Kent asks already starting to pull his arm away.

"I'm fine. Don't go." Kent smiles and settles back around me. I'm close enough to hear a small sigh escape his lips. "Honestly, I'm nervous." I don't say why out loud, but I'm hopeful he's reading the situation the same as I am. As far as moments for first kisses go, this one is kind of perfect. Now, I need the courage to make to happen. My nerves are all based on my own possible ineptitude. I've never done this before, I don't want to screw it up.

First, I need to look at him long enough to give me a chance for this to happen at all. He won't kiss me if I keep looking away.

I force my eyes to stay locked on his, trying to convey my meaning in how I'm looking at him.

"I'm nervous too. Somehow, I've managed to get a date with this gorgeous girl, now she's letting me hold her close to me. I'm going to mess this up at any second."

"That's my life pretty much all the time. Just one stray thought away from ruining everything."

"You've been perfect. That first day I saw you, I knew you were someone I wanted to talk to. You've blown me away every day I've seen you since then. You have nothing to worry about."

I don't say anything because all thoughts have left my head. It seems like he's even closer to me now, like he's inching his way forward without appearing to move at all.

I'm not sure how I get up the courage, but I make myself move my head forward just the tiniest bit, angling it as I go.

This is happening.

Everything else falls away when his lips touch mine. At first, it was just the softest graze against my bottom lip but soon we're completely connected, my whole body is tingling.

Before I can let myself worry about anything, like where I'm supposed to put my hands or how much I'm supposed to move my mouth, Kent pulls away.

For second we stay there, inches from one another, eyes locked. Then he whispers, "Well, I think it's safe to say neither one of us screwed that up."

I giggle, it's enough to erase any of the tension without ruining the magic of this moment.

"No. I think we can do better." I bite my lip and move toward Kent yet again, eager to see what else we are capable of.

CHAPTER 27

STANDING behind the curtain for my cue to go on stage, I'm fully aware of everyone who is on the other side of the curtain. Knowing that Kent's out there with the other half of the class, and that Mr. Sullen let me sneak Reece and Rhiannon in to see my exam performance as well, there's a good chance I made a major mistake. I'm about to embarrass myself and I would be better off if a third of my family wasn't here to see the humiliation in person. Over Christmas, I'd gotten it in my head that I'd be more confident having them here, but it only makes the stakes seem higher.

Kent's and Jen's performances already happened, they did a classic take on *Alice in Wonderland* with costumes that obviously exceeded the budget they were supposed to use, which resulted in some decent acting. Kent's group managed to make the classic story much more violent than the original.

So far, three different people in my performance have forgotten their lines. So at least the bar isn't set all that high for my couple of lines as the king of hearts.

In the end, our group decided to gender swap *Alice in*

Wonderland. I'm not exactly sure what kind of statement we're supposed to make, but it's been fun if nothing else.

And so, the trial begins. I do my best to look confident as I walk onstage with everyone else. Most of the people from the last scene have disappeared, hiding themselves in the small area available to us offstage in the classroom. I can practically feel almost twenty sets of eyes on me directly, even though someone else is talking right now, so the feeling of everyone watching me could be all in my head.

I'm here now, and this is happening. Besides, somehow my drama grade ended up being my best of the semester, at least going into exam. If I can manage not to screw this up, I might actually have something to show for myself. Not a new potential career option, but still almost impressive showing in the class that everyone probably thought I would drop out of as well.

Before I can overthink it, I'm saying my lines and gesticulating in what I hope is a dramatic fashion, pleading with my deranged spouse to spare the young boy who has shown up in our kingdom to wreak havoc unknowingly.

I end up getting my head chopped off and breathing a sigh of relief when my turn on stage is finally over. I do not understand how this plot twist ended up in our version of the script, since I had very little to do with that. Instead I did most of the visual stuff for our group. If nothing else, our version of Wonderland looks awesome.

I fish my phone out from where I'd been hiding it in my costume, and take a behind-the-scenes picture to send to Nadine later. Rhiannon has also promised to take pictures of my big moment to share with our parents, or for me to accidentally delete so no one can ever see them ever again.

The lights come up, and it's all over. Our group disperses after an enthusiastic round of applause from the audience. A few people are shooting my sisters weird looks, but I guess people at school don't get to see more than a couple of us together at any time. I rush over to them as they are talking with Kent.

"Well, that's finally done." I lean my head against Kent's shoulder before he pulls me into a hug.

"You did great."

I glance at my sisters for confirmation and find Rhiannon making a face. I can trust her not to lie to me. "You didn't embarrass yourself." she says, grinning.

"I'll take it. That's all I was going for. Thanks for coming guys, you should probably go before the class wraps up."

They say their goodbyes and disappear back out into the hallway, off to eat their food in the limited time they have left in their lunch period.

"Don't listen to them." Kent says. "I thought you were awesome."

"I definitely wasn't, but that was a lot of fun."

"Still happy that it's over?"

"Oh yeah."

"I'm still holding onto hope of you joining drama club next semester. We've even dragged Rosie out a couple of times, I'm not giving up on you yet."

Drama club starts at the beginning of the next term, when the drama classroom becomes a music classroom and Mr. Sullen becomes an English teacher until the new school year.

As though summoned by my thoughts, our teacher joins us, Jen in tow. I'm pretty sure Frank is still somewhere in the back, taking off his costume. He had been banking on being the cheshire cat before we went with our gender swap idea. Instead, he ended up as Dinah.

"Well done." Mr. Sullen says, clapping slowly. "We had

a great showing this year. I hope you will all be back next year for our junior level course."

I smile politely, but I don't commit one way or the other. I've kind of loved taking drama this semester, but the idea of doing it when there are other, non-public speaking oriented classes available to me still seems like a foreign concept. Somehow, I suspect I'll give in.

If nothing else, Mr. Sullen has become one of my favorite teachers. I'm already hoping I can rework my schedule a little next semester to have him for English along with Frank.

The five of us don't have lunch together for our next set of classes next term, but I've been still lucky enough to end up with Kent and Rosie plus Reilly and Rhiannon. I don't think hiding out in the library will even be an option for me again anytime soon.

And, even better, I get a different teacher for my science class next semester too.

CHAPTER 28

I'M ALREADY LIKING the Valentine's Day Festival way more than I liked the Halloween one. A couple months after getting together with Kent, I'm still a giant ball of sappy emotions from everything from the heart shaped streamers, to the punch and the kissing booth in the town square, speaks to my soul. I *love* love.

Even though Kent and I are couple now, we still go to the festival with Jen, Rosie and Frank. Or at least we were supposed to, Frank has decided not to make an appearance. More specifically, he's promised us that there is no amount of money we could have paid him to get him to go.

We wander around the square, eating heart-shaped chocolates on a stick and, once again, I'm on the lookout for my family. My parents aren't here this time around, choosing to use the opportunity when most of us were out of the house to have a date night of their own, going to a restaurant together in the next town over. Reece is here with her now second Fairview boyfriend. This one, Tom, has lasted for three weeks already. From the way she talks about him, I'm a little surprised it hasn't ended already. I wouldn't be surprised if she was holding out until after the Valentine's Day festivities. Both she and Reilly are here with a big group of friends.

Rhiannon, who broke up with Derrick after he bailed from coming to see her for New Year's Eve, is staying home to enjoy having the house to herself. Though I'm at least a little tempted to call and check in... just to make sure she's really there.

"Have I mentioned how much I love your hair?" Kent asks. All four of us somehow convinced our mother to let us re-dye our hair a little earlier than planned, so we would have everything looking it's best for Valentine's Day.

As a result, Kent *has* mentioned it, multiple times. Instead of going with the pink streak I'd once imagined, I actually ended up going a little bolder. The top of my haircut is still its natural color, but the entire lower half is a deep and vibrant purple. Reece has now gone almost fully blond, and Rhiannon has toned down her red look but just a little. This time round, Reilly decided to mix it up and add in a few highlights to her own look. Somehow, people still confuse us for one another.

"Stop it, I'm blushing."

"You really are." Rosie points out. "You make it seem like he barely ever complements you. Kent, that is not how you treat a lady. You should be telling Reagan every day that she is the prettiest girl ever."

Now I am blushing, so hard my face must be bright red. Rosie is completely teasing both of us. It was only last week that we managed to tone things down enough that she stopped giving us a hard time, especially when we were constantly complimenting one another. Even I can admit that we were getting a little ridiculous. "Actually, I have good news. Completely unrelated to how attractive I find Reagan."

"Oh yeah?" I ask, giving Kent's hand a squeeze of gratitude for the distraction.

"Well, my mom went to high school with Mrs. Bishop, the lady who runs the animal shelter. If Reece is still looking to get in for volunteering, I can talk to her."

It takes me a second to figure out what he's saying. "Really? That's amazing!" If I can do anything to help Reece find something to get her feet planted here in Fairview, I'm open to the idea.

"My mom gets that she owes your family a bit of a favor."

"Why? Because she showed up on our doorstep on her first day in town looking for new story?"

"Unfortunately, no. I think it's because she's planning to do more of the same in the future." Kent grimaces.

I want to ask what he means, but before I can, I see my sisters and their friends appear from around the corner. They're both easy to spot, even within a crowd of nearly a dozen people. It's like I have an extra sense when it comes to them.

Soon enough, our group merges with theirs, and I'm one of three nearly identical people in a crowd. At the first opportunity, I pull Reece aside.

"Were you still interested in volunteering at the animal shelter?" I ask.

"Not an option." Reece answers, her smiling falling away instantly. "Maybe, by the time we're seniors I'll make enough of an impression around here to try again. But probably not."

"What if I had an in? Or specifically, Kent does. Would you be interested then?"

"Ummm... yes. I would be interested! Forever grateful too. Have I mentioned that Kent is my new favorite person?"

"Hey!" Tom says from behind her, pulling her backwards for a kiss. Reece rolls her eyes. Yeah, right. She's loving the attention.

If nothing else, it's nice to see Reece really start to find herself again. Things didn't go how she'd hoped at first, but I'm starting to suspect that next year will be when she really shines.

As everyone else goes off for more food, I finally have my first chance of the day to be even somewhat alone with Kent. My boyfriend.

Crazy.

His fingers are tangled in mine as he pulls me closer to him, until my body is pressed right up against his. At first, I feel a little weird, knowing the whole town can see us, but Kent only places a kick kiss on my forehead before taking a step back.

As we separate, I take in the busy town around me. Just like Halloween, it feels like everyone is here at the same time, even though this is probably only a fraction of the town's population.

"Psst," Kent whispers in my ear, sending a shiver running through me. "What's on your mind?"

"I was just thinking... I'm glad we moved in Fairview. I actually kind of like it here."

Kent leans forward and gives me another quick kiss, this time on my lips. "I'm glad you're here too." he says as we separate.

Yup, I'm definitely going to love living here.

ABOUT THE AUTHOR

Kellie Sheridan, writing as Kellie Bean.

Kellie lives in Ontario, Canada with her husband and their labradoodle, Piper. And because one dog is never enough, she frequently hosts other canine visitors as a dog-sitter.

When not playing with puppies, Kellie runs Patchwork Press, along with writing her own books for young adults. Her life is basically all dogs, all the time, and she wouldn't have it any other way.

Learn more at kelliesheridan.com